The

Arabs

The

Arabs

A Compact History

Francesco Gabrieli

Translated by Salvator Attanasio

HAWTHORN BOOKS, Inc.
Publishers   New York

First Printing, April, 1963

H-0405

$\mathcal{P}$reface

THE aim of this modest volume is to give a summary account, yet one which is as accurate and up-to-date as possible, of the political vicissitudes of the Arab people from their beginnings up to the present day. Because of the broad dimensions of the historic process, still in motion, and the vastness of Arabic cultural patrimony, I have preferred to give primarily a political outline here, against the background of a sober cultural framework which can be further developed in a later work.

Without going too deeply into the subject, this political history touches upon the great religious phenomenon of Islam under the sign of which the Arabs inscribed their name on world history. The relation between the history of the Arab people and that of the Islamic religion and civilization is one of those points that the educated public needs to have clarified. We have tried our best to make this clarification in the following pages. But even after precisely establishing the connection and distinction between them, I cannot eliminate a small sense of dissatisfaction that seizes me in the presence of my work: although I had limited myself to an outline of national history in an attempt to condense the enormous amount of material in a brief compass, there are still too many names and dates which are unfamiliar to the average reader, too many histories of dynasties, and too little concerning economic and social facts. Experts will understand my dissatisfaction along with the justification for this imbalance, the reasons for which are to be sought in the very nature of the native sources on which I have primarily structured my outline, and in the state of the research—still in its initial stages—being conducted in the economic and social history of the Arab-Moslem Middle Ages, large areas of which are still *terra incognita*, only now being explored. In other respects, the political vicissitudes, the succession and co-existence of governmental formations, which in the oriental Middle Ages are essentially dynastic formations, constitute a necessary frame for the picture—the first lines of which have barely begun to be traced. Indeed, the modest and essential aim of this volume is to provide just such a frame. Whether within this frame I have also succeeded in tracing some lines and grasping some particulars of a more personal vision of men and events, is a matter upon which specialists will have to judge.

I dedicate this attempt at an outline history of the Arab people to the fond memory of Ettore Rossi (1894-1955): Arabist and Turkologist of eminent distinction, excellent authority on the Arab and Moslem world, but above all a friend of unforgettable nobility and goodness. It is a very slight token of my appreciation of how much I have learned from him in the field of scholarship and from his example of the honesty and dignity of life: *fa-inna llaha la yudi'u ajra l-muhsinin.*

—Francesco Gabrieli

Table of Contents

List of Illustrations

1.

The Pre-Islamic Arabs

THE Arabs entered the mainstream of history with Mo-hammed and with Islam in the seventh century after Christ. But before this time, which compels even school books to make a rapid foray into the deserts of Arabia, there was a thousand-year span of Arab history, less famous and less revolutionary in character. Nevertheless, it was of a notable importance among the events of the ancient world.

The first mention of the name of this people, whose etymology is obscure, appears in an inscription of the Assyrian king Salmanasar III, 853 B.C., while the names of persons and places, clearly referring to Arab races and centers occur in many biblical passages and in Genesis itself.

To these oriental sources must be added the citations of classic authors, Aeschylus, Herodotus, and later Eratosthenes and Strabo, and of other Greek and Roman savants belonging to the time in which the Arabs and Arabia had entered into the ambit of scientific knowledge, of exploration and of trade with the Graeco-Roman world. These classic and oriental sources, with the epigraphical evidences *in situ* which we shall discuss presently, constitute the base for a scientific reconstruction of the ancient history of Arabia. Deserving of much less credence, indeed of none at all according to a radical criticism, are the abundance of accounts—largely

1

of a fantastic and legendary character—that Arab tradition itself provides regarding its more distant pre-Islamic past. This consists of the copious self-styled historical, genealogical and anecdotal materials gathered by Arab-Moslem philologists, chroniclers and antiquarians. Pure legend, or the caprice of chance and scholarly systematization, which are irreconcilable with the meager but certain aforementioned data of non-Arabic origin, usually lie underneath the apparent richness and precision of these sources. Nor are some recent attempts at a re-evaluation, albeit accomplished with great learning and serious scientific method, wholly convincing in this regard.

What cannot be rejected, however, is the fundamental fact basically underlying the indigenous historico-genealogical tradition: the distinction between two large ethnic groups in the bosom of the Arab peoples, one northern, the other southern. In broad lines it corresponds to the double aspect of the history and civilization of the ancient Arabs as must now be outlined here: a history and culture of peoples who in the north were essentially nomads, and of a sedentary and agricultural civilization in the south. And in this sense the genealogical distinction can be interwoven with the ethnographical and sociological distinction on which the great fourteenth century Arab historian, Ibn Khaldùn, established his whole view of history with respect to the world known to him: namely the distinction between Bedouins (*ahl al-badw*) and town-dwellers or sedentaries (*ahl al-hadar*), in whose reciprocal actions and reactions he saw the course of civilization unfold. Obviously the double distinction just referred to can be accepted only with great discretion and in a wholly summary manner: the "southern" tribes in the classification of the Arab genealogists, did not all have their centers in the south of the Arab peninsula. Rather, they often appeared in northern and central Arabia, intermixed with northern tribes with whom they shared the language, a rudimentary culture, and in many cases nomadism. On the other hand, just as there was no lack of Bedouin elements in the south, stable settlements with the beginnings of civil life of a more advanced character are to be found in Arab antiquity in the north, and also outside of the peninsula proper, among Arab peoples whose southern origin is not always certain. It must be admitted that profound upheavals and migrations (to which learned Arab tradition also offers some historical clues) already altered that primitive ethno-geographical division in antiquity without, however, completely cancelling the validity and the consciousness of this division. The fact remains that southern Arabia, the *Arabia felix* of the classic writers (who thus translated the indigenous name of Yemen, perhaps erroneously from an etymological viewpoint), had its own history in the ancient period with its own character, completely apart from the monotonous and obscure happenings of the Arabs in the north. While it is to the northern Arabs, rather, that we should look for the antecedents of the appearance and of the mission of Mohammed, the history of the Arabs in their totality cannot ignore the splendid and closed chapter of South-Arab civilization which archeological exploration and epigraphical interpretation has revealed to us for almost a century. Monumental remains, still awaiting adequate excavation and study, and an impressive epigraphical heritage attest to the fact that in Yemen—between the first millennium before and the first centuries after Christ—there was a flowering of governmental formations of a monarchical type, of an advanced and complex social life, of an essentially commercial activity, and a settled and refined way of life. The succession and, in part, the coexistence of several states in southern Arabia is confirmed by a comparison of the archeological and epigraphical data with the accounts of classic authors. These authors knew and described precisely this Arabia, and it was this they had in mind when they celebrated its *beatae divitiae*, simply inconceivable in the squalid deserts of the north. First of all should be mentioned the people of the Minaean kingdom (with its capital Qarnaw—present-day Main) in northern Yemen, who extended their commercial influence well north of Yemen, as far as northern Hijaz. The period of their greatest flowering can be placed between the eighth century and the third century before Christ. They were followed by the kingdom of the Sabaens, which in fact already coexisted with them. Its capital was in Maryab (present-day Marib), which has been raised to a symbol of this whole ancient Arab civilization through the biblical narrative of the visit of the Queen of Sheba to Solomon. Under Augustus, a Roman expedition commanded by Aelius Gallus (25-24 B.C.), hazarded an attack against this kingdom, at the peak of its development, but was forced to withdraw before its impregnable fortresses. Owing to the preponderance within the Sabaean kingdom of the Himyar clan (the *Homeritae* of the classics), the later period of this kingdom was called Himyarite (already in the first centuries of our era). After having experienced a first Ethiopian invasion in the fourth century A.D., it finally succumbed to a second intervention of Christian Ethiopia into its affairs when the Himyarite king, Dhu Nuwàs, having embraced Judaism, began to persecute the Christian communities of South Arabia with a neophytic zeal. At the invitation of the native feudal barons, the Ethiopian occupation (A.D. 525-75) was followed by that of the Persians. Later came a period of anarchical independence, until all Yemen peacefully passed over into the orbit of nascent Islam.

It is customary to sum up the vicissitudes of ancient *Arabia felix*, which stretched over more than a millennium, in the Minaean—Sabaean—Himyarite succession (other minor kingdoms like those of the Qatabanians and Hadramawt are attested to by classic tradition, and confirmed by epigraphs and coins). It has passed into history wholly permeated with the fragrance of its spices which constituted its principal trade and source of wealth. These spices (frankincense, labdanum, myrrh) were intensively cultivated on its soil thanks to a most highly developed agricultural technique. They were then convoyed, together with the products of India and of Somalia, towards the Mediterranean basin. The whole life of the state, headed by an hereditary king (*Mukarrib*) assisted by a council of dignitaries, was based on this commerce placed under the patronage of the native deities. These deities formed a rich pantheon, where we find the well-known Semitic, astral divinities of Astarte, Sin, Shamas and still others, served by a powerful and well-organized sacerdotal class. The south Arabian epigraphs, the only written documentation which came down to us from that epoch and civilization, are our primary source regarding the structure of public life, the religion and the cult, the solid and, probably, monogamic family structure, the economy and the law. Engraved on slabs and rocks and fashioned in monumental characters, completely different from the north Arabian script and in a language notably divergent from it, they preserve the authentic voice of a society and of an historical period of which the subsequent Arab-Islamic tradition has lost every precise remembrance. For a dismaying hiatus separates these authentic testimonies, laboriously collected and studied by orientalists in the course of the last century, from the fantastic genealogies and events that Moslem antiquarians intertwine on the Yemenite *Tubba* (their name for those very ancient kings). All the coincidences, synchronizations and reconciliations that Semitic studies have been able to establish between this direct documentation and the other sources, connect the south Arabian epigraphy with the extra-Arab accounts (Graeco-Roman and Oriental) rather than with the fantastic native antiquarianism of the Moslem era. The latter, in turn (and this is quite significant as regards its worth) continued within Arab literature in the popular narratives and the fabulist literature of the type of *A Thousand and One Nights*. It does not seem unwarranted to conclude that, without the recovery of the western antiquarianism and epigraphy, every precise notion regarding south Arabic civilization would have totally vanished among later generations.

The aromas and the precious woods which the south Arabian kingdoms in part produced on their soil, and in part forwarded as a port of call for overseas trade, arrived in the Mediterranean through a double route: one was entirely by land, and from southwestern Arabia it went through Transjordan to Palestine and Syria. The other, which was primarily reserved for the trade with India, went up the Euphrates from the Persian Gulf. After the merchandise was unloaded in the emporium of Dura-Europos, it was then sent on to Syria, from the east, along the caravan routes across the desert. Both roads created the fortune and the power of two other Arab states, which were not closed in the splendid isolation of those of Yemen, but gravitated within the orbit of the Hellenistic and Roman world. At Petra in Transjordan, the ancient seat of the biblical Edomites, the kingdom of the Nabateans flourished from the fifth century B.C. They were without doubt Arabs by race and language (although it cannot be strictly ascertained from which stock), but depended for their culture on the more civilized Aramaeans. In fact their official language was Aramaic, as appears from the inscriptions. The alphabet too was of Aramaic derivation, from which later the north Arab or, in brief, the Arab alphabet was to evolve.

At the time of its greatest flowering the Nabatean kingdom controlled a zone extending from the Gulf of Aqaba to the Dead Sea, including a part of northern Hijaz. After becoming a vassal state of Rome in the first century B.C. (Pompeius visited Petra in 65 B.C., and the expedition of Aelius Gallus started out from a Nabatean port), it ended up by being absorbed by the latter when Trajan, in 105 A.D. created the *Provincia Arabia* with the capital in Petra itself. The grandiose architectural ruins, still visible here, the inscriptions and the coins preserve the memory of this Arab state which maintained its independence for two centuries in the shadow of Rome.

More dramatic is the history of the relations with Rome of the other Arab state of Syria, the equally aramaicized Palmyra (Tadmur in Arabic). Here also a population of Arab origin, at least in part, had strongly felt the effects of the Aramaic and Hellenistic influence, as appears from its impressive monumental residues, from its inscriptions, and from its cults. It controlled the transport trade because of its position along the caravan route from the Euphrates to Syria. The principal activity of the kingdom appears to have revolved around commerce and banking; in addition it also hired out its celebrated archers as mercenary troops. In the long duel between Rome and the Parthians, it chose to side with Rome. In consequence it received privileges and honors until the good fortune of one of its leaders Odenathus (in Arabic Udhaynah), who had been elevated previously by Rome to the title of *Corrector Orientis,* induced him to attempt the foundation of a dynasty and an independent state. The ambitious program was continued after his death (267 A.D.) by his equally ambitious wife Zenobia (in Arabic Zaynab, but which Arab tradition knows rather in the form of az-Zabbà) on behalf of her son Wahb Allàh. After an ephemeral triumph, the intervention of Aurelian in 273 destroyed the dreams of the Queen of Palmyra. She ended her days in exile in a villa in Tivoli, while her city abruptly fell into a rapid decline. Zenobia is the only personage of Arab proto-history whose memory Arab tradition has preserved, albeit in distorted form by the fable according to which she perished in vengeance for another Arab king whom she had put to death.

While the impressive ruins and the classic sources speak to us of Petra and Palmyra, only the epigraphy urges us to remember some other small states of the north, formed and dissolved in the desert before the growth of Islam.

Such, for example, is that of Lihyan in northern Hijaz with its center at Dedàn (present-day el-Ola). At first it was subject to south Arabic Minaeans and later became autonomous. It is known to us only through its copious inscriptions, written in an alphabet of south Arab type, but in a northern Arab language. It seems to have been at the acme of its power in the first centuries of the Christian era, when the rival Nabataean kingdom disappeared. But it, too, vanished on the eve of Islam, in the sixth century. Its importance lies in the fact that, in contrast to Petra and Palmyra, which were both located outside the Arab Peninsula and widely open to foreign cultural influences, it represents the most ancient pure Arab state that we have been given to know in northern Arabia, independently of the sedentary civilization of the south of which, at the beginning, it was also a tributary.

UP to now, in outlining the vicissitudes of the ancient Arabs, we have had to put to one side their national tradition, which has very little to do with their most ancient history. Coming now to the heart of Arabia, that is to the life of the desert, we can again draw closer to the Arab sources. Although these sources are of a much later origin, they reflect a reality which has remained unaltered for centuries against the background of an immutable nature. This is tantamount to saying that we now leave the *ahl al-hadar*, the inhabitants of Yemen or of Petra and Palmyra, and we enter into the kingdom of the Bedouins. Let us make clear at the outset that the Bedouins were also involved in the history of those inhabitants. But they constituted its fluctuating, marginal element, backward in a civil sense, from which the commercial, political and warrior elites who formed the backbone of those states clearly distinguished themselves. Between the third and the sixth century of the Christian era, the power of Rome waned in the north as did the prosperity of the Yemenite states in the south. It was at that time that the relations between the inhabitants and nomads in the whole area of the Arab world underwent a profound change: the original nomadism regained ground; we do not know too well when and how, but it swallowed up state formations like the Lihyan, and spread out almost over the entire peninsula and north of it, up to the borders of Byzantium, the heir of Rome and of Persia. Both the great empires tried to secure themselves against the barbaric tide by favoring the formation of new buffer-states, among the Arabs themselves, on their frontiers. On the Byzantine border these were the semi-nomad Ghassanids, vassals of Byzantium, which bestowed upon them the title of "Phylarchs" or tribal chieftains, while the Lakhmids, stationed at Hirah on the Euphrates, served as tributaries of the Great King who sat in pomp at Ctesiphon. The history of these two little states, which maintained themselves up to the beginnings of the seventh century, that is up to the immediate eve of Islam, can finally be reconstructed from Arab as well as Syrian and Byzantine sources: they both represent the transition from the civil life of Syria and Mesopotamia to the pure nomadism of the Syro-Arabic desert and of central Arabia. For their nomad co-nationals they were the antechamber of civilization; for the Byzantines and Persians that of the desert. Therefore foreign cultural elements, of non-Arab languages and customs and religious faiths, filtered into the world of the nomads, breaking up its monotony, and bringing some variety and embellishments to their squalid life. Both the Ghassanids and the Lakhmids were Christians (a Christianity of a quite tepid and superficial character, naturally) and the Bedouins watched their rites, convents and hermitages which were part of their religion with a deferential awe which changed into a Bacchic enthusiasm upon tasting the wine of the adjoining taverns. This relative softening of customs did not prevent the Ghassanids and Lakhmids from being mutual enemies, like their respective patrons, and from reciprocally exterminating each other conscientiously. The great days of their wars, like the famous one known as the "Day of Halimah," the figures and the adventures of those rulers like the various Harith of the Ghassans, Numàn and Mundhir of Hira, live on in the songs of the Bedouin poets, magnified by a naive fantasy out of all proportion to the modest reality. What is real is the fact that for a couple of centuries the Ghassanids and Lakhmids equally carried out the political function assigned to them, and the historico-cultural function of being mediators between the advanced civilization of Hellenistic-Roman-Western Asia, and the primitive living conditions of pre-Islamic Arabia.

Upon delving more deeply into the latter, we find nomadism in its pure state. This does not mean that there were not some stable settlements even in the interior of the Peninsula, which were destined for an illustrious future, like the two Hijazan centers of Mecca and Medina and some agricultural colonies, primarily Jewish, in northern Hijaz. But these were little islands lost in the ocean of sand, of steppe and rock, among which roamed the *Scenitae*, the tent Arabs, in a monotonous alternation of seasons and pasturages. Here the social organization pivoted around the tribe, further structured into its various subgroups. The only bond and code was tribal solidarity (*asabiyyah*), and the duties of collective responsibility, of protection of the client and the guest and of vengeance which were connected with it. At the head of the tribe was the freely elected *Say yid*, or sheikh, whose limited powers of authority and of prestige were of a moral character more than anything else. He was the leader in battles (substituted sometimes by a military chieftain or *rais*), concluded peace-treaties and settled blood feuds. Violation of tribal solidarity without effecting an affiliation with another organized group was a sure augury of death in the struggle of all against all for survival. The raid (*razzia*) with the attendant skirmishes, which tradition sometimes magnifies into epic battles, was a recognized law in the relations between tribes. The long, murderous wars of pagan Arabia were born of raids or of personal affronts which coinvolved whole tribes because of the aforementioned code. The war of Basùs, for instance, started over the killing of a camel, and that of Dahis was named after a famous war-horse, for which brave warriors fell in combat, at once spurred on and bewailed in the songs of the poets. The sacred months offered the only respite in the state of perpetual war, among which that of *Rajab* is renowned, as also are the rites of the pagan pilgrimage to Mecca.

From time immemorial the character of the Bedouin, which has remained substantially unchanged down through the centuries, was formed in this literally and figuratively harsh climate. Some in the East and West have idealized it, others have unjustly depreciated it more than necessary. At its base lies an unrestrained individualism, a proud consciousness of oneself and an aversion to every authority and hierarchy which was, and is, reflected in the anarchic particularism of the individual tribes. The individual does not live entirely apart by himself simply because this would make it impossible for him to survive (nevertheless in the poetry and in real life there was no lack of attempts and boastings in this sense), but he

turns away from every social organization that goes beyond
the ambit of his own tribal group. Bending under the lash of
a cruel nature, intent upon the daily satisfaction of his limited
material needs, ready when necessary for plunders and blood-
shed, he nevertheless feels as a part of his *muruwwah* or
Arab *virtus*, of his primitive ethical ideal, the magnanimity
of renunciation and of giving, above all as regards hospitality.
Hence the celebrated hospitality and generosity of the Arabs,
the legendary example of which pagan antiquity exalted
in Hatim at-Tai, and which urban civilizations of all times
have enjoyed and admired. Alongside this stands the jealous
pride in one's own freedom and dignity, faithfulness to the
tradition of the homeland, courage and sobriety. But this
courage wanes easily where success of the first surprise may
be lacking, the sobriety surrenders to the unleashing of the
lustful passions as soon as a favorable opportunity for feasting
or booty presents itself. For the Bedouin, the two highest
goods of life (*al-atyabani*) remain food and woman. Comparison with the mortifying restrictions and undervaluation
to which we see woman subjected later in the civilization
of Islam certainly influences our judgment of the high position
of woman among the pre-Islamic Arabs. There is no doubt
that in the free life of the desert (also, in the Islamic era)
woman was valued and honored quite otherwise than in
urban life. But, even considering certain barbaric pagan customs like the burying alive of new-born infants which has
left a famous echo behind in the Koran as wholly isolated
cases, it is not necessary to yield to naive idealizations in
drawing the image of the Bedouin woman. Outside the
fugitive flower of youth, in reality she was and is a beast of
burden for man, and an object of prey and of pleasure for
as long as the flower remains. This does not exclude the fact
that the *Jahiliyyah*, or Arab paganism has known women who
were eminent because of their virtue, counsel, magnanimity

and poetry; and indeed many more of them than the my-sogynist Moslem society can boast of.

We have already made several fleeting references to poetry, and in fact it constitutes our principal and suggestive, but sometimes deceptive, source for reconstructing the material and spiritual life of the ancient Arabs. As they themselves have so well called it, it is the archive of their pomp, the depository of their memories, which otherwise would be con-secrated to oblivion because of the rare use of writing, and in the main the genuine spokesman of this their most ancient epoch. Nevertheless, though it is a precious document for the reconstruction of their material life, it must be used with a certain caution as the expression of their moral and senti-mental life for the reason that it has come down to us in a form already rigidly stylized. For example, sentimentalism in the relations between the sexes, which it seems to reflect, gives us probably a highly conventional and one-sided image of reality, and in general, its whole restricted and monotonous subject matter leaves out, or stylizes, aspects of the real which elude a precise knowledge on our part. With all that, we must always see in it a conspicuous image, perhaps indeed the only image perceptible to us of Arab spirituality in its first phase, the choral "voice of a people," which is all the more instructive the more we can listen to it without any romantic infatuations. Rejecting sceptical views of a hyper-critical character that have recently come to the fore, we see in pre-Islamic Arab poetry an authentic product of this pagan era, of the nomad, semi-nomad and sedentary Arabs of the north and center of the Peninsula (a south Arabic literature besides the inscriptions, if ever there was one, has been completely lost, and as we already mentioned at this time the southern tribes had a language, centers and modes of life in common with those of the north).

Into this poetry which, let us make clear, more often does

not give us the whole reality rather than a false one, the Arabs of the fifth to the seventh century A.D. (these are its chronological limits) poured the record of their laborious life, of their ideals, aspirations and passions. They portrayed themselves in their eternal wandering, which often broke cherished bonds of love, in the company of their faithful camels and chargers, in the hunt for wild animals of the desert, in the excitement and ardor of the fray, in the joy of their gross banquets. One by one they numbered their wells, their oases, their meager pastures, they echoed their tribal conflicts, fratricidal wars, the praises and vituperations of single individuals and tribal groups, their scanty ethical laws according to the ancient Semitic and human norm of "an eye for an eye, a tooth for a tooth." And they mixed the primitive emotions of their souls, their elementary reflections upon the value and the destiny of man, on the value and the burden of life, and on the fate of mortals with a most minute analysis of the external world, which we often find opaque and oppressing.

THE religious impulse among these Arabs of the north, especially the Bedouins, seems to have been weak and primitive before the extraordinary experience of Mohammed came along to push it socially to the first plane. After having defeated Arab paganism, Islam spread a veil of abomination over its very memory. By utilizing the late accounts of historians and antiquarians, and verses of ancient poets, the authenticity of which is not always sure, Semitic study, not without hard work, has been able to gather those "remains of Arab paganism" which were the subject of a classic work by Wellhausen. At the base of the paganism there appears a polydemonism with elements of fetishism and animism (not totemism, however, as was once maintained). The pagan Arabs of the north worshipped a rich pantheon of deities, to whom a legion of demons, or good or evil genii (*jinn*) were subordinated. The features of the deities however, were developed only slightly; just as little developed—or indeed not at all—was their plastic representation. Some of them, as in southern Arabia and in general in the whole Semitic area, bear the character of astral deities: such as Allàt, goddess of the sun (the *Alilat* of Herodotus) and al-Uzza (literally "the Most Glorious One") who originally was the personification of the planet Venus. A male lunar deity was lacking in contrast to the South Arabians. Other deities personified abstract ideas, like Manàt, the goddess of dire fate and death, and Wadd, the god of love. Others had an exclusively local importance, like some idols of the Meccan Kabah above which rose the venerated image of Hubal. The name and perhaps the very concept of Allah (the God), destined to take the place of all the other deities, does not appear to be unknown in this pagan pantheon, although he was still far from assuming the place that the future was reserving for him. According to some, at first he was probably naught else but an apposition to the names of the individual gods (for instance, to the Meccan Hubal) who then assumed his own character, supplanting the name to which he stood in apposition. But others, either because they are influenced by the theory of primitive monotheism, or because of the testimony provided by the ancient Arabs themselves, see therein a vague supreme God of fate, already standing out in the pagan era against the background of the minor but more concrete and nearer deities. In fact some of them were connected with him, and the aforementioned goddesses Allàt, Manàt and al-Uzza in Mecca were held to be Allah's daughters.

These and many other divine beings were worshipped by the Arabs in very simple idolatrous forms: rough stones and rocks, in accordance with a litholatry of which the Black

Stone of the Kabah is the most conspicuous example, and trees and springs. Numerous sacred places, some of a pan-Arab character and others of a purely local character, induced the cult of the faithful. Rather than by actual priests the cult was developed with the assistance of "guardians" (Sadanah) of sorcerors and seers along with animal sacrifices and libations, with mantic acts among which consultation by means of arrows was pre-eminent, and with pilgrimage rites. Most celebrated among the latter, and the only one destined to survive in Islam, was that of the sanctuary of Mecca with its pious stations and processions, and the throwing of apotropaic stones. The favor of the deity was entreated exclusively in terms of this life, since to the extent that we are able to perceive, this paganism was lacking in a clear and solid faith in the Beyond. An eloquent testimony in this regard is the poetic elegy of the dead, whose magnanimous gestures are celebrated, thus perpetuating their fame. But no account is taken of any other afterlife, nor is it expressly denied. When an embryonic concept of the world beyond the grave and of corresponding retribution does flash up in some poets, we cannot be certain as to whether this involves an isolated personal attitude, under foreign influences, or retouchings and interpolations effected during the Moslem era.

The possibility of the first hypothesis is confirmed by the fact that, alongside the prevailing polytheism, pre-Islamic Arabia was aware of both the great monotheistic religions of western Asia whose influence it underwent in various measure, so that without them the rise of Islam would be unthinkable. Judaism had penetrated the Peninsula for some time, probably after the last diaspora under Hadrian. Flourishing Jewish colonies had been established in Yathrib (the future Medina where indeed at a certain time the Jews must have enjoyed political predominance), as well as in a series of fertile oases of northern Hijaz (Wadi I-Qura, Khaibar, Fadak, Taima).

We have already seen how Jewish proselytism had already been victorious in southern Arabia to the point where it provoked Ethiopian intervention because of the persecution of Christians. It must, however, be made clear that this Judaism of Arabia contained little, or nothing at all, that was pure in an ethnic sense; rather it was a matter, at least in the sixth or seventh century—during which time we have a better knowledge of it—of Arab elements who were judaized religiously. Linguistically and culturally, however, they were not greatly distinguishable from the rest of their co-nationals. The poetry attributed to these Jews, for instance, hardly differs at all from the pagan poetry that has come down to us, beginning with the language. Rather, it is to be observed that, here as elsewhere, the Jewish or judaized nuclei preferred sedentary occupations, agriculture, artisan trades and commerce, and left the deserts to the Bedouins. The pure Bedouins despised them, as they despised all sedentaries in general, except when they turned to them for their products and their technical skills. All these Jewish communities of Arabia appear to us in the unfavorable light of Moslem polemics, which fought and persecuted them and ended up by expelling or exterminating them. An echo of the misery and grandeur of Israel reaches us from that remote tragedy.

Alongside Judaism stood the Christianity of Arabia, with features that ethnically and culturally were not very superior, in the Monophysite and Nestorian confessions which the two rival versions had actively spread there. The small Ghassanid and Lakhmid states on the border, outposts of the civilization on the edges of the desert, were also Christian, as we have seen. Various clearly Arab tribes, like the Tanùkh on the border of Mesopotamia, the Taghlib, the Kalb and the Hanifa, were also entirely or prevalently Christian. The south of Arabia also largely knew Christianity, sealed with the blood of the martyrs of Najràn. All these Christian communities of Arabia were a modest and superficial branch of the Christianity of the Orient: ignorant of theological profundities and subtleties, they reduced their faith to rites and symbols and external usages, to simple devotional acts and—if we are to believe Arab poets—to a small-scale wine trade. Gilded crucifixes, luminous icons, lamps from hermits' cells which brightened the darkness of night, goat-skins of good wine sold to avid Bedouins is all of ancient Christianity that struck the fancy of the poets (here, however, the aforementioned one-sidedness of their documentary value still holds). Above and below these externals, we must also postulate an influence of ideas, if not of dogmas, of ethical experiences and forms of Christian asceticism, upon a receptive minority of the surrounding pagan peoples. These were experiences and ideas, of which the aforementioned hints of eschatology and theodicy among some poets may well be the echoes, in competition, of course, with the parallel Jewish influence, and above all the singular phenomenon of the Hanifs.

In pre-Islamic Arabia the latter were isolated personages, but merited as a group a collective denomination. Unsatisfied with the crude native polytheism and equally alien to the acceptance of Jewish or Christian monotheism with all its dogmatic baggage, they remained faithful to the fundamental religious idea that monotheism expresses. Living apart and in a state of meditation, they sought the divine with a noble spiritual disquietude. Because of this presentiment and search, Islam rightfully considered them its precursors; naturally, however, once Islam arrived at a full consciousness of itself it absorbed or rejected them. And the Hanifs, whether they were para-Christians, para-Jews or para-Moslems, decided to enter or re-enter one of these faiths, or they persevered in their simple and bare deism. They disappeared when there was no more room in the Arab Peninsula for the worshippers of Allah without the recognition of the correlative Prophet.

But, we repeat, they were the leaven and a vital presage of Islam (odes are indeed attributed to some of them, like the poet Umayyah Ibn Abi s-Salt, which would give us a Koran *avant la lettre;* they are certainly a falsification, but a significant one), and their presence is perhaps the highest feature of religion in pre-Islamic Arabia.

IT is difficult to trace a line of development for the destinies of the nomad Arab world, in contrast to the settled kingdoms of South Arabia, and the small dynastic states on the northern border. If history is development and becoming, the desert has no history. The almost complete impossibility of chronologically ordering the dates of the tradition concerning its guerrilla wars and raids, and the thousand picturesque episodes of Bedouin life (often material for an epic rather than a chronicle) corresponds to a more substantial static state of that primitive society and its resistance to evolution. Occasionally there appeared on the surface some effort at overcoming the sterile anarchy which was the ordinance of desert life. Such was the attempt, the only one to our knowledge after the disappearance of the Lihyanite kingdom, to overcome tribal provincialism by giving place to a more ample regrouping under the hegemony of a single race; an attempt headed by the South Arabian tribe of the Kindah, one of whose families, between the end of the fifth and the beginning of the sixth century, succeeded in organizing a kind of confederation of the various tribes of central-eastern Arabia. But the ephemeral Kindite hegemony soon fell apart because of the prevalence of centrifugal forces. Only the echo of it remained in the poetry of the last scion of that ambitious race, the "errant king" Imru' l-Qays. Another milestone in the uniformity of Bedouin life was the resistance that a tribe on the northern border, the Bakr, offered to the king of Persia, defeating his troops in the battle of Dhu Qar, much celebrated in the annals of Arab pride but difficult to fix in the chronology (beginnings of the seventh century).

A glimmer of evolution naturally appeared in the inhabited centers. The pre-Moslem history of Yathrib, later to become Medina, was completely taken up by the disputes between the two tribes, the Aws and the Khazraj of southern origin. After having stripped the Jewish element, at one time dominant in the city, of its power, they wore themselves out for a long time in a fratricidal conflict, attested to as usual by the poetry no less than by antiquarian tradition (the "Day of Buàth" famous among the Medinese war annals, which ended with the victory of the Aws). This war-weariness was certainly not unrelated to Medina's invitation to Mohammed, in which his function of arbitrator and peacemaker was implicit. Finally the seeds of an evolution that could be pursued historically achieved a greater consistency in Mecca, which was certainly the largest urban center of all northern and central Arabia. Here, on the eve of the birth of the Prophet, the Quraysh clan held undisputed hegemony; they held political power, the most important posts, both social and sacred in character, which were connected with the pilgrimage, and finally the economic power, nourished by the caravan trade, the profits of which were in turn invested in it. This Quraysh hegemony was not very ancient. About a century before Mohammed (if the uncertain chronology fixed in five generations by the genealogists can be thus expressed) a member of the Quraysh, the semi-legendary but also semi-historical Qusayy, had conquered for his tribe the primacy which was first maintained in the sanctuary by the rival Khuzaah tribe. Thenceforward the Quraysh had practically administered that "merchant republic," as the Meccan state in the pre-Islamic era has been felicitously called. Given over entirely to its commerce, but no less piously devoted to its Kabah, filled with idols, and to the native traditions of which it was the center, Mecca constituted the heart of Arabia in the sixth century. And it jealously watched over its economic and religious primacy, without ever thinking of extending it into a political imperialism. A particular upsurge of patriotism was provoked by the famous episode of "the Elephant" in the year 570, which a later synchronism had coincide with the birth of the future Prophet. At that time an Ethiopian army under the command of the Ethiopian governor of Yemen, Abraha (let us recall that Axumite Ethiopia had set foot there in 525) moved against Mecca. But before reaching the city the army was decimated by an epidemic and forced to return. The episode later was echoed in a celebrated *sura* of the Koran, which attributes the defeat of the impious invader to providential intervention. Stripped of its supernatural features and of religious polemic, it has been considered by modern historical research as an Ethiopian attempt to assure the control of the important position of Mecca for the northward-moving traffic. And some scholars have also speculated that the expedition of "the Elephant" (so-called because of the presence of a pachyderm among the Ethiopian forces) was part of a more extensive plan, in alliance with Byzantium, to attack rival Persia from Arabia. The expedition failed, however, and in it Meccan patriotism saw a sign of the favor of its gods, while the monotheistic faith of Mohammed was to attribute the defeat entirely to the grace of Allah. Other episodes of the Prophet's youth are linked with the facts of the external and internal policy of his native city. But a summary consideration can omit it, limiting itself to noting that on the eve of Islam the most complex and advanced human aggregate of the Peninsula lived in the city of the Quraysh. The hour of the south Arab kingdoms, of Petra and Palmyra, had passed for some time in the history of Arabia. Now the future was being prepared there, in Hijaz.

THUS terminated the pagan prelude in the history of the Arabian people. Whoever compares it with what followed, which gave the Arabs a primary role on the stage of the world, and inspired high thoughts and high works, not only to an exceptional man emerged from their bosom, but to an entire élite which for several generations gathered and promoted his word, cannot but notice the leap that the destinies of this people assume here. The rhythm of its life, until then weak and dispersed, was about to find a unity, a propulsive center, a goal; and all this under the sign of religious faith, of a revolutionary penitence in contrast with the meager spiritual life led by the Arabs up to then. No romantic love for the primitive can make us fail to recognize that without Mohammed and Islam they would have probably remained vegetating for centuries in the desert, destroying themselves in the bloodletting of their internecine wars, looking at Byzantium, at Ctesiphon and even at Axum as distant beacons of civilization, completely out of their reach. Instead, a few decades later they were knocking on the portals of these states with a call that was at once peremptory and ineluctable.

With all that, several positive values assert themselves in the wretched life of the *Jahiliyyah*, even to the most sober historical judgment. We deliberately restrict its ambit to that Arab world of the north, nomadic to a great part, from which we see the new faith develop, thereby leaving the silent empires of Saba to their closed isolation. In the Arab ambience, no matter how primitive or semi-barbaric, man's struggle for survival has assumed a virile aspect, an awareness of the human condition—along with a pride in it—which cannot but impress us as striking. It was expressed in the Bedouin ideal of individual freedom and dignity, of hospitable generosity, of contempt for danger. And it was translated in the force and value of the word, rhymed in poetic meter or put into abundant prose, operating with efficacy in the councils of the tribe. It alone was capable of assuring immortality to the ephemeral individual by celebrating his magnanimous works. In short a breath of humanism, primitive and crude, but nevertheless unmistakable, pervaded Arab paganism in its higher manifestations. It is engraved in its poetry, which remained an unsurpassable model in the very centuries of Islam, in its epic traditions, in its incisive maxims and in its proverbs dense with a practical wisdom. If it was ignorant of a deep and evolved religious life and an advanced culture, the *Jahiliyyah* equally was ignorant of pietism, the mechanization of faith and of science, the narrow dogmatism in which Islam stiffened the life of the peoples who embraced it, and in part that of the Arab people itself. We say in part because something of the deepest Arab soul escaped its grasp, and maintained itself in the perilous freedom of the native desert. Not all Arabism can identify itself and recognize itself in Islam, to which nevertheless it owes its greatest affirmation in history.

2.

Mohammed and Islam

BETWEEN the second and third decade of the seventh century Mecca was the scene of an event that was to give a new course to the history of the Arab people. One man's individual, unrepeatable achievements asserted themselves into the destinies of his people; he transformed them, endowed them with a great potency and set them on the path to lofty destinies, perhaps beyond every expectation of the protagonist himself. Islam is a phenomenon that transcends the history of the Arabs, but which has its root and the generation of its irresistible initial expansion among them. Arabism and Islamism coincided for about two centuries, from the first half of the seventh century to the first half of the ninth.

The Islamic faith was pushed forward in western Asia and in the Mediterranean basin on the points of Bedouin lances, to the gallop of Arab horses. Later, this correlation between the Arabs and Islam was to break when the capacity for expansion and hegemony of a people was to reveal itself inadequate to the unexhausted expansive power of its faith. If Arabism was forever to remain Moslem almost in its totality, Islam was to continue its march among peoples along other paths and with other bearers of its message. Nevertheless, it too was to preserve some indelible mark of the Arab ambience in which it was born.

While recalling both the life and work of Mohammed, we shall not forget to consider both from the point of view of their dependence on the Arab world which brought them into being. Therefore we shall give particular emphasis to the link that bound the Prophet to his people, to the national element. Of late, this element in Mohammed, in which he fused the disparate influences and materials of his inspiration, has increasingly been accorded greater appraisal.

Afterwards, in a rapid evaluation of Islam, we shall underline precisely that which it has preserved as specifically Arabic, thereby justifying its consideration in the framework of this book, which is not a religious, but a political and national history of the Arabs.

The only certain source relating to the life of Mohammed is the Koran itself, followed immediately by the canonical biography (*Sira*) as it was formed in the beginnings of the second century of Islam. It found its classic expression in the *Life of the Prophet* by Ibn Ishàq (died ca. 767), which has come down to us in a somewhat reduced and annotated edition by Ibn Hishàm (died 834), and in extracts from the most ancient chroniclers like Tàbari (died 923). Other important sources are the "Book of Military Expeditions" (*Maghazi*) of the Prophet by al-Wàqidi (died 822), and the great biographical collection on his Companions (*Tabaqàt as-sahaba*) by Ibn Saad (died 899). In modern times radical criticism has inclined, perhaps excessively, to invalidate the historical worth of all these sources, judging them to be hagiographical combinations and deformations. A more tempered critical examination must always make use of them with vigilant caution and recognize, especially for the more remote period of Mohammed's life, that we know very little outside of that which is drawn directly from the Koran.

Strictly speaking, we do not know the very year of the Prophet's birth: the synchronism with the "Year of the Elephant," i.e., 570, can be accepted in an approximative way; indeed some scholars have sought to reduce it almost by a decade. Doubt has also been expressed, wrongly we think, regarding the name Mohammed itself (which etymologically means "the much praised one"), a name not unknown in pre-Moslem times. What is certain is his origin in the Quraysh clan of the Banu Hashim. Mohammed was the posthumous son of the merchant Abdallàh, esteemed but not rich, who died during a journey far from his native country, and of Aminah, who herself left the child an orphan when he was barely six years old. The boy grew up first under the care of his paternal grandfather Abd al-Mùttalib. Later he was entrusted to an uncle Abu Talib, father of that Ali who was to become one of his most faithful first companions, then his son-in-law and finally his fourth successor as Caliph. What is certain among the facts of the youthful life of Mohammed prior to his vocation, the broad purposes of which were effected between his thirtieth and fortieth year, are his marriage to the rich widow Khadijah, for whom he had also traveled and traded, and his contacts with Christian elements of the desert and, perhaps, of Syria, and with Hanifs. They have been embellished by tradition but contain a historical core of a highly probable character. All the varied elements of the religious life of Arabia, as we have outlined above—urban and Bedouin paganism, Christianity and initially Judaism to a minor degree, vague conceptions and monotheistic aspirations—found acceptance, elaboration and a reaction in the receptive spirit of this man. We know little about his crisis which erupted around 610, in the visions and in the "voices" of his holy retreat on Mount Hirà.

Of the two types of inspiration which tradition has bequeathed to us, the visual and the oral, it is quite difficult to determine which may have been the first and the one that prevailed in the initial phase. Later, he named the angel Gabriel as the celestial creature who appeared to him and, with irresistible force, imposed the monotheistic assertion contained in the most ancient koranic versicles; the same creature was considered as the normal means for transmitting the subsequent revelations. The fundamental concepts of this monotheistic assertion, in the first phase, were the repudiation of the native polytheism, in order to exalt the only Allah above and against every other divinity (some casual attempts at a compromise were quickly withdrawn and overcome), the imminent judgment with the inescapable final retribution of good and evil, praise of God the Creator and of His marvels, and the certain resurrection beyond the grave. All the more ancient koranic *suras* play upon these themes over and over again, and they reflect at one and the same time the nascent polemics and the struggle with a hostile ambience. In fact, the new preachment offended the native traditions and piety, sincerely felt in at least some Meccan circles. At the same time it also irked the elementary rationalism which found the concept of life after death repugnant, as well as the material, economic interests of that mercantilistic oligarchy which was naturally conservative. The notion that Mohammed's message was primarily social in character and aim, is a fantasy of the positivistic and Marxist historiography and its current obdurate practitioners. What is true, rather, is that the new theological and eschatological conception, like primitive Christianity, nourished itself on the discontent over the injustice of which the earth is full, and with its supra-mundane hopes it preferably attracted to itself those who had suffered most from this injustice. Mohammed's first followers were recruited above all among the humble, petty artisans and merchants, buyers, slaves—not without the cooperation of that which we shall call the Meccan middle class. But from the ruling class, from the Quraysh aristocracy came a resolute and gradually ever increasing rigid opposition. Then and later the Prophet, to be sure, tried to gain the latter to his cause with approaches that were hardly in keeping with an intransigent social reformer, but only the clear indication of his triumph, which occurred very much later, succeeded in disarming the aristocracy of its resistance. In those first years the resistance was dogged, although bloodless, consisting essentially of vexations, repulses and mockery, which at one time culminated in an attempt to place the innovator and his small community beyond the pale. The boycott was broken through the intervention of authoritative members of his own clan in which, though they were pagans, the inherited law of the solidarity of blood still spoke loudly: but the situation in Mecca at one moment seemed so untenable that it induced part of the small community to migrate beyond the Red Sea, to Ethiopia facing Arabia. The more or less authentic speech which tradition places in the mouth of those refugees in the presence of the Negus aptly summarizes, albeit with some polemical exaggeration, the import of the more ancient preachment of Mohammed: "O king, we were a barbarous people of idolaters, who committed shameful misdeeds, despised the ties of blood, violated the obligations of hospitality: a people among whom the stronger devoured the weaker. Such were we until God sent us an apostle from our very bosom, whose descent, veracity and continence are known to us: and he called us to God, to recognize Him alone and to worship Him, repudiating the stones and the idols which we and our forefathers worshipped in His stead. He has ordered us to be truthful, to render loyally the deposit confided to us, to respect the ties of blood and of hospitable protection, to abstain from illicit acts and from shedding blood; he has forbidden us to indulge in any turpitude and deceit, to devour the goods of the orphan and to calumnify honest women, he has commanded us to worship

God, and to place nothing beside Him, to observe canonical prayer, the legal alms, the fast. We have believed in him, we have followed him in the precepts which he has brought to us from God; hence our people have become hostile to us, and have persecuted us . . ."

In comparison with many other methods of persecution, suffered and later even practiced by a new faith on the march, those employed by the Quraysh towards young Islam may seem mild enough: this does not remove the fact that the Prophet certainly lived through many bitter and anxiety-ridden hours during that vigil. It dragged on for about a decade and terminated, as is known, with the decisive act of his career; he abandoned the city of his birth with all his followers in order to establish himself and his community in Medina. This "hegira" of September 622 marks the beginning of a new era not only in the Moslem calendar, but in the personal history of Mohammed, and in that of Arabia and of Islam.

THE hegira was not a sudden brain storm but a decision which had ripened by means of soundings and negotiations exchanged between Mohammed and the Medinese which went on for at least two years. In fact the first convention, leaving out still earlier contacts, of al-Àqaba (a hill near Mecca) goes back two years before. Here twelve Medinese, in the presence of the Prophet, took the oath, the so-called "act of homage of the women": a pledge, that is, of monotheistic faith, of ethical duties in the Moslem sense, and of obedience which did not yet involve obligations of war. A year later in the same place there followed "the act of homage of war" which a group of seventy Medinese swore in the hands of Mohammed, thereby recognizing him as their religious and military leader, and pledging themselves to fight at his side up to the shedding of blood. The hegira of the Islamic community from Mecca was carried out bit by bit, and it culminated with the departure of the Prophet himself.

Mohammed arrived in Medina with actual powers and a prestige still far removed from those he was to have about a year after his sojourn there. The Arab-Jewish population was not exactly at his feet from the very first moment, and it is proof of the Prophet's political ability that he knew how to become master of the situation. Besides the Aws and the Khazraj who had summoned him and who certainly must not have all been for him from the first moment, there were in Medina three Jewish tribes, who though no longer enjoying hegemony had not yet been degraded to the status of helots. Soon, relations with them became difficult. A short time after his arrival the Prophet indeed tried to improve such relations, not only with the Jews but among all the various parts of the community (*Muhajirùn* or Meccan Emigrants, his fellow citizens, *Ansàr* or Supporters, i.e. Medinese Moslems, residual pagans, Jews) with the "Medinese Constitution" which is at once a precious historical and juridical document, and the most ancient authentic sample of Arab prose that has come down to us besides the Koran. But it was not long before relations with the Jewish element and the latent Medinese opposition worsened: the Prophet moved towards the Jews expecting to find among them persons prepared to acknowledge the value of his monotheistic message. Instead he ran into their closed and ironical exclusivism, into the cavilling hostility of their rabbis. They were joined by those whom he labeled as "hypocrites" (*Munafiqùn*), lukewarm laggers who by not coming forth into an open struggle undermined the dedication and the solidarity of the believers with their mute defeatism. The situation was difficult and of an emergency character in the overpopulated city and in the face of hostile

Mecca: recourse to the ancient Arab weapon of the raid became a vital necessity.

The first blood was shed in a none too honorable episode—during the truce of the sacred month, which the Prophet allowed to be violated. Later he both condemned and justified the violation by ambiguous koranic versicles. But the baptism of fire of young Islam took place one year and a half after the hegira, in March 624, at the battle of Badr. Here the Moslems, led by Mohammed collided with the Meccans, who had hastily rushed out of the city in order to lend assistance to a caravan that Mohammed had tried to attack. This minor clash had major consequences. For the first time Arabs fought against Arabs of their own blood but of different faith. The annals of militant Islam were inaugurated. Here fell its first martyrs. The manner of the division of booty was also revealed for the first time by this victory. In Medina the Jews very soon were to feel the counter-blow, and one of the three tribes was expelled from the city. The Meccans took their revenge a year later in a new clash which could have meant the annihilation of Mohammed; instead it was only a trial of adversity which the Prophet knew how to combat, and easily overcame with an admirable pliability and a persuasive efficiency. The Meccans were guided by an able military chieftain, Khalid ibn al-Walìd, who in the future was to become the "Sword of Allah." They attacked the flank of the Moslems, who were intent upon the booty after the clash, hurling them back and scattering them. Mohammed himself was slightly wounded, but the pagans did not exploit their victory and the believers were able to re-enter Medina undisturbed. This time, too, the second tribe of Jews had to bear the costs of the event, and in a short time it also was compelled to leave the city. The offensive of the Meccans, now engaged in open warfare with the exile, undertook its greatest effort in 627, a memorable date because Bedouin elements, above all of the Ghatafàn, joined the city's contingents: the "Confederates," as the Koran calls them. From a local quarrel the dispute between the two cities of Hijaz began to assume a Hijazan if not a pan-Arabic importance; the nomadic world began to participate in it, and to take sides as its more or less immediate interests counselled. The Moslem propaganda was now acting upon the Bedouins with alternate results of conversions, repudiations and apostasies, the balance tilting in favor of the Prophet as, little by little, he asserted himself in Medina. The Meccans now directly put the enemy's nest under siege with all the urban and Bedouin forces they could muster. But it was a very weak blockade lasting only a few weeks, during which a rudimentary moat was dug by the Medinese. It was lifted after a few skirmishes without obtaining anything. Rather, it served Mohammed much more, enabling him to complete his liquidation of the Jewish element of Medina: during the siege, the Banu Qurayzah, the last remaining of the original three tribes, had had some contacts with the Quraysh without, however, daring to open direct hostilities against the Moslems. This potential fifth column now had to be exterminated. After the besiegers retired, the Banu Qurayzah were in turn besieged by the Prophet in their quarter, forced to surrender, and subjected to the judgment of a Medinese arbitrator (of the tribe of the Aws their ancient ally, but fanatically dedicated to the Prophet, who, moreover was dying as the result of wounds received during the siege, and therefore already in sight of the joys of paradise . . .). He handed down a death sentence, as Mohammed desired, and the massacre of several hundreds of men and the reduction to slavery of women and children, crowned the victory of Islam over the vain efforts of its enemies.

From a moral point of view the blood-bath of the Banu Qurayzah and the individual murders of single adversaries, which preceded and followed that massacre, constitutes the most painful episode of Mohammed's career. But, alongside these stains, which are such only in accordance with an ethics that was neither of his people nor of his time, it would be wholly unjust to leave in the shade the work of long duration with which, meanwhile, he went about constructing his religious law and his state. The simple Moslem theology was already completely formulated in the Meccan period. Now it was a question of regulating the relations between what was recognized as divine and human, the position of the chosen Apostle of God among men, and the duties of the latter towards Allah and his Prophet. From the beginning Mohammed had felt himself as an Arab messenger to his people of those same substantial truths which other Prophets before him (Jesus was the last of the series and his immediate predecessor and precursor) had been commanded by God to reveal to their people. This cyclical conception of the prophetic dignity permitted him to present himself not as the destroyer but the perfector of the other religious laws, such as Judaism and Christianity, from which he again took up its basic monotheism, restoring it, as he maintained, to its original purity. Thereby the Arab Prophet completed the work initiated by his predecessors going as far back as the biblical Abraham, the common ancestor of Israel and Ishmael, i.e. of the Jews and the Arabs themselves. But in the more mature conception of Mohammed, the native Peninsula came to assume an ever-increasing central and preponderant function. Abraham himself, the first venerated monotheist, was supposed to have founded the cult of the Meccan Kabah, later profaned through the idols. Therefore the faces and hearts of the believers in prayer should turn to the Kabah, which was now to be reconsecrated to the cult of the only Allah. The institution of such a new *qibla* or direction of the prayer in a national sense, which already in the second year of the hegira replaced the original direction of Jerusalem, was the most brilliant and revolutionary act accomplished by Mohammed in the elaboration of his message. It was integrated with the annexation of the pagan pilgrimage to Mecca, which followed soon thereafter, with which act the Prophet incorporated the principal pan-Arab rite of the pagan era into his faith. Hence from that moment on there was no longer a struggle of the dissident, of the rebel innovator against the city of his birth. Instead there was the filial longing of the Reformer and Purifier to liberate the fatherland from the filth of idolatry, to restore to it its sacred function as a religious and social center, as a common destination of pilgrimages for all the sons of Ishmael. Islamist scholarship has correctly seen in this conception the milestone of consolidated Islam, and along with it the key of its sweeping success after it had overcome the crises of the Medinese siege.

THE stages of this success are marked between 627, the fifth year of the hegira, the year "of the Confederates" or "of the Ditch" (the defensive moat dug at Medina), and the beginning of 630, the eighth year of the hegira when Mohammed and his victorious faith made a triumphal re-entry into Mecca. In 628 he attempted to force the situation which was still not yet ripe, by moving with too few forces against his city. But the feverish preparations which the Meccans made for resistance induced him to enter into negotiations which culminated with the compromise of Hudaybiyah, a notable example of his political pliability and also of the ascendancy that he had now acquired among his followers. In fact the Prophet maintained a singularly conciliatory and deferential attitude towards the emissary of the Meccans; he accepted formulations drawn up by protocol which were almost humiliating, and conditions which were all else but that of a conqueror:

namely, to postpone a brief pious pilgrimage to Mecca until the following year, not to receive any further deserters and to pledge himself to a ten year truce. This apparent capitulation strongly disturbed the Prophet's closest companions, above all Omar, the future second Caliph and Mohammed's alter ego throughout the Medina decade. But the Prophet, blending gentleness with authority, knew how to reaffirm his prestige; indeed even to increase it a little later after an expedition against the Jews of Khaybar, who even this time were the scapegoats at every good or bad stage of his career.

The pilgrimage to Mecca, which had been negotiated at Hudaybiyah, took place in the following year without incident. Then, the situation rapidly took a precipitate turn. By now most of the most valiant and influential Quraysh—the whole general staff of young Islam—had gone over to Mohammed's side: from the most faithful companions of the first hour, Ali, Abu Bakr, Omar, to the future great captains of the conquests, Khalid ibn al-Walìd, Amr ibn al-As, Saad ibn Abi Waqqàs. The Omayyad Abu Sufyàn ibn Harb, who had conducted the struggle against the Prophet remained in Mecca— up to then irreducible—as the moral, if not constitutional, head of the pagan mercantile republic. And even Abu Sufyàn capitulated (according to some he had already capitulated with previous secret agreements) when in January of 630 Mohammed, breaking the pledges made (a pretext was soon found to denounce the treaty of Hudaybiyah), moved in force against his natal city. It was little more than a military parade: at the eleventh hour Abu Sufyàn also went over to the victor's side, all resistance crumbled, and the Prophet, at the head of an enthusiastic army of emigrants, supporters and Bedouins, found himself the master of his city from which he had furtively departed seven years before. Moslem tradition portrays the scene with epic simplicity. Mounted on a camel Mohammed advanced towards the Kabah, which he ordered to be opened and cleared of the idolatrous clutter, and pronounced solemn words which declared dissolved every bond to the pagan era and inaugurated the new era of Allah. Moreover, with a most notable moderation in victory, sentences against his enemies were limited to a very few serious cases, forgiving even some who had cruelly offended him in his affections and prestige. In contrast to the pitiless harshness of which he showed himself capable in struggle, the hour of triumph saw him magnanimous, either because this responded to a *bone fide* gentleness of his spirit, or because it was a sapient political calculation which turned out to be fully justified.

Destiny reserved him two years of life yet after the conquest of Mecca which brought the duel with his tiny native land to an end. And in the space of two years his horizon widened to include all Hijaz, all Arabia, and even areas beyond the borders of the Peninsula. The Bedouins until then had looked upon the conflict between the two cities with divided feelings, in part feeling repugnance against novelty that threatened to subvert so many aspects of the customs of the country, in part subjugated by the superior personality of the Prophet; they were flattered by his liberalities, intimidated by his threats, and here and there affected in their intimate being by his simple and austere word. Success, a decisive element, in the end induced almost all of them to rally to his side, as the political leader of Arabia if not always as the Prophet and religious legislator. The tribes of the desert had been bound to him by a series of embassies and of treaties, before and after his entrance in Mecca. The elements that remained hostile, who rallied around the pagan Hawazin, were routed at the battle of Hunayn, shortly after the conquest of Mecca. The murder here of the old knightly sheikh Duraid ibn as-Simmah was almost the symbol of the death blow to Arab paganism.

But the victorious Prophet already looked further than cen-

tral and southern Arabia (Yemen also had received his cate-
chists and representatives). Before entering Mecca, he had
sent a body of the faithful towards the north, to the border
with Byzantium in Transjordania. And the bloody defeat
which befell them at Muta, in that venturesome expedition,
seemed to spur him to a new punitive expedition which he
himself led, in the year 9 (631), towards the borders of Syria,
and which was brought to a halt at Tabùk by the heat and a
crisis of fatigue and discouragement among his faithful. Destiny did not allow the Prophet to see Islam's victory over the
Rum. But in the same year 9 he attended to the definite formulation of the obligation of the faithful to make war on the
infidels, and to keep them away from the holy places of
Arabia. The permanent exclusion of non-Moslems from the
sacred territory of Mecca and Medina is commanded in versicles of the koranic *sura*, which was then emanated, relative
to it. This is also true of the concept of the religious *bellum
perpetuum* of Islam against pagans and "People of the Book,"
i.e. Jews and Christians, among whom later the Zoroastrians
were included. These "People of the Book" were admitted to
the bosom of the Moslem community as tolerated tributaries,
but Islam's theoretical vow to wage war against their states
remained firm. Mohammed in his last years is supposed to have
addressed messages to the heads of these infidel states, the
emperor of Byzantium, the king of Persia and the Negus of
Ethiopia, inviting them to embrace Islam. But we may legiti-
mately doubt the authenticity of these messages, at least as
they have been handed down by tradition. It is certain that
the universalism of his doctrine, doubtlessly at first limited to
his city and then to his country, must have appeared more or
less explicitly in the consciousness of the Prophet, little by
little, as an unexpected success assisted the propagation of the
faith proclaimed by him. But in the only certain document

regarding him that remains, the Koran, this evolution did not find formulations of a character so peremptory that would exclude every doubt on this score.

From Medina, where he had returned after his Meccan triumph, he reappeared once more in his natal city in the tenth year of the hegira (the first months of 632) in order to personally conduct the Moslem pilgrimage there; the year before he had been represented by the faithful Abu Bakr. This was the "Pilgrimage of Farewell," where, with the solemn words of the last revelation, the Prophet declared his mission accomplished, and proclaimed that the grace of Allah had now entirely descended on his people with Islam. Thereafter he retired once more to faithful Medina, among his *Ansàr* or Supporters, towards whom he maintained to the last the pledge of unbreakable solidarity assumed in the distant days of al-Àqaba. One of his last acts that has been passed on to us is the visit to the Medinese cemetery and his sermon over the tombs of his dead companions, "Greetings," he said, "O people of the tombs! Blessed are you for this state, in respect to that of the living. Behold, the tempests advance like shreds of dark night, one following upon the heels of the other, one worse than the other . . ." The presentiment of the imminent end courses through these, as in all the last words and acts of Mohammed: and the end came after a brief illness, on June 8, 632, as he nestled his head in the lap of his favorite wife Aishah. He did not or he could not make a political testament and he did not designate the one most worthy to succeed him. He expired invoking "the high Companion of Paradise," the same one who had appeared to him perhaps twenty years before in the solitudes of Mount Hirà.

THE medieval occident saw in Mohammed the dragon who was lacerating the bosom of the universal Church, which hardly three centuries before had emerged victorious over paganism. That he too, the Prophet of Arabia, had fought his battle against the paganism of his native land could not diminish the rancor against the founder of a faith which in a few decades was to cause Christianity to lose vital positions in Asia and in Africa. Hence the famous accusations of imposture, base cupidity and hypocrisy that were hurled at Mohammed during the Christian Middle Ages. For the followers of his faith, on the other hand, he was and is the chosen of God, the seal of the Prophets, the model of every virtue. A man, as he consistently affirmed himself to be, he was elevated to the superhuman sphere only by esoteric speculations and popular superstitions. Yet he was considered, just as he wished, a man of exception (not in the obvious historical sense, but in a religious and juridical one) with special prerogatives because of his most special contact with the divine. A consideration of the position of Mohammed in the faith of his community would lead us astray from the argument of this book, no less than would an analysis and evaluation of his faith itself, Islam, insofar as it is a universalist religion and civilization. What matters to us here is to fix the character of the Prophet as a son of his people, and to discern how much he brought of what is specifically Arabic to its construction, together with evident foreign influences. These problems quite rightfully enter into even a most summary history of the Arabs, of their function and contribution to the history of civilization.

Like every great reformer and innovator, Mohammed was strongly rooted in the race and in the tradition from which he emerged, at the same time surpassing it with his genius. We must not forget that his origins were in the urban Arab ambience which explains certain of his characteristics, and certain divergences from the Bedouin mentality. The practicality and concrete realism of the "mercantile Republic," his country, are reflected in the very conception of the relations of God with man, which are those of master and servant, but also those of a "buyer" to a "seller" of the soul in a transaction in which Allah proposes and man may or may not accept a good business deal. It has been noted that the images and terminology of trade have left their impress on a good part of the Koran, its ethics and theodicy. The most exalted eschatological vision, the most transcendent representations of the divinity are translated into the most concrete images (the famous Koranic anthropomorphisms), corresponding to the slight capacity for abstraction of the Prophet and of his audience: a primitiveness and concreteness which was entirely Arabic, and urban Arabic to boot. On the other hand it cannot even be said that the old monotheistic concept which arose on his crude translations was an absolute novelty for the age and times of Mohammed—as we have seen—prepared as they had been by Judaism and Christianity, and by the phenomenon of the Hanifs. What was uniquely Mohammed's was the shattering profundity of that revelation and the heroic will to broaden it from an individual experience into a message for the multitudes, into an active, ever-present norm of life.

The whole ancient history, or that which is believed to be such, of his nation was relived by him in the light of his discovery or rediscovery of the only God (in Arabic *tawhìd*). Allah was not only the creator and Lord of the universe, but the one who had already addressed himself to the Arab people with messages that had gone unheeded, even before he sent them the last Prophet. The Arab populations of Ad and Thamùd, who had despised the warnings of previous envoys, had experienced Allah's wrath and therefore had incurred the supreme punishment. In fact the history of the Prophecy, according to Mohammed, ran along a double line, Hebraic and Arab, in order to unite in the common progenitor Abraham and Mohammed himself. And just as God had already spoken to the unbelieving ancestors of the desert, so had He manifested his mercy to the Meccan forefathers by letting the most venerated sanctuary rise among them—through the work of Abraham (which later was profaned by idolatry), by promoting their welfare with the two annual seasonal caravans, and by diverting Abraha's impious attack from Mecca. Finally the last seal of His benevolence was his sending of the Arab Prophet, of an Arabic Koran to His people, foretold by the previous envoys, indeed by a divine compact and convention of all the Prophets in heaven. The *gesta Dei per Arabes* which were to be sanctioned by subsequent history were prepared by a clearly arabo-centric view of the relation of God to the world. On the other hand, to this solidarity of Mohammed with his people, felt if not explicitly theorized as a chosen people, and stimulated to accept its particular honor and the divine invitation by adherence to Islam, stood opposed not only the obvious anti-idolatry polemic of the Prophet, but his firm ethical and intellectual repudiation of the pagan mentality which created a rupture between the new history and the ancient Jahiliyyah. Pagan pride and individualism are condemned no less than its idolatrous cults; poetry, the greatest expression of its spirituality, is devalued and distanced from the new inimitable masterpiece as the Moslems consider the sacred Book, even in terms of its expressive and formal aspect. Mohammed was denied the gift of poetry, at least that type of poetry which we have seen rise to canonic value and forms in the pagan era. The attributes of poet fastened on him in Mecca by adversaries made Mohammed indignant no less than that which accused him of being an obsessed teller of unlikely tales and a visionary. With that he expressed his repugnance against a form of spiritual life profoundly rooted in his people, which even Islam could not eradicate. That sense of individual worth, genealogical pride, poetry, all that which we have called rudimentary Arab humanism, summed up in the pagan term *muruwwah,* was cast aside, as a pagan residue to be extirpated, by him and after him in favor of the new religious value of the *din*, incarnated in Islam. The entire subsequent spiritual history of Arabism was to reflect something of this contrast between a non-extinct pre-Islamic element, ingrained in the race, and the more mature fruit of the religious experience of the Prophet, relived and deepened by the following generations.

But undoubtedly it would be anti-historical to exaggerate and intensify this contrast. To admit, this notwithstanding, a substantive consonance of the Prophet with the spirit of his people, and to discern therein a trace of the composite edifice of Islam, is a thesis rightfully propounded by modern scholarship and originally developed by the Italian scholar Michelangelo Guidi. While at first the tendency was to resolve Islam almost wholly into its dogmatic and cultural elements of foreign origin (the Hebraic-Christian monotheism, the eschatology and demonology and more recently the very form of the revelation, which has been compared to the Syrian hymnology and homiletics), Guidi and others have placed the emphasis on the compromise between such undeniable foreign influences and the national tradition, which was realized in the mind and work of Mohammed. The genius of compromise, which assisted him in so many difficulties of his stormy career, seems in fact to have been one of the characteristic traits of that complex personality. It permitted him to solidarize with his people in the very act of proposing to them the most radical religious intellectual and moral metanoia; and to "arabize" in depth (even at the price of historical falsehoods, from which arose a new history) conceptions and institutions of non-Arab origin, figures of history or of the Semitic religious myth which had so far been entirely alien to the children of Ishmael. He infused sacred Hebrew and Arab history with the violence and arbitrariness of his genius. The compromise was realized with such a profound persuasive efficacy that it gave the illusion of something entirely new, original and irreplaceable. There was no compromise on one point alone, nor could there be any without destroying the value of that message at its base: the intransigent affirmation of divine unity, affirmed with a rigor that charged Christianity with polytheism and regarded itself more monotheistic than Judaism. The greatness of the religious and political genius of Mohammed, the secret of his soul which remained at once Arab and universal, lies in compromise down the whole line, save for that fundamental exception.

In its turn Islam, insofar as it is a creation detached from the person of the Founder and developing its own life down through the centuries, has preserved its tenacious Arab background even when it became a universalistic religion, to a measure incomparably greater than Christianity has preserved the Jewish ambience from which it emerged. Even after they declined from their ephemeral hegemony, the Arabs retained the glory of having provided the raw material for the new faith, the cradle and tomb of the law-giving Prophet, and the language of his revelation. The latter in substance is also wholly impregnated with Arab elements, and conditioned by the Arabic life of that seventh century. It is crammed with allusions to, and echoes of, contingent factors which find their explanation only in the Arab history and chronicles of that time. To this day the nomenclature, the religious and juridical terminology of the whole Islamic world has remained Arab. And the Moslem generations, even those ethnically most distant and foreign, still maintain an ideal and material contact with Arabism, of the past and present (consider the continuing immersion into Arabism constituted by the pilgrimage), which only the dissolution of the Islamic faith itself will be able to bring to a halt. Moslem universalism was never able to dispense with these ties which link the religion of Mohammed to his country and his people.

3.

The Caliphate and the Conquests

FOR a short time the disappearance of Mohammed plunged the Medinese community, which continued to form the directing nucleus of young Islam, into a crisis. It was necessary to provide a successor who, without being able to inherit the untransmittable religious prerogatives of the Prophet, would be his continuator as the political head of the society of believers: the vital organism which Mohammed had formed under the sign of the Islamic faith should not die with him. After stormy hours due to competing individuals, ambitions and tendencies (the Ansàr Medinese presented their candidate, while another candidacy was already that of Ali, the cousin and son-in-law of the Prophet), Omar's energetic intervention prevailed, supported by Abu Bakr and by the other authoritative "Companion" Abu Ubaidah. At the tumultuous council held in the headquarters of the Banu Sàidah in Medina, Omar, almost as a surprise, imposed Abu Bakr as *Khalifat Rasùl Allàh,* Vicar or Lieutenant or Successor of the Envoy of God. Like so many events and institutions, the Caliphate was born of an improvisation.

With the election of Abu Bakr the principle was established that the Caliphate or Imamate (Imàm in this case is a synonym of Caliph) had to remain in the Meccan clan of the Quraysh from which Mohammed came. But at the same time the elective character of the post was sanctioned, as that of the *sayyid* or chief of the tribe had been in the pagan society, by rejecting the legitimist claims of the family of the Prophet (*Ahl al-Bait*), personified by Ali. The double principle, of the "Imams of the Quraysh" and of their at least formal election, was always observed in the institution, throughout all its history, in the bosom of orthodox Islamism. And when the Ottoman Sultans many centuries later—the Caliphate being already extinct—tried to resuscitate it and arrogate the dignity to themselves, the rule that it could not leave the Arab tribe of the Prophet always invalidated their claim on the basis of strict Moslem law.

With Abu Bakr, one of the oldest and most faithful Meccan "Companions" of the Prophet rose to the leadership of the Moslem community. He was also related to Mohammed, being the father of his favorite bride Aishah (Mohammed's first wife Khadijah had died before the hegira). Abu Bakr was a man of balance, honesty and loyalty, as indicated by the epithet *as-Siddìq* ("The Veracious") which tradition has bestowed upon him. Though mild in spirit, he was inflexible in keeping custody over the precious legacy that had been entrusted to him. This was seen in the manner with which he attended to the first task that history imposed upon him, namely to defend the unity of Islam and of the Medinese state from the dangerous secessionist movement of the tribes of Arabia, the so-called *riddah*. In fact, upon the death of the Prophet, many Bedouin tribes refused further obedience and tribute to Medina, turning away from the faith of Islam which they had but recently accepted, according to the version of Moslem historiography. Or, rather, with the disappearance of Mohammed they considered themselves as released from a purely political and personal bond of subjection to him, as modern criticism interprets it. This interpretation, essentially correct, cannot ignore, however, the competing religious movements

that sprang up in Arabia in these years, following the successful example of Mohammed, indeed sometimes contemporane-
ously with and independently of him.

"Prophets" who failed rose here and there among the Bedouins. As is to be expected, Islamic tradition has for them
only scornful epithets, descriptions of scandals and abomina-
tions, the fate commonly reserved to the vanquished. Yet the
traits of one of them at least, "Musàilimah" of the Banu Hanifah, were not all contemptible and have been transmitted to
us by his very enemies. They reveal an ethical and ascetic tem-
per, influenced by Christianity even more than Mohammed
himself. Fragments of his revelation, composed like the Koran
in rhymed prose, rich in images and oaths, and some allusions
found in the oldest pagan polemic against Islam have even
induced the supposition that rather than an imitator of the
Meccan prophet, Musàilimah might have been an inspiring
model instead, in a way concerning which we are entirely in
the dark. Now they are all vain conjectures because victorious
Islam has erased every trace of these unfortunate rivals or
epigoni of Mohammed, relegating their memory to infamy.

Medina acted with fire and sword against them and also
against secessions inspired purely by political and fiscal motives. Abu Bakr sent Khalid ibn al-Walìd to put down the
revolt of the *riddah*. Khalid had been the pagan victor at the
battle of Uhud, but upon coming over to Islam's side later,
he was to become one of the most illustrious military chiefs in
the age of the conquests. Khalid separately defeated the Asad
and Ghatafàn with their prophet Tulàihah, then the Tamìm,
whose valorous chief Malik ibn Nuwairah he killed after the
surrender, and finally the Hanifah following Musàilimah. The
latter, who for some time had entered into a politico-religious
alliance and, it seems also a conjugal one with Sajàh, the
"prophetess" of the Tamìm, in the end fell with all his fol-

lowers at the bloody battle of Aqrabà in the Yamamah (central-eastern Arabia). This, in 633, sealed the end of the secessionist movement of Arabia. The age of the *hanifs*, of solitary
thinkers, of religions anterior to and in competition with Islam
was now forever finished (Christians and Jews were totally expelled shortly thereafter). The faith of Mohammed, even only
superficially accepted and practiced by the Bedouins, now
was to install itself in his native country with no rivals. After
thus bloodily suppressing the secessionism of the desert, all
Arab forces were now available for the greatest adventure.
They were to go over and beyond the borders, towards which
the Prophet had already pointed in his last years. There they
were to bring his word together with the hegemony of his
people. The grandiose phenomenon of the Arab conquests
which placed this people in contact with the higher civilization of the Mediterranean and western Asia, has engendered
the marvel of historians and sociologists due to the dispro-
portion between the means employed and the results achieved
in so short a time. Small armies of Bedouins (from time to
time no more than ten thousand men), poorly armed, devoid
of any ancient military traditions and of advanced methods of
assault and siege, in a few years routed the armies of two great
powers like the Byzantine and the Sassanid Empires, wresting
rich provinces from the former and destroying the latter to
its very foundations. They spread out hundreds and thou-
sands of miles from their homeland and succeeded in founding
a unitary state. The fact that this state managed to endure for
more than a century, before falling apart under the weight of
its very expanse, is a marvel in itself. The secret of such a
tremendous irresistible force has for long been seen in the religious enthusiasm which Mohammed must have kindled in his
co-nationals. According to this view, the formula of the Moslem faith *la ilàh illa llah, Muhammad rasùl Allah* ("there is no

other God but Allah, Mohammed is the Envoy of Allah") had been the "open Sesame" that swung the disconnected portals of those empires wide open, and let loose the multiplication of the virginal energies of the Arabs. The historiography of about a half century ago (Caetani, Becker) opposed an economic and social thesis to this "religious" one. The Arabs, only haphazardly and superficially united by Islam, in reality were supposed to have swarmed out of their Peninsula under the irresistible need for new homes, new sources of sustenance and wealth, in the face of the progressive impoverishment of Arabia, which had gradually become arid in contrast to the very different climatic conditions of the prehistoric age. Both these theses, in their restrictive character, seem to neglect a part of reality. In truth religious enthusiasm or fanaticism was not the sole motivation of the Arab expansion, the last of the great Semitic migrational waves that started out in a documentable historical era from the Peninsula. Arab historiography itself already points to the presence of more material motives, albeit obliquely through observations that are imputed to enemies. But even giving the proper weight to the latter (without, however, accepting the very dubious theory of the desiccation of Arabia in a documentable historical age), we cannot underrate the importance of the ideal motive as positivistic historiography was wont to do, relegating it from a dominant to an accessory cause, to a mere pretext and semblance. For many of those first Arab generations Islam was a veritable profound revolution, a total remolding of life, a sublimation of all their physical and moral energies for a common cause with a supra-worldly aim. It may not have been such for Khalid or Amr ibn al-As or Abu Sufyàn and other political and military chiefs of the conquests who were of more frigid temperament. But it certainly was such for an Abu Bakr, for an Omar, for a great part of the Arab élite who listened to the message of the Prophet in his own living voice, who worshipfully preserved the image they had of him, and who in their Arab faith felt the divine grace at last descend upon the poor people with its call to new lofty destinies. Areligious or irreligious nationalism is something wholly modern. In the seventh century A.D. the Arabs were invested, or more exactly, impregnated with a credo which established ideals higher than those instinctive ones of wealth and plunder. They were, however, set along a path that also managed to gratify such instincts. And while the latter certainly must have prevailed among the more primitive Bedouins, a higher ethical consciousness enkindled by Islam must have animated the ruling class in the age of the conquests. This ethical consciousness, to be sure, permitted them to regard the infidel enemy with aversion and contempt, but in the name of something superior to the naked, crude spirit of oppression. Whether mechanistic historiography, oriented towards a crude economic and class-minded view, likes it or not, this "something" had been infused by Mohammed in the so humanly fragile spirit of his people. And we can recognize in it a vital function in the psychology of the great Arab victories, of the disordered and marvelous epic of their conquests. In order to explain the latter, next to the strength of the victors, it is certainly necessary to account also for the weakness of the vanquished: the ethnic and religious heterogeneity of the conquered provinces with respect to their centers (monophysitic Egypt and Syria with respect to Byzantium, Mesopotamia with respect to Persia), the economic and fiscal oppression practiced by them on alien peoples or on the depressed classes, and, for Persia in particular, the political and social decadence into which the Sassanid state had fallen for several decades. It was now reduced to a shadow of the empire which at one time had resisted both Byzantium and Rome. Nevertheless, after adding

up these and other addenda, something is still lacking from
the sum, the final result. This something cannot be sought for,
save in a religious consideration of history.

THE beginnings of the conquests were all else but spectacular, and can hardly be distinguished from simple frontier raids.
If governmental initiative, that is, the express mandate of the
Caliph, can be recognized for the three Arab columns which
in 633 penetrated into Palestine and Transjordania, it seemed
to be entirely lacking for the first contemporaneous operations
in Mesopotamia. Here the local chief of the Banu Shaibàn
Arabs, al-Muthanna ibn Hàrithah, seems on his own initiative
to have attacked Hirah, the ancient residence of the Lakhmids
of the Euphrates. Here, after that bufferstate had already
been extinct for about a decade, direct Persian domination had
ensued. Hirah surrendered when Muthanna was joined by
Khalid ibn al-Walìd, a veteran of the repression of the *riddah*.
For a short time the latter directed the operations that developed on the Euphrates from that first conquest. But in 634,
on the orders of the Caliph, he handed over the command of
Mesopotamia to Muthanna, and in a memorable march across
the desert he entered Syria on the flank of the Byzantines, who
were engaged in a confrontation with the Arab invasion from
Palestine.

Here a series of lightning-like successes (the battles of
Ajnadain, Baisàn, Fihl) very quickly placed all Palestine and
Syria into the hands of the Arabs. Damascus capitulated in
635, at the very moment when the besiegers were taking it by
assault. Khalid concentrated the direction of the operations,
in which Yazìd ibn Abi Sufyàn, Amr ibn al-As and Abu
Ubaidah had distinguished themselves, in his own hands. And
in August 636, in a decisive battle on the Yarmùk (a tributary

of the Jordan, south of Lake Tiberias), he faced the counter-offensive mounted in force by the emperor Heraclius. The memorable day, which ended with a splendid Moslem victory, gave the Arabs the definitive possession of Syria. Damascus, which had been evacuated, was re-occupied, Jerusalem surrendered in 638, and Caesarea, the last remaining Byzantine stronghold, in 640.

Men succeeded one another. It was no longer the Caliph Abu Bakr who came to inspect the conquests of Syria. Instead this was attended to by his successor Omar, who came from Medina in 637. He replaced Khalid with Abu Ubaidah, but this same valiant "Companion" to whom the Caliphate might have belonged one day, was soon carried away by the plague of Emmaus. The work having been accomplished, the arabization and islamization of Syria remained a permanent acquisition. The brilliant Khalid ibn al-Walìd, removed from command by Omar's severe and jittery authority, ended his days shortly thereafter in obscurity, in Syria itself or in Arabia. But the great conquest remained forever linked to his name, as well as the proud title the "Sword of Allah." From northern Syria the Arab wave was then to reach the upper Euphrates and Armenia. The Taurus mountain chain barred the way to Asia Minor, which the Arabs were never destined to occupy except for fleeting raids.

The campaign against Persia was developed during the same years as that in Syria. This great campaign, from the modest and almost private beginnings in Hirah, was to lead to the destruction of the Sassanid state. The first phase is summarized in the name of al-Muthanna, the valorous military chieftain to whom Arabism largely owes the conquest of Iraq. During a three-year preparatory guerrilla war on the Euphrates, the Arabs experienced some serious reverses (the "Battle of the Bridge"), but with the victory of Buwaib they consolidated themselves in the Babylonian provinces. The equivalent of Yarmùk for the conquest of Mesopotamia, however, was the battle of Qadisiyya near Hirah (636 or 637). Here, in three days of tenacious struggle, the Arabs, under the command of Saad ibn Abi Waqqàs (Muthanna had died of wounds a short while before) crushed the imperial Persian army and opened the way for themselves to the capital Ctesiphon. Here, where the Roman legions could never establish a stable foothold, entered the Arabs of the desert, victorious beggars who pounced with an ingenuous greed upon the luxuries and treasures of that refined civilization. Beaten once more at Gialulà, Yezdegerd III, the last Sassanid sovereign, initiated the sorrowful retreat towards the Persian highland plateau, abandoning all Mesopotamia to the enemy. But the Arabs were ever at his heels, and at Nehavend near Hamadàn, in 641 or 642 (the chronology of these campaigns is thorny with contradictions and difficulties) a second and last battle on an open field decided the fate of the Sassanid Empire. The Arab commander fell during the fighting, but his successor wrested victory from the foe. After then all organized resistance from the central authority ceased, and the Arab penetration continued its conquest, one by one, of those cities and fortresses which still opposed the invasion. It took, however, no less than a decade (651) to complete the operation, which came to a halt in the border district of Khurasàn, the future base for operations in the direction of Central Asia. At the end of this decade (651), the nephew of the proud emperors, of the Shapurs and of the Chosroes, ended his wandering flight and was assassinated near Merw. The Mazdean state of Persia was extinguished forever in this tragic end of Yezdegerd III, who later was to be greatly mourned in the national epic. Minor state formations, personified by feudal lords of the Caspian regions (Mazandaràn, Gilàn), maintained their independence for some time, continuing the national religion and culture there. Everywhere else in the rest of Persia Mazdeism decayed rapidly, although not being wholly extinguished. But the national tradition underwent a kind of eclipse before the language and faith of the invaders. When the Iranian language and tradition began their renascence two centuries later, Persia, on the religious side, was to a great part already Islamized. Her reaction to the invaders was expressed, rather, in heretical ferments in the very bosom of Islam, instead of in a revivification of the national religion.

In the decisive decade from 632 to 642, Egypt was the third target of the conquests, and from Egypt they moved towards North Africa. The Arab conquest of Egypt is linked to the name of Amr ibn al-As, another improvised military chieftain of great martial qualities but with an even greater political ability and sagacity, that has become proverbial. At the end of 639, with an authorization granted reluctantly by the hesitant Caliph Omar from Palestine, Amr showed up on the Egyptian frontier, at the head of a few thousand horsemen. The Byzantine resistance was even weaker and more uncoordinated than in Syria, and undermined by treachery to boot. In fact, it is not possible otherwise to qualify the conduct of the patriarch Cyrus (the "Muqauqis" mentioned in Arabian sources, formerly bishop of a see in the Caucasus, and who now exercised civil powers in Egypt). At a rather early stage this patriarch entered into negotiations with the Arabs, who had been the victors in 640-41 at Babylon near the site of present-day Cairo, and who had come up from the Delta to attack Alexandria. Thanks to the accommodating attitude of "Muqauqis," the strongly defended Egyptian metropolis, which furthermore was opened to help from the sea, was vacated in the summer of 642, after a year of siege. With the surrender of Alexandria, and its recovery after a temporary Byzantine return in 645, all Egypt was practically in the hands of the invaders. If the Melchite Cyrus had represented the interests of the sovereign of Byzantium so badly, the Monophysitic Coptic population of Egypt had even less cause to worry about them. Hence the Arabs could establish themselves there almost without opposition, and vigorously begin to exploit it. From Egypt Amr ibn al-As looked out upon Marmarica. But his successor was to proceed further down the long road of the Occident. This was Abdallàh ibn Abi Sarh whom the third Caliph Othmàn put in the place of the conqueror. The career of the latter, however, was by no means finished. Indeed his ability to worm himself into the winning side in the subsequent period of the civil war, was to restore him to the governorship of the province of the Nile until his death.

Thus in a decade the Arabs of the Peninsula had spread themselves everywhere over the "fertile Crescent." Members of the same tribe which had roamed the desert in the times of the Prophet now fought guerrilla wars and conducted predatory raids in the name of Islam, on the one hand in the Persian highland plateau, and on the other in the reefs along the Libyan coast. The lands which were to form the heart of the Arab-Moslem empire, Syria, Iraq, Persia, Egypt, received orders and obeyed governors sent from Medina, the capital of a state which was at once theocratic and Arabic. Tumultuous, unsystematic conquest, in which the share of conscious human wills and energies did not appear to be higher than that of fortune and chance, was now followed by consolidation, and the creation of a political, administrative, economic order, in which religious precepts and interests and worldly prejudices, and purposeful wisdom, merged into a disconcerting, but nevertheless fruitful cooperation.

ALTHOUGH aware of the dignity of their new faith, and of the theoretical right and duty to propagate it, the Arabs at that time did not think of imposing it by the sword, and not even by means of a relentlessly hammering propaganda. To be sure they imposed their political domination with the sword but it does not appear that they exerted special pressures of proselytism towards subjugated Christian and Zoroastrian populations. Their most pressing concern was to regulate the relations between victors and vanquished, between believers and infidels, wholly to the advantage of the former naturally, but without violently wresting the latter from their beliefs and their ways of life. The Koran had already sanctioned a *modus vivendi* with the "People of the Book," i.e. the followers of religions with their own written revelation (Christians and Jews to which later the Zoroastrians were assimilated). These could coexist with the believers, in an obvious position of inferiority or tolerated subjection. This principle was applied on a grand scale in the conquests, leaving freedom of person and cult to these infidels. Indeed they were extended protection (*dhimmah*, whence their title of *dhimmi*) against the payment of a definite tribute. This consisted in a personal tax (that later was specified under the name *gizyah*), and in a land tax (the *kharàj*, but the two terms were promiscuously used in a more ancient epoch), while Moslems had to pay the state only the "legal alms" or *zakàt*. The state-owned lands and those abandoned by the proprietors in the conquered provinces became the direct property of the Islamic state, in addition to the koranic fifth of the movable booty. All the others, which in theory would have been divided among the individual combatants, were left to their ancient owners against payment of the aforementioned land tax. The State, which collected the tribute, passed on military stipends or pensions, almost as though they were dividends from those properties, to the combatants. In order to do this it was necessary to compile rolls or lists of combatants (*diwàn*). This was the great administrative novelty introduced by the Arabs, who up to then were little accustomed to bureaucratic regulations, as well as the bookkeeping and accounting procedures required by the fiscal system. In this first phase, however, the victors left it in the hands of the respective Byzantine and Iranian bureaucracies. They continued to use their own languages for this purpose, and acted as intermediaries between the non-indigenous taxpayers (individuals and communities) and the victors. An Arab functionary (*amil*) naturally stood at the head of the financial services in the various provinces alongside the political and military governor (*wali*). The governor was nominated by the caliph and deputized, among other things, to preside at the prayer of the believers in the chief town of the province. On the whole, it was a simple and elastic administrative structure peculiar to a young and improvising State which did not hesitate to make use of every pre-existent mechanism in order to assure itself quick and certain revenues. These flowed into the coffers or public treasury (*bait al-mal*) of Medina, patriarchically administered by the first caliphs.

According to tradition, the lines of this grandiose and simple organization of the conquests go back to Caliph Omar ibn al-Khattàb (634-44), whom Abu Bakr designated as his successor when he was at death's door. Omar ruled the nascent Arab empire in the crucial decade of its formation. Modern criticism sees here an overenthusiastic reconstruction of the past, and attribution to an individual of achievements and institutions that really developed slowly and gradually. But even if we admit this to a certain extent, it is still a merit of Omar's impressive personality that he polarized on himself the memory and the feeling of later Moslem generations, as one of the most eminent among the four "orthodox" or "well guided" (this is how the Arab *rashidùn* is usually rendered) caliphs who formed the golden age of Islam. On the "Day of Jàbiyah," in 637, while inspecting the army near Damascus, which had been victorious over Syria, Omar is supposed to have fixed the principles of the organization which also remained, as an example, for the other provinces. Thus the formation of the "rolls" of military pensions, the fixing of the Moslem era from the hegira, and the title "Prince of the Believers" with which thenceforth the Caliph was hailed, are all attributed to him. His demiurgic action set its stamp on the whole growth of the young Arab empire, just as his austere figure dominated that first era which was still so rich in personalities of great prominence. Although not among the very first to embrace the faith of Mohammed, indeed he had embraced it after having at first been its dogged adversary (which justifies the otherwise incongruous title of "St. Paul of Islam"), Omar, on the eve of the hegira and later in the Medinese decade, was the right hand, the animator, sometimes even the stimulator and contradictor of the Prophet (recall the episode of Hudàybiyah), towards whom he preserved a true and tried loyalty and devotion.

After Mohammed's death, having pushed forward the older and more authoritative Abu Bakr, he sustained his work during the two years that the latter survived the Master, and he gathered up his legacy when Abu Bakr was laid beside the Prophet in the Medinese tomb. At that time, in 634, the movement of the conquests had already begun. Starting out from tenuous and uncertain beginnings, it grew larger little by little, like an avalanche that swells while moving along its path. Omar followed their victorious march from Medina, and as much as the difficult and slow communications permitted, he organized and dispatched reinforcements to the captains operating on the various fronts. He imposed his authority on every new conquest and on his colleagues, no matter how prestigious (see the case of Khalid ibn al-Walìd), bowing only to the merits and priorities of the faith. As defender of the discipline of the Law against lasciviousness and personal aggrandizement, it is said that he did not hesitate to strike his own son who had transgressed against the norms of the *Shariah*, and his famous *dirrah* or riding-whip was ready to come down without ceremony on the guilty no matter how highly placed. But tradition does not only report acts of severity and violence on his part. The harsh caliph who led a simple life was capable of running out at night carrying a sack of flour on his back, upon hearing the cries of hungry babies, of helping the mother to cook the food, and of getting on all fours to play with children until satiated and comforted they serenely surrendered to sleep; or, with a companion of watching over the baggage and animals of transient travelers in the little guarded Medinese market-place. There is an inexhaustible supply of anecdotes about Omar, although admittedly they reveal an idealizing tendency. He who senses the truth that *on ne prête qu'aux riches* will always discern, behind the idealization, beyond every anecdote or edifying judgment attributed to him, a nucleus of indubitable reality which places the second caliph among the loftiest figures engendered by Arabism and animated by the faith of Islam. His rough frankness, to which all compromise and all hypocrisy seems alien, has served to make even non-Islamic modern historians see the more complex and sometimes ambiguous figure of Mohammed in a better light. The fact that Mohammed was able to gain the total devotion of a man as frank and austere as Omar has counted for much in the judgments that have been passed on the Prophet.

In November of 644, when he was still this side of sixty, Omar suddenly disappeared from the scene, the victim of an assassination. Behind the strictly private motive of that deed (a complaint regarding tribute had not been accepted by the Caliph), a less confessable political motive has been suspected. Tradition gives clues which show that behind the instigators stood highly placed and important Moslems who had become impatient with that patriarchal dictatorship. The doubts and suspicions, very weakly grounded for that matter, will never be clarified. Certainly the disappearance of the "Farùq" (the "Discriminator of Good from Evil," according to the current interpretation of the surname) was a serious loss to the Moslem community in those years of dizzying development. It is impossible to say, with the history of "ifs," what the destinies of the Arabo-Islamic state would have been if that untamed but equitable and disinterested energy had remained longer at the helm. In the light of what followed, it is licit however to conjecture that the selfish particularisms, the ancestral and individual ambitions, the old and new cupidities would have been further bridled, and the era of the *fitnah* or civil discord would not have been opened, among so many successions of unhoped for triumphs, in the very generation of the Companions of the Prophet.

ON his deathbed Omar entrusted the nomination of a successor to a council (*shura*) of six eminent Moslems who were to pick him from among themselves. They were all old Companions of Mohammed, his son-in-law and cousin Ali, Talhah and Zubayr, Abd ar-Rahmàn ibn Awf, Saad ibn Abi Waqqàs and Othmàn ibn Affàn. The latter was a member of the aristocratic Quraysh family of the Banu Umayyah, the only member of it to have embraced Islam in the years of the vigil, when his kinsman Abu Sufyàn headed the pagan opposition. Now, naturally, they were all Moslems, and ready to make a grab at power. Omar is also supposed to have recommended to Othmàn, as well as to the others of the *shura*, that if elected they were not to place their familial clan "on the necks of the Moslems," just as he had kept his own kinfolk, the Banu Adi, from commandeering the high offices of the state. But Banu Adi were obscure Quraysh folk of second degree. When, with the election of Othmàn, the noble and wealthy Banu Umayyah had one of their own at the summit of the Moslem community, it was difficult to resist their pressure to occupy the key posts of the Empire. Othmàn was a man of sincere piety and personal rectitude, but he lacked entirely his predecessor's energy. Shortly after his rise to the Caliphate, Omayyads and their friends, whose past as Moslems was indeed everything but exemplary, were at the head of the provinces (Muàwiyah ibn Abi Sufyàn already for some time in Syria, Abdallàh ibn Amir and Walìd ibn Uqba in Iraq, Abdallàh ibn Abi Sarh in Egypt). Othmàn's cousin, the future Caliph Marwàn ibn al-Hakam, was his most intimate advisor. This nepotism, like all nepotism based on blood and patronage (*nasab* and *walà* to use the Arab terminology), may have had its justification in a leader's need to support himself on elements known and faithful to him, and to give unity and an organic character to the administration. Like every other nepotism on the other hand, it offered an excellent motive for opposition, for disappointed ambitions and for moralisms that had been offended.

The center of the opposition to Othmàn was constituted by Ali, who had been supplanted for the third time, and the no less ambitious Talhah and Zubayr, the "Mother of the Believers" Aishah and the pietist milieux of humble social origin among the Companions who were scandalized to see power in the hands of the ancient aristocracy which only yesterday had been pagan. But it reluctantly submitted to this outrage for more than a decade before exploding into open revolt.

Despite the Caliph's very weak personality, the twelve years of Othmàn's caliphate (644-56) constituted the development and the continuation of the expansionist policy of Arabism, begun in Omar's decade. The spectacular rhythm of the conquests was slowed down somewhat, but they were further consolidated and enlarged. Arab penetration of eastern Persia continued (the surrender of the Iranian metropolis of Istakhr, near ancient Persepolis took place in 650 and, as we have seen, 651 is the date of the end of the last Sassanid, Yezdegerd III). Armenia was subjugated by expeditions under the command of Iyàd ibn Ghanm and Habìb ibn Màslamah. In northern Africa, Abdallàh ibn Abi Sarh pushed forward up to Tripoli and to Tunisia (Ifrìqiya), while in south Egypt he came into contact with Christian Nubia. But the assault of the Arabs on the sea was, perhaps, the most salient fact of this period, which in general constituted a hiatus between the first and second phase of the conquests, as was to take place under the Omayyads. The initial aversion of the Bedouins for the sea, which is documented by significant testimony, was quickly overcome when the victors looked out upon the Mediterranean from Alexandria and from the coasts of Syria. In 649 Muàwiyah conquered Cyprus from Syria, and shortly thereafter one of his lieutenants arrived for the first time in Sicily on a raiding expedition. The year 655 saw the first great Arab naval victory, with the battle of Phoenix on the coast of Licia, where the combined forces of Muàwiyah and Abdallàh ibn Abi Sarh routed a large Byzantine fleet, and inaugurated Arab supremacy of the sea in the eastern Mediterranean. Was this really the event that broke the continuing unity of the ancient world, according to Pirenne's well-known thesis? We cannot go deeply into this problem here, the solution to which, as formulated forty years ago by the Belgian historian seems rather one-sided and oversimplified. What is certain, of course, is that the entrance of the Arabs on the Mediterranean scene is a factor that cannot be underrated. By dismantling the hegemony of Byzantium in the eastern Mediterranean, by wedging itself between the two basins of this sea across Tunisia and then Sicily, they undeniably destroyed the preexistent balance of forces between East and

West, without however succeeding in cutting the Byzantines entirely out of Italy. Nor, as we shall see, were they able to complete the reduction of the entire Mediterranean to an Arab lake. Yet the mere fact that this new maritime power looked out in force on the ancient *mare nostrum*, with a people who had so far been totally alien to it in language, culture and faith, must already appear as a tremendous innovation.

The victors meanwhile went about settling themselves in the conquered provinces. Gradually they attached themselves to the soil, and abandoned the nomadism in which many had lived until then. The most conspicuous social phenomenon of these first decades, alongside the arabization—not total however—of the large preexistent urban centers (such as Damascus and Jerusalem, Antioch and Alexandria), was the creation *ex novo* of other centers which became the metropoles of medieval Arabism and of Islam. These new Arab cities were born of the military camps (*amsàr*) which the victors established in the conquered regions, and which from improvised billets evolved into stable urban centers. Such were the two centers of Basra and Kufa in Iraq, which were to have a function of such great importance in the Arabo-Islamic political, social and cultural life of the first centuries. Such also, was al-Fustàt, founded by Amr ibn al-As in Egypt, the first nucleus of future Cairo. It was here that Arabism assumed its urban countenance, hardly prefigured by the more modest aggregates of Mecca and Medina. It was also here that the science, culture and art of Islam developed to a great extent. But, under Othmàn, around the middle of the seventh century, this process was barely in its beginning stages, and Kufa and Basra which were to give him and his successors so much trouble were still formless human agglomerations, encampments rather than cities, swarming with an Arab throng of "warriors"

(*Muqàtilah*), Koran readers (*Qurrà*), tradesmen and artisans, and the usual fluctuating wave of Bedouins. In the chaos of the first expansion, Omar had sought to trace the first lines of an order and a governmental organization. Othmàn, with much less brilliance and energy, but with just as much good will, had tried to continue that work, basing himself on his nobiliary general staff, for whose collaboration he nevertheless had to pay in some way. Measures with respect to economic and agrarian policy, which were of enormous import for the further destinies of Moslem society, can be traced back to Othmàn and to his counselors. The initial prohibition imposed on Arabs to own lands outside Arabia (the so-called *fai* or booty, which, insofar as it was real estate, theoretically was the common property of the victors) was tempered with land grants (*qata'i*), especially in Iraq, which set off the formation of great landed estates and of big capital, and the correlative class hatred. The Omayyad clan, naturally, was the first to take advantage of these concessions, and the nascent urban proletariat the first to resent it. Here as everywhere in Arabo-Islamic society, economic motives mixed with, and often sincerely draped themselves in, ideal motives, and social protest was formulated in ethical-religious terms. The popular class of the *Qurrà* or Reciters of the Sacred Book, the powerful caste which felt itself to be the depository of the letter of the Revelation, of the authentic spirit of Mohammed and of the first Islam, was wounded in its sensibilities and privileges by the institution of that which, nevertheless, remains one of Othmàn's greatest merits vis-à-vis the legacy of the Prophet: namely, the compilation and canonical fixation of the Koran, which was carried out at his behest around 650. All these motives fed the slowly maturing but continuous discontent of the opposition, openly or hypocritically instigated by some of Othmàn's very electors (Ali,

Talhah, Zubayr). And after skirmishes between turbid ele-ments in Iraq and in Egypt, the situation came to a head in 656.

In the spring of this year groups of malcontents and rebels launched a march that was to converge on Medina from the provinces. The Egyptians, who were the first to arrive, were the protagonists of the dramatic events which led to the as-sassination of the third Caliph, and the first laceration of the Moslem community. Disarmed at first by the mildness and accommodating attitude of Othmàn, who promised to satisfy all their grievances, the rebels had already started on the way back when they intercepted an order of the Caliph to the governor of Egypt, instructing the latter to arrest and punish the leaders. They returned in a fury to demand the reason for this from Othmàn who denied authorship of the order, which was probably a provocative falsification perpetrated by his own enemies. But with a dignified firmness Othmàn refused to abdicate. He was then besieged in his modest resi-dence in Medina for several days, while the instigators—be-ginning with Ali—hypocritically stood aside and the assistance that had been invoked from Syria did not come in time to liberate him. In June 656, the irreparable was accomplished: the rebels broke into Othmàn's residence (it is the sorrowful "Day of the House" in Arabic historiographic tradition) and they murdered the successor of the Prophet, at that moment intent upon reading the Koran, which was stained with his blood. The era of the civil wars had been ushered in.

THE murder of Othmàn finally opened the path to the caliphate to Ali ibn Abi Talib. The cousin and son-in-law of the Prophet had been waiting for that hour for twenty-four years, with the accompanying recognition of his moral, if not juridical, rights to the succession of Mohammed. A formal designation on the part of the latter, later the strong-point of Shi'ite legitimism, seems never to have been brought forward as a claim by Ali himself. But the manner in which he came to power, stained by blood, was bound to poison this tardy recognition. What measure of moral co-responsibility (excluding a material and direct one), he may have had in the drama of the "Day of the House," is something which passionate partisanship on both sides has never allowed to be ascertained. Certainly while still protesting his innocence, he could not and did not wish to strike at those who were directly responsible, and thereby expose himself to the accusations of the hostile party. The latter was personified by the Omayyad clan, itself attacked in the shape of its kinsman the Caliph. The Omayyad clan in the name of the ancient tribal law of blood-vengeance and of the Islamic dignity of the Caliphate demanded punishment of the guilty. The Omayyad governor of Syria, Muàwiyah ibn Abu Sufyàn, very soon appeared as the leader of such a vindication. He refused recognition of, and obeisance to, Ali in the name of "vengeance for Othmàn," which had become the slogan of the anti-Ali opposition. The son of Abu Sufyàn had inherited his father's intelligence, energy, and flair for politics and he had known how to make a wholly devoted domain out of the ably administered province of Syria. The hope of winning him over through persuasion failed, and all that was left to Ali was the test of arms. At the end of this same year, 656, having moved his residence from Medina to Kufa in Iraq, the new Caliph already had been compelled to settle scores with another branch of the opposition. This was led not by the Omayyads but by his two former associates Talhah and Zubayr, with whom Aishah, the widow of the Prophet, also joined forces. The "Battle of the Camel" (so-called because of Aishah's camel which served as a war-chariot or palladium for her followers) cleared the ground of Ali's rivals. Talhah and Zubayr fell on the battlefield; Aishah, taken prisoner, with all due deference was sent back to Medina and restored to private life. But the struggle with Muàwiyah turned out to be much more difficult. Facing one another at Siffin on the upper course of the Euphrates, battle was joined (July 657) after much temporizing. Ali and his lieutenant Malik al-Ashtar almost had victory in the palm of their hands, when an episode took place which, from a simple stratagem of war, was to change itself into an apple of discord, pregnant with consequences for the entire history of older Islam.

On the advice of Amr ibn al-As, the cunning ex-governor of Egypt who was on Muàwiyah's side, the latter had copies of the Koran raised on the lances of the Syrians who were already about to give ground, thereby appealing to the sacred Book for a settlement of the quarrel. This gesture made an enormous impression on Ali's army, composed in great part of fanatical *Qurrà* or Koran Readers, and Ali very soon was forced by them to suspend the struggle and to listen to the enemy's proposals. These were to submit the causes for the conflict to the judgment of two arbitrators, in the letter or in the spirit of the Koran. Arab historiographical tradition has created an enormous muddle of contradictory data concerning how such causes were then formulated, the real task and power of the arbitrators, the place, date and the course of the arbitration itself, which modern research has not yet succeeded, and perhaps will never succeed in clarifying. The arbitrators were faced by two, interwoven but distinguishable, problems: in the first place the legitimacy or illegitimacy of Muàwiyah's vendetta action, starting out from the judgment of whether Othmàn had been "wrongfully" killed or with good reason. Secondly, and almost obliquely, the question grafted on to it as to who was the most worthy to be invested with the Caliphal dignity, a dignity which was disputed with Ali by his adversaries because of the "moral question" in which it had been ensnared without an explicit candidacy having yet been advanced on the part of Muàwiyah. According to various sources the site of the arbitration was now one now the other, of two localities in northern Arabia, Dumat al-Jandal or Adhruh (and there are also those who think that both meetings may have taken place, in two phases and in regard to those two different problems). The real meeting, and in our judgment probably the only one, took place in Adhruh, in January 658, i.e. six months after the interrupted battle of Siffin. Muàwiyah's arbitrator was his faithful Amr ibn al-As, Ali's arbitrator was the unfaithful Abu Musa al-Ashari, who had been forced on him by his own partisans. He was an old Companion of the Prophet, and probably a man of sincere piety but scant political ability. Even if we disregard the grotesque particulars of tradition, he certainly yielded in the face of the astute Amr's verbal dueling, even though his positive program was certainly not unconditionally favorable to Ali. The arbitration proceedings were concluded entirely to Ali's disadvantage, his own representation having consented to declare him deposed from the Caliphate, although it is not exactly certain if an explicit proclamation on behalf of Muàwiyah was advanced from the other side. In short, the inconclusive result again submitted the question to the test of arms, but in the meantime Ali's political and military position had greatly deteriorated.

In fact his acceptance of the proposed and imposed arbitration had created a sudden split in his own camp, which broadened into the first real politico-religious schism of the Moslem community. One part of his warriors of Siffin, and among these were several who at first had forced him to accept arbitration, experienced a crisis of conscience when the "appeal to the Koran" appeared to them for what it actually was, an appeal to judgment and humane interest for settling the dispute, a game which Muàwiyah and his followers showed they could play very well. The cry *la ḥukma illa li-llàh* (the judgment only to God) which at first seemed equivalent to the acceptance of the Syrian invitations to judge according to the Koran, later became the slogan of those, who rejecting all human intervention now recognized the obligation to fight the rebel Muàwiyah in a precept of the Koran itself, the word of God. They recognized, and at the same time, they demanded this recognition from Ali himself, namely that he had erred (indeed "sinned" in their theological language!) by acceding to the Syrian proposal. This was the beginning of the famous Kharijite schism which was to stain Islam with blood for more than a century, and often constituted the foremost problem of caliphs and governors. The Kharijites (the disputed etymology of the name seems to mean "rebels, activists," rather than "secessionists" as has been for so long repeated), deserted Ali, even when he invited them to resume the struggle after the futile arbitration. They deserted him because they considered him an impenitent sinner for having refused to recognize the error, the sin committed, as they had done, and for continuing the struggle more in the name of his personal interest (and here they were not wrong) rather than "for the cause of God." Withdrawing from his ranks after Adhruh, they developed a rigoristic and ultra-democratic conception of the Caliphate, freed of every link and prerogative of race and accessible through election "even to an Ethiopian slave." And they wrapped themselves in a fanatical puritanism against all the remnant Islamic community, whether it was pro-Ali or pro-Omayyad, which they judged as "infidel" and as such, to be fought pitilessly to the last drop of blood. This explosion of politico-religious extremism is the most disconcerting phenomenon of the origins of Islam. Almost incomprehensible in more rational and temperate times, perhaps it is less so in our own time with its irrational mysticisms and its "religious" fanaticisms.

With the rapid spread of Kharijite terrorism, which immediately began to rage in Iraq, Ali was forced to intervene. Against them he directed all the forces that had remained loyal to him and which he at first would have wanted to use against Muàwiyah. At Nahrawàn, not far from Kufa, he in fact inflicted a bloody defeat on the Kharijites (July 658), which, however, did nothing else but sow the seeds for their new propaganda, creating new converts and martyrs. Here Ali's ever vacillating energy came to a halt. Not having quickly succeeded in dragging his followers back against his rival (it seems that a formal proclamation by Muàwiyah in Syria had taken place in April, 658), he was no longer given a chance to confront him on the open field. For two and a half years, immobilized in Iraq, which had remained loyal to him but which was already drenched in the blood of the Kharijite guerrilla warfare, he had to stand by and watch the progressive affirmation of Muàwiyah, who increasingly gained ground in the various provinces of the Empire. In those years Amr ibn al-As reconquered Egypt for the Omayyads, eliminating, through poison, Malik al-Ashtar, whom Ali had dispatched there as governor. Thus this man who had been among the first to answer the call of Mohammed, whose blood he perpetuated through his wife Fàtimah, who had fought valiantly in battles of the faith, and who then had to wait so long for his hour to come, now saw the longed-for legacy crumbling in a sterile struggle of equivocations, deceits, and betrayals. In January 661 the sword of a Kharijite struck him dead during an *attentat* against him in the Kufa mosque. Death was almost a liberation for the disappointed and embittered Ali, deserted by all save for a group of his faithful followers. Fortune beyond the grave was to compensate him for so bitter a life, when his figure, which politically had been a failure, was super-humanized by the faith and the superstition of his party (the "Shiah of Ali" or simply "Shiah") and elevated to the spheres of the supernatural and the divine, even higher than his initiator and Prophet.

4.

The Arab Empire

MUÀWIYAH succeeded in founding a dynasty in his family, the Banu Umayya or Omayyads, who held the Caliphate and the Empire for ninety years. The history of the Omayyad century or of the "Arab Empire," as Wellhausen called it in his classic book, has come down to us tendentiously disfigured by Moslem tradition, which is almost wholly inspired by Abbasid rivals and successors. On the other hand, an opposite tendency of idealization prevails in modern historians, whether they be laymen like Wellhausen or anti-Moslem ecclesiastics like Lammens. Certainly the forces and the persons at work in the Omayyad period seem closer, more understandable and more human to us than those appearing in the following period, as they seem more noble and magnanimous to us. The religious element was not at all absent, nor confined to a function of pure opposition. But it certainly did not appear as the first order of business as in the preceding and following times. Thus the reproach leveled against the Omayyads by the pietist tradition, which holds that they transformed the sacred Caliphate into a *mulk* (a profane kingdom), is not without a basis of truth, although exaggerated by their hostility.

For once Muàwiyah and his successors, under the sign of Islam, managed to unite the Arab people, a hegemonic element in the tremendously vast territory created by the con-

quests, into a single organism. That Arab monarchy which
the Bedouin tribes had for so long rejected and which up to
then had dissipated itself in the small vassal states along the
frontiers or in the ephemeral sovereignty of the Kindah, now
found itself ruling the immense body of the Arab-Moslem
state from Damascus. In the days of its greatest power recourse was had to the Omayyad Caliphate in matters concerning justice from India to Spain, and its orders and representatives were respected and feared from one end of the Empire
to the other. These Omayyads also regarded themselves as
heads of the Moslem community and of Arabism (Omar had
already called the Arabs *maddat al-Islàm*, the raw material of
the new faith), and, except for Omar II, as the deliberate ad-
vocates of Arab primacy within that community. In the Arab
world itself they naturally were very sensible to their family's
predominance and exerted themselves to maintain it, and in
an alternating struggle they tried to substitute the Arab principle of succession between brothers by that of succession by
direct lineage. The forces against which they had to struggle
were, firstly, traditional Arab particularism, the centuries-old
repugnance of the Bedouins for governmental organization
and discipline; secondly the pietist tendencies in the opposition which could not without scandal see the supreme Islamic
power in the hands of a race that had been alien or flatly hostile to the birth and affirmation of the faith. From here came
the food with which these tendencies throughout the century
nourished every anti-Omayyad movement from the puritan
Kharijite to the legitimist Shi'ite and to their Abbasid heirs
and supplanters. The struggle of the central power, of the
major Caliphs, supported by faithful and valiant collaborators,
against these centrifugal forces, was one of the salient aspects
of the period we are discussing and it is woven into the glorious event of the conquests which resumed their impetuous
course under the Omayyads. This struggle ended with the

defeat of the dynasty and of that which it had represented, the national primacy of the Arabs in the Moslem state. But it died not without both dynasty and people (which were later so blindly to contribute to its defeat) first writing, for almost a century, the most Arabic page in the history of Islam and in the immense area in which the faith was first spread.

With the Omayyads the patriarchal character of the Caliphate under the four "orthodox" Caliphs gradually evolved into a type of monarchy tending to an absolutism of a kind which was then to be perfected under the Abbasids, and which corresponded to the well-known characteristics of ancient oriental monarchies. Under the Omayyads it could only take its first steps, and to the Byzantines the Caliph still appeared only as a *primus inter pares* among the great tribal chieftains, his partisans and rival advisors. But the direction towards which the Omayyads themselves tended was certainly that of absolute power, and in this sense their Abbasid successors can well be called their heirs. It seems to us that the fundamental difference between the two dynasties and the two states consisted in the fact that the Omayyads always felt themselves as the conscious champions of Arabism, while for the Abbasids (ethnically no less Arabic, indeed in genealogy they were even closer to the family of the Prophet) this ceased to be a living dominant force, a primary element of their policy, supplanted by other races and by a different social organization. In the long run would the Omayyads themselves have abandoned that national principle and support, if after less than a century they had not been overthrown by the lapse of that support because of internal discords? The example of their transplantation to Spain, where they too in the end were forced to lean for support on Berber and other alien elements also, is not a definitive proof because for them that very transplantation signified losing contact with the geographical ambience and the ethnic reserve of their race. Leaving vague theoretical speculations behind, we can fix the following principle on the basis of events that really occurred: for the Arabs, the Omayyad century, in the frame of Islam, represented their greatest affirmation in history. But the consciousness of this fact, which remained vague in them, was not enough to make them sacrifice their innate egotisms and rivalries, which soon broke the unity of their state and drove them from the political primacy which the spread of Islam by force of arms procured for them.

THE son of Abu Sufyàn had already been put by Omar in the government of Syria, the conquest of which he had participated in under the orders of his older brother Yazìd. Twenty years of sapient rule had won him the attachment of the Arab element stationed there. This was subdivided into the four *jund* or military districts of Palestine, Jordan, Damascus, and Hims (a fifth, the district of Qinnasrìn or of northern Syria was added later). With these faithful Arabs of Syria he had revolted "to revenge Othmàn," and though winning more with diplomacy than with force he had preserved unfailing support for every future policy of his in the Syrian *jund*. Ali's assassination in 661, due to a multiple Kharijite murder plot in which Muàwiyah himself barely escaped, rid him of his rival, who moreover politically was in a desperate plight. Thus, after purchasing neutrality from Ali's first born son al-Hasan, acquiring the latter's renunciation of every legitimist claim, Muàwiyah could attend to the pacification and organization of the Islamic state, which recognized him as Caliph. In this task he had as a collaborator an able politician of uncertain origins, Ziyàd, whom he did not hesitate to recognize as his brother, i.e. as the son of Abu Sufyàn, so as to win him over to his cause and to detach him from Ali's. Ziyàd ibn

Abihi ("son of his father" as the genealogy designates him with a significant vagueness) very soon concentrated the government of Iraq into his own hands, having also jurisdiction over the vast territories which had been conquered in the East. Here Ziyàd restored order and obedience to the new sovereign with a firm hand. In truth this order and obedience were of a superficial character, since throughout the whole Omayyad century Iraq was the fountainhead of Kharijite and Shi'ite opposition, while Syria remained the residence and stronghold of the Caliphs. To his twenty-year rule of the Syrian government as Prefect, Muawiyah added another twenty as Caliph. And when he died in 680 the fruit of his strenuous labor—in which he did not shrink from being assisted by Christian counsellors and functionaries—seemed to be assured. The Moslem state was pacified internally, there was a further victorious expansion abroad (in 669 his son Yazìd had conducted an expedition against Constantinople itself), and the succession was retained in the bosom of his own family, with the *baia* or recognition of Yazìd, which the Caliph had wrested from the Arab chieftains with infinite patience and calculated munificence. The memory of Muàwiyah and of his proverbial *hilm* (a mixture of intelligence, patience and finesse) has remained alive among Arabs down the centuries: averse to shedding blood where money, pardon and even a drop of poison could suffice, an excellent judge of men and of their weaknesses and passions, amiable and flexible—he was inflexibly fixed to his ultimate purposes. All in all he remains one of the most attractive personalities of Arab history, before whom not only the Jesuit Lammens but everyone who esteems human intelligence and ability must bow.

The arduous and fragile character of Muàwiyah's achievement became evident immediately upon his vanishing from the scene. Yazìd, his son, had not inherited all the rare qualities of his father: far from being that monster of impiety and deprav-

ity which the pietistic tradition has made of him, he himself
was otherwise cunning but without his father's exceptional
experience and habitual caution. Moreover, as the friend of
luxury, of art and of poetry (unforgivable faults in the eyes
of the bigots), he found himself the prey of resurgent Shi'ite
legitimism on the one hand, and of the competing ambitions
of former Companions, or sons of Companions, on the other.
Husayn, the other son of Ali and Fàtimah, hence a grand-
son of Mohammed, unlike his older brother had not re-
nounced his claims to the Imamate, and upon Yazìd's accession thereto he let himself be induced to lead a revolt. From
Medina he came to Kufa where soon, however, he was isolated with a small group of followers. After being surrounded
by police forces of the Omayyad government of Iraq, he was
killed following a brief skirmish at Kerbelà (October 680),
thereby shedding the blood of the Prophet to the horror of
the pious. Yazìd, who had not desired Husayn's death, was to
bear the curse of sacrilege for all posterity. But for the moment the revolt of Abdallàh ibn az-Zubayr, the son of Ali's
former companion and rival who was killed in the "Battle
of the Camel," appeared even more serious politically. At
Husayn's death he proclaimed himself Anti-Caliph, and he
was immediately recognized as such in Hijaz where the tradition of the Companions and the animosity against the Omayyad
"usurpers" was much more alive. A Syrian army was forced
to intervene, defeating the Medinese at the gates of their city,
then proceeding to the siege of Mecca, where Ibn az-Zubayr
had shut himself up. The siege of the holy city, which was
bombarded and burned, continued for two months when at
the end of 683 news arrived of Yazìd's untimely death, and
the besiegers withdrew.

Muàwiyah II, Yazìd's young son, also died after a few
weeks, and in the anarchy that was unleashed the Caliphate
seemed, for an instant, to slip from the hands of the Banu

Umayyah. The rivalry between northern and southern Arab tribes had a great part in the public disorders which then broke out in Syria; later it was to prove fatal for the Omayyads, as well as for the destinies of all Arabism. The northern Qays proclaimed their support of Ibn az-Zubayr, while the southern Kalb, to whom Muàwiyah and Yazìd were bound with matrimonial unions, rallied to the defense of the dynasty. Their candidate, however, was not Yazìd's son but old Marwàn ibn al-Hakam, Othmàn's former secretary and cousin, who belonged to a different branch of the Omayyads. With Marwàn, acclaimed as Caliph at the assembly of Jabiyah (June 684) and confirmed on his throne by the victory of Marj Rahit which smashed the rebellious Qays, supreme power passed from the Sufyàn (Muàwiyah's branch) to the Marwanids who were to preserve it in the East up to the end, and later in Spain (where indeed the Omayyads are more often called Banu Marwàn).

The old but able and energetic Marwàn died after ruling less than a year, before he could undertake—from Syria—the reconquest of Arabia and of Iraq, which had recognized the Anti-Caliph Ibn az-Zubayr. The reconstitution of the unity of the Empire was a task that fell upon his son Abd al-Malik, whose caliphate (685-705), with that of his son and successor Walìd (705-15) marks the apogee of the Omayyad era. Upon the accession of Abd al-Malik to the throne of Damascus, Ibn az-Zubayr consolidated himself in Hijaz. He held Iraq with the lieutenancy of his brother Musab, who in Kufa had suppressed the Shi'ite revolt headed by Mukhtàr (685-86), an agitator who had launched the uprising in the name of the Alid Mohammed ibn al-Hanafiyyah. Musab ibn az-Zubayr was defeated at Dair al-Jathliq by Abd al-Malik (691) who thus recaptured Iraq. But the subjugation of the anti-Caliph of Mecca required a new long siege and bombardment of the holy city, and a general attack under which Abdallàh ibn

az-Zubayr fell heroically (692). Only then could Abd
al-Malik return and make entire disposition of Muàwiyah's
legacy and attend to the reorganization of the Empire from
Syria. The name of this Caliph is linked to the introduction
of Arabic as the official language of the administration, which
until then had been Greek or Pahlavi according to the provinces. His name is also associated with the minting of the first
coins with Arab legend, and with a whole series of other
measures reaffirming Arab supremacy and the authority of the
central power.

His right arm in this enterprise was a *homo novus*, al-Hajjàj
ibn Yusuf who was born in Taif (Hijaz). This obscure school
teacher evinced his talents as a warrior during the siege of
Mecca, and as a statesman who ruled with an iron hand in the
administration of Iraq (from 695) and in all its oriental dependencies (from 697), which, like Ziyàd before him, he
held with viceregal powers up to his death. There is a porten-
tous quality about his work under Abd al-Malik and al-Walìd
because of the gravity and complexity of the tasks, and the
pitiless energy expended in fulfilling them. Iraq ever remained
a nest of latent rebellion, a testing area for all the activities
of the opposition. After the suppression of Mukhtàr's revolt,
the Shiah devoted itself to underground subversion which
was to re-explode only later in the Kufan revolt headed by
Zayd ibn Ali (740), and finally broaden out into the Abbasid
revolution. But at that time Kharijite terrorism was the real
scourge of Iraq, indeed of all the eastern part of the Empire.
In those decades the Kharijites were Hajjàj's principal problem in connection with the maintenance of public order.
They were subdivided into a number of factions more or less
clearly differentiated in beliefs (more often characterized by
the name of their individual politico-military leaders), all
making use of the common tactic of armed insurrection, of
the lightning raid, and of murder. He faced them sometimes

in person, frequently through his lieutenants, among whom emerged the Azdite al-Muhallab ibn Abi Sufrah, who in a tenacious guerrilla campaign succeeded in routing the Azraquites with their leader Qàtari, the intrepid warrior-poet. Another terrible Kharijite revolt was that headed by Shabìb, who for a moment threatened al-Hajjàj in Kufa itself. But the inflexible Omayyad governor weathered every storm. The most serious one of all, no longer of merely local import but which threatened the security of the whole State, was the revolt of Abd al-Rahmàn ibn al-Ashath in 701. The latter was not a Kharijite, but a valorous general on the eastern front, who had carried Moslem arms to the extreme southeast part of Iran, to Sigistàn. Because of a quarrel with his superior Hajjàj, he was forced to march towards the west in open revolt. Beaten several times at first, Hajjàj faced the rebels in a battle at Dair Jamajim near Kufa, and then on the Dujail river, where he succeeded in dispersing them. Ibn al-Ashath fled to Sigistàn, ruled by his ally, who cemented the alliance by sending his head to Hajjàj. When the Caliph Abd al-Malik died, the great governor of the East preserved his prestige with his successor Walìd during the decade of whose reign he could concentrate his indomitable energy on works of peace: such as the foundation and the development of his new residence in Wasit, the reorganization of the drainage and irrigation system in Iraq, and the care lavished on the vulgate of the Koranic text, which had found its final and canonical formulation under Othmàn.

THE crisis of 656-60 which brought the Omayyads to power, and that which erupted at the accession of the Marwanid branch, were only partly reflected in the movement of the conquests. The distance of the frontiers, the slowness of communications, and the necessary autonomy of action of the local military chiefs only slowed down the expansive force of the Arabs without ever compromising it, and this force was still a long way from having arrived at its greatest possibilities. Energetic and capable sovereigns from Damascus, or a Hajjàj from Iraq, gave new directives and certainly stamped some undertakings with a new impulse. But in general it was the initiative of the chieftains on the periphery who pushed the conquests forward, except that later they had to give an account to the central authority, and give up or resume the command in obedience to sovereign orders. Northern Syria was the theater of operations directly under the control of Damascus, it being the jumping-off place for the chronic guerrilla war against the Byzantines. Here the barrier formed by the Taurus mountains for centuries checked Islam's advance in Anatolia, and soon offensive operations were reduced to occasional seasonal raids (*sawàif*) more for the purposes of harassing the enemy and grabbing a booty than for stable territorial conquest. This does not take away the fact that Asia Minor was crossed and recrossed by Arab armies in the Omayyad century, and that Constantinople itself was menaced several times, by land and sea, by Omayyad arms. We have already seen in 669 the expedition headed by Yazìd, Muawiyah's son and future Caliph. Another major effort was attempted later, under the Caliph Sulaymàn (715-17), under the command of the latter's brother, Màslamah, one of the most experienced generals who had distinguished himself in the holy war. This siege also failed because of the energetic resistance organized by Leo the Isaurian, and this was the time when the Arabs came closest to the coveted prey. But they were not destined to conquer the second Rome for Islam. On the other hand the eastern Mediterranean was crossed by the Arabs who had absolute superiority over the Byzantine fleet. The latter failed to recapture Egypt, nor was it any more successful in defending the Mediterranean islands, Cyprus, Rhodes, Crete, and Sicily itself, from Moslem raids. At the same time the great terrestrial operations in the East and West were resumed, and the stable conquests expanded in a second phase.

The base of the expansion eastwards was the Khurasàn province in northeastern Iraq, whose governor was sometimes autonomous and sometimes subordinated to the governor of Iraq. We are particularly informed about the martial events that were developed from here beyond the Oxus River as well as about the internal disputes of the Arab tribes stationed here in the greatest historical work on ancient Islam that has come down to us, namely, the annals written by Tàbari (839-923). When the Arab garrisons of the Khurasàn were not dissipating themselves in sterile conflicts over old rivalries and genealogical antagonisms, the governors led them into the holy war against the infidels, the Iranians and Turks of Transoxiana (*Ma warà an-Nahr*, ancient Sogdiana).

Guerrilla warfare on the frontier developed into a virtual conquest under Qutaiba ibn Muslim (704-15), who with force and with crafty and disingenuous diplomacy subjugated the Turko-Iranian petty monarchs of Samarkand and Bukhara, and roamed into Farghanah and on Shash (modern Uzbekistan) beyond the Jaxarte. These were the extreme points reached in the direction of the East by the Arab conquest, which then had to call a halt because of the very tough resistance of the Turkish element, which had supplanted the Iranians in those regions. The conqueror Qutàiba, who had risen in revolt against the Caliph Sulaymàn who had succeeded Walìd, was killed in a military tumult. His successors maintained the line along the Oxus river for almost thirty years, coping with the Turkish pressure until the internal crisis of the Khurasàn and the Abbasid revolution which was its consequence momentarily suspended external operations in that sector. Further south, still under Hajjàj and Walìd, the Arabs had for the first time set foot in India, infiltrating across southern Persia and Baluchistan into the region of Sind at the mouth of the Indus. But that region, almost severed from the rest of the Empire, did not have a direct development. Hence the conquest and Islamization of India belongs to another epoch and to a people other than the Arabs.

The development of the second phase of the conquests in the West was much more impressive. While Abdallàh ibn Abi Sarh, under Othmàn, had reached Tripoli, the real conqueror or rather the first scout of the Maghrib, under Muàwiyah, was Oqba ibn Nafi, who at an epic pace advanced along the whole coast of northern Africa to the ocean. In terms of a stable conquest we can speak only of that of Roman Africa or Ifrìqiya, modern Tunisia, where he founded the camp city of Qairawàn. Central and peripheral Maghrib (modern Algeria and Morocco) were at that time more raided than solidly held; the weak Byzantine rule was rapidly eliminated; but still the Arabs were not able to break the proud resistance of the indigenous Berber element. The insurrection of the Berber chief Kusaila, to which Oqba himself succumbed south of Biskra in 683, was but the first of a cycle which was protracted for several decades, culminating in the great revolt of 740-42 which for a moment placed in doubt the destinies of Arabism in the whole of North Africa. It recovered after making a supreme effort, thus saving Ifrìqiya for the Arab Empire and the rest of the Maghrib for the faith of Islam, albeit no longer under the direct administration of the Caliphs. Moreover, it should be noted that the Berbers were driven to rebellion not as pagans or Christians but, rather, under the sign of heterodox dissidences in Islam itself, above all Kharijism. Here as elsewhere, religious formulas covered up deeper ethnic and economic causes of discontent, which we must now illustrate. But let us first conclude this rapid sketch of the expansion of Arabism by recalling its passage on European soil. Still under Walìd's happy caliphate, Tariq ibn Ziyàd and Musa ibn Nusayr in 711 managed to cross the strait, which from Tariq took the name Gibraltar (Jebel Tariq, the Mount of Tariq), and began the conquest of Visigothic Spain. Thereby they opened up one of the most brilliant chapters of the Arab diaspora and of the civilization related to it, which we shall have to discuss separately.

Thus in Damascus, Walìd and his successors up to Hishàm (under whom at least westernmost Maghrib escaped from the central authority) found themselves at the head of a gigantic empire, such as nobody within or without Arabia would have been able to imagine a century before. The Arab people provided the directing cadres to the immense conglomeration of the most disparate peoples, who in less than eighty years had bowed to its supremacy. But the latter was not considerable in terms of a pure and simple manifestation of force; below and above the force, stood the law and the duty of the faith, of a creed which presented itself with a distinct universalistic stamp. As such, by denying every racial exclusivism, it offered a theoretical basis of equality to all its converts, citizens of a single Moslem community. This fundamental contrast, between the instinctive will to power and exploitation, and the supranational character of the religion accepted and spread by the conquerors, was the crucial problem of the Arab Empire in its brief life. Sovereigns and administrators labored mightily to resolve it until a solution was imposed upon them by the course of events, by the forced abandonment—an effect of the Abbasid revolution—of that nationalism which had also been the raw material and the marching wing in the spread of Islam.

The most burning aspect of the problem was economic and fiscal; the Moslem State drew its greatest revenues from the tribute of the subjugated infidels, in the first place the personal

tax or poll tax, and the land tax. In theory conversion to
Islam should have freed every neophyte from such obligations, and this consideration suffices to make us understand
why only a slight proselytizing pressure was exerted by the
Arabs on conquered peoples, especially in certain places and
periods. In reality proselytes, who at that time embraced the
new faith for reasons which were essentially, if not exclusively, fiscal, universally complained that they were still unjustly burdened with the taxes after conversion. The poll tax
was the most characteristic tribute of the non-Moslem subject.
But the land tax also harshly weighed down on the agricultural population which often was reduced to such desperation
that it abandoned its own fields and flocked to the city, pro-
voking prohibitions and repressive measures from zealous governors like Hajjàj. Nor did the economic aspect exhaust the
problem: equality with the victors on the juridical and moral
plane was claimed by the new converts, called "customers" in
Arab (*Mawali*), colliding here also with Arab racial pride,
which in practice never bowed to acknowledge the universalistic postulates of its own faith. This was the source of a permanent hardship which nourished the revolts of a national and
social character. Ultimately it nourished that final rebellion
by which the Omayyad Caliphate was overthrown.

Intermittently the historical texts furnish us with accounts,
sometimes unclear or contradictory, of this conflict which,
nevertheless is visibly profiled in its fundamental lines. The
papyri offer us a more systematic and direct documentation
as regards Egypt. For some periods at least (for example the
government of Qurrah ibn Sharìk, 710-14), they shed light on
the systems of the financial administration, the organization
maintained along the lines of the pre-existent Roman-Byzan-
tine set-up, the severity of the taxation and the many superimposed abuses. The fiscal reform introduced by Omar II

(717-20) aimed at making a decisive turn on this point. This pious Caliph and man of good will felt the need to satisfy the juridical and moral exigencies of the faith by reconciling them with the financial interest of the State. The main features of the much discussed reform introduced by Omar seem to have been the following. First there was fiscal equalization between the new converts (non-Arabs) and Arabs, the neophytes being unburdened of the poll tax which was replaced, as for all believers, by the legal tithe (*sàdaqa* or *zakàt*). The second feature was the levying of the land tax, independently of the religion of the proprietor, but giving the tenant-farmers who had become Moslems the option to exempt themselves from the tax by leaving their plots and coming to live in the cities without being further prevented from doing so. Finally there was the prohibition of any further concessions to private persons of land belonging to the State, that had resulted in the formation of great individual landed estates to which Othmàn had given the first impulse in the form of the *qatai* or *sawafi*, akin to the Byzantine *emphyteuseis*. Omar's measures have been variously judged, and if judgment must be made in terms of their practical efficacy it can only be negative. In fact even after Omar we know of complaints and public disorders over poll taxes unduly demanded from converts (for example under Hishàm in Transoxiana and in Africa), and all the subsequent development of landed estates and of the regime of feudal holdings in Moslem society which is in obvious contradiction to the letter and spirit of the Omarian reform. It remains a memorable effort (we certainly know more about its inadequacies than about its practical actualization and the momentary advantages obtained) to resolve the crisis on the economic-social level and in the moral sphere connected with it. But in reality this could be resolved only as it was later—by changing the very foundations of the state and by placing Arabs and non-Arabs on the same level not only in their juridical and fiscal status, but in their common condition as subjects of a bureaucratic absolutism.

In the field of spiritual life and culture, the Omayyad era was still purely Arab, but in it there already sprouted the first germs of that which later was to be the great Arabo-Moslem culture of the following era. Poetry, which the Arabs felt as a national pride and treasure, was in full flower, but already new spirits and forms began to stand alongside the traditional ones because of the burgeoning urban life and the first contacts with foreign cultures. The great Omayyad poets constitute the transition between pure Bedouin poetry and the new style, while in Hijaz a love poetry flourished with an autonomous development. The turbulent political life, questions of public law and even religious polemics were expressed in verse, as appears from the Shi'ite and above all Kharijite propaganda. Whole pages of the political, social, religious history of the epoch are deducible from the verses of the contemporaries which complete the historical tradition as Lammens has brilliantly shown. Towards the end of the dynasty literary prose also made its first experiments among the circles of the *Kuttàb* or secretaries of the Caliphs. But the foundations of "science," in the Moslem sense of the word, were laid alongside the literature, namely, the study of the Koran and of the *hadìth*, the juridical interpretation and the first deepenings of theology. All this incipient intense activity was accomplished under the Omayyads primarily in Medina, which had remained the depository of the prophetic tradition even after having lost its primacy as a capital, and to a lesser degree in Damascus where heterodox theological tendencies took root, and in the *amsàr* of Iraq, Kufa and Basra, where grammar and philosophy were to flourish in the first Abbasid period. Egypt with North Africa, and the Iranian regions, were still sterile, or seemed to be, in the scientific field, though they were destined to a great future in this regard. What was now being accomplished in all these peripheral regions was the slow fusion among the Arab newcomers and the indigenous cultures and populations from whose amalgamation Arabo-Moslem culture and science were to emerge. The Omayyad period shows us the very first fruits of such contact in the field of art, in the few surviving monuments as the Great Mosque of Damascus and the caliphal palaces in the Syrian desert, Qusair Amra, Mshatta and Qasr al-Hair. All these arose under the influence of the Syro-Byzantine precedent, and Hellenistic artistic tradition which the Arabs had received here almost passively in this first period before combining and modifying it with other elements. The Arab culture of the Omayyad era, centered in the triangle formed by Arabia, Iraq and Syria, had the freshness and acerbity of youth: it was a tenuous flower, which was to yield its opulent fruit only after the disappearance of the Omayyads.

FOUR sons of Abd al-Malik ascended to the throne of Damascus in less than twenty years after his death: the first one al-Walìd, who still enjoyed the fruits of Hajjàj's devotion and energy ruled for a decade (705-15) and saw the most distant triumphs of the conquests from Transoxiana to Spain. Then his brother Sulaymàn, whom tradition depicts as a slothful hedonist, ruled for two years. He further committed the mistake of upsetting the internal policy of his brother by persecuting the creatures of the deceased Hajjàj in favor of their Muhallabite rivals. He was followed by the interlude during which Omar ibn Abd al-Azìz or Omar II (717-20), ruled. The latter stood outside direct descendance from Abd al-Malik, and was a cousin of Sulaymàn. The intrigue of a learned jurist, fond of conflicts, had obtained the designation for him from the dying Caliph. Omar II was the only Omayyad whose memory has been spared the condemnation which has been hurled at the whole dynasty in the pietistic and philo-Abbasid tradition that has come down to us. He was a man of sincere, intimate dedication, with a scrupulous desire for justice who was inspired by his great namesake of Islam's heroic age. We have seen his honest attempt, which in itself was not at all Utopian—no matter what may be said about it —to heal the imbalance between the arrogant pride of the hegemonic race and the equalitarian spirit of its faith. His attempt failed in a purely politico-economic jurisdictional sphere, but Islam has rewarded him by making Omar II a model of the ideal sovereign. After three years, there was a return to the remaining sons of Abd al-Malik, who had been kept from the throne momentarily, with Yazìd II (720-24). Yazìd II also seemed to have succumbed to the destiny of names, by repeating the frivolous character of the name-sake son of Muàwiyah and reviving the condemnations which the latter had drawn upon himself. By once more inverting Sulaymàn's policy, and showing himself hostile to the Muhal-labites, he provoked their revolt in Iraq (721). He had to send the best sword of his dynasty, his brother Màslamah to quell the uprising. (Among all these sons of Abd al-Malik Màslamah perhaps was most worthy of the throne. But he was always excluded, being the son of a slave girl and because of Arab racial pride which was to fall away completely under the Abbasids).

The suppression of the Muhallabite revolt, and the exter-mination of that illustrious, but restless, and intrigueful race, which provoked the resentment of the whole northern Arab element to which it belonged, was the achievement of the caliphate of Yazìd II who in the anecdotes about him is remembered more for his favorite concubines and his dissi-pations. Fortunately for the Omayyads, Yazìd II in 724 was

succeeded by another brother, Hishàm, and in the twenty
years of his reign the Arab Empire experienced the last noon-
day splendor before the storm.

Hishàm ibn Abd al-Malik was a man devoid of any physical or moral attractiveness; he was a harsh and tight-fisted administrator without the charm of Muàwiyah, or the majesty
of Abd al-Malik or of Walìd. But he knew how to appreciate
the legacy that had come into his hands, and how to watch
over it and defend it tenaciously. He was able to make use of
another faithful and intelligent servant, Khalid al-Qasri, for the
important position of trust in Iraq. Like Ziyàd and Hajjàj the
latter was a *homo novus* and no less than they served well for
the preservation of peace and for the material prosperity of
the country entrusted to him. After the Muhallabite revolt,
and in a period of relative surcease from the Kharijite guerrilla
warfare, Iraq enjoyed a breathing spell under his rule. Governors of different worth and ability succeeded each other in
the province of Khurasàn, always in conflict in Transoxiana
with the Turks, while other Turks (the Khazars) threatened
the Moslem frontiers from Armenia and the Caucasus. They
were thrown back only after arduous operations conducted
by eminent military leaders like Màslamah and Marwàn ibn
Mohammed, the future last sovereign of the dynasty. The
formidable revolt of the Berbers flared up in the West at the
time of Hishàm, and the Caliph sent expedition after expedition from Syria to put it down. Many succumbed before
Hànzalah ibn Safwàn saved the destinies of Arabism in the
Maghrib (742) in a battle near Qairawàn. In far-off Spain,
Arabs and Berbers, old and new recruits, scuffled with each
other in an alarming anarchy. Destiny reserved the task of
terminating this situation precisely to Hishàm's descendants.
This parsimonious and sober-minded Caliph, who was most
jealous of his authority, firmly ruled the Empire from his
favorite residence Rusafa in the Syrian desert, the splendid

remains of which are preserved in modern Qasr al-Hair. The Empire was not enlarged under him (in the distant Frankish West, at Poitiers, the Arab wave, for the first time, flowed back from the furthermost points that had been reached). But it was preserved strong and united, at least in appearance. Having died in 743, Hishàm could not gratify his desire to leave the throne to one of his own sons, and he had to maintain the order of succession arranged by his predecessor Yazìd, in favor, precisely of the latter's son, Walìd ibn Yazìd. He was an impatient heir, exasperated by a subterranean ill-feeling towards the reigning uncle, and by uncontrolled passions. With him was ushered in the final crisis, in which the fortunes of the Omayyads and of the Arab state were to collapse together.

WALÌD II was not made for politics: he hardly let himself be seen in Damascus, and remained in his residences in the Syrian desert, giving himself completely to revelry and poetry. The most iniquitous and stupid act of his reign was to have allowed Hishàm's faithful governor, Khalid al-Qasri, to perish amid cruel and sadistic torments. This Khalid al-Qasri had fallen into disgrace under his predecessor but had been living undisturbed until then. Khalid's death and Walìd's conduct, wholly dissipated and violent in character, rekindled the hatreds around the throne. A conspiracy was hatched among the Caliph's own kin, and it exploded in Damascus in April of the year 744, bringing to power a son of Walìd I, Yazìd, while Walìd II was captured in flight in the Palmirene, and killed. The same year of 744 saw four Caliphs rapidly succeed one another in Syria, from Walìd II to Yazìd III who died after a few months, to the brother of the latter Ibrahim who was recognized only in northern Syria, and to

Marwàn II who was to be the last Omayyad of the East. He was a nephew of the first Marwàn, who up to then had remained far removed from dynastic disputes, intent upon governing the frontier provinces and on the wars related to them. He had acquired an exceptional military experience in long campaigns in Armenia and in the Caucasus under Hishàm, which he also applied to military reforms of an organic and a tactical character (a professional army, and combat in closed formations in place of the disordered open order of the Arabs). In the chaotic situation created by the death of Yazìd III, he stepped forward, basing himself on the Qays and other north-Arabian tribes in the north of Syria. He was proclaimed Caliph in Damascus in December 744, but he immediately transferred his residence to Harràn in Mesopotamia and for two years he led a strenuous struggle on many fronts, against defections and revolts proliferating on all sides.

Syria itself rose against him, supporting another Omayyad claimant, Sulaymàn ibn Hishàm, whom Marwàn had to defeat in Hims. Meanwhile Shi'ite and Kharijite insurrections followed one upon the other, the most serious of which was that of the Kharijite Dahhàk ibn Qays ash-Shaibani, who after taking over Kufa held out there for almost two years, also advancing against northern Mesopotamia. As soon as he was free of other troubles, Marwàn crushed this insurrection in September 746, leaving the final liquidation of the movement to the new governor of Iraq. At the end of this year the valorous and tenacious Omayyad believed himself to be the master of the situation in Syria, Mesopotamia and Iraq, when a new threat arose in the East. It was to render futile the work accomplished until then, and bring him and all his dynasty crashing down into ruin.

The new fact was the entry on the scene, or better the passage to the level of action in Khurasàn of Abbasid subversion which had already been working clandestinely for decades to undermine the bases of the Omayyad state. The Abbasids, that is the descendants of Abbàs, the Prophet's uncle, were Hashimite just like the Alids: i.e. belonging to the same clan of Mohammed, although deprived of the closer blood link which Ali had contracted with the Prophet by marrying his daughter, Fàtimah. In a first phase, they were mixed up in general legitimist current of the opposition to the Omayyads, in the name of the blood-rights of the Banu Hashim, which was the denomination they shared in common with the Alids. In the revolts with which these latter had several times claimed such rights (from that of Husayn to that of Mohammed ibn al-Hanafiyyah, and to that of Zayd ibn Ali), the Abbasids had remained in the background. But they themselves soon initiated the activity in an ambiguous competition with the cousins who were Ali's descendants, in order to uproot the power of the "impious" Omayyads. The Abbasid tradition, instead, fixed a regular cession, at a determined moment, of rights from the Alid side to them as the leaders of the legitimist movement. This is supposed to have been the much-discussed "testament of Abu Hashim," a real investiture with which this son of Ibn al-Hanafiyyah, upon dying in 716, is supposed to have transferred his rights and powers to the Abbasid Mohammed ibn Ali. Whatever there is to think of this formal cession, in the last decades of the Omayyad caliphate the Shi'ite and Abbasid subversion continued along parallel lines, often intersecting. It seems that Caliphs and governors, even the most energetic and alert, underrated the danger of these intrigues. Perhaps they were also deceived by the relative ease with which typically the Alidic insurrections had been put down, in contrast with the bloody Kharijite guerrilla warfare. It is certain that Abbasid subversion was able to branch out from Iraq to the eastern provinces, especially in Khurasàn, where it found a favorable reception in the autochthonous "customers" or *Mawali*, the same element on which Mukhtàr's Shi'ite revolt in Kufa had based itself sixty years before. Then as now, the latter were non-Arab Moslems discontented with their inferior economic and social position. Thus Hashimite legitimism, born in a frankly Arab ambience and operating on behalf of an Arab race, nourished itself in an Iranian ambience of social resentments and repressed national ideals of that conquered people, forged in the crucible of mystical messianic beliefs and an ardent religious fantasy. But if the Iranian *Mawali* furnished the shock troops for the Abbasid revolution, all Arabs cannot be considered as having been strangers or hostile to the movement. Not only were its instigators and beneficiaries Arabs, but part of its most convinced propagandists (like some of the *Nuqabà* or Apostles who were deputized by the Abbasid claimant to the leadership of the cause), its military leaders who led the movement to victory (primarily the Tayyit Qàhtabah ibn Shabìb), and part of the fighting forces themselves were Arabs. It must be concluded from this that the politico-religious theme of anti-Omayyad legitimism produced the fraternization between Arabs and non-Arabs in the revolution, and that whereas the latter, more or less, consciously pursued ethnic and social demands, the Arabs did not realize that they were sacrificing their national hegemony to their resentments and fanaticisms. Most of them did not realize this, but some far-seeing minds were aware of it like Nasr ibn Sayyàr, the last Omayyad governor of Khurasàn. He pointed out in his urgent poetic appeals to the Caliph for assistance, when the conflagration was about to destroy everything, that "the killing of Arabs" was the final aim of the revolt.

The Arabs of the Khurasàn had conscientiously destroyed themselves in tribal struggles, seditions and secession, all of which were to the advantage of the Abbasid movement. The direction of this movement was assumed there around 746 by

Abu Muslim, an obscure personage of Persian descent whom Ibrahìm, the Abbasid pretender to the throne, had sent from Kufa to the eastern province with full powers.

When in the summer of 747 he unfurled the black banners of the Abbasids near Merw, the forces and the authority of the valiant Nasr ibn Sayyàr were already strongly compromised by the chain revolts with which he had until then struggled in his province. Not only did the *Mawali* answer the Abbasid appeal *en masse*, but also the southern Arab tribes and the cognate group of the Rabia responded, while only the northern group of the Mudar remained loyal. The marshalling of Marj Rahit at the advent of the Marwanide branch was now upset and the southern Arabs, who had gone over to the opposition after the extermination of the Muhallabites, were now among the most fervent anti-Omayyads. The veteran Nasr vainly tried to arrest the movement at the beginning with insufficient forces. After being defeated, he had to flee towards the West and died in flight, glimpsing the outline of the catastrophe which he had foreseen and tried to exorcise. The advance of the rebels grew like an avalanche, rolling towards the West, without a single military leader of worth being found who could bar their path with adequate forces. Màslamah ibn Abd al-Malik had disappeared from the scene since 738, and the Caliph himself, Marwàn, had hardly caught his second breath after the bitter struggles of the preceding years. In September 749 the "Blacks" entered Kufa without striking a blow, and in November of the same year, after the Alids had been unmistakably set aside, the new dynasty was proclaimed in the capital of the opposition. The first Abbasid Caliph was Abu l-Abbàs, the son of Ibrahìm, the claimant to the throne. The surname of as-Saffàh with which he has passed into history can be interpreted either as "The Bloody One" or as "The Generous One," and the facts speak more in support of the first etymology.

Only at this point, after half of the Empire had already been lost, did Marwàn II face the enemy in person. It is difficult to evaluate by what errors of judgment or material obstacles that expert and energetic warrior let the decisive two years (748-49) go by without an adequate intervention on his part. In January of 750, at the head of a modest Syro-Mesopotamian army, on the Great Zab, a tributary of the Tigris, he encountered the Abbasid forces under the command of as-Saffàh's uncle, Mohammed ibn Ali. Marwàn's Arabs, undisciplined and quarrelsome to the end, fought poorly, and their rout was a decisive one. Syria, which Marwàn had alienated by transferring the Caliphal residence to Mesopotamia, did not give any effective support to the last Omayyad, and surrendered to the victors almost without resistance. Marwàn traversed Syria with the Abbasids at his heels, and from Palestine he sought refuge in Egypt. Here in upper Egypt or in Fayyùm his pursuers caught up with him and put him to death. But even before this the Abbasid terrorists had made massacre of his family, hunting down and slaughtering Omayyads (sadly notorious was the slaughter of Abu Futrus near Jaffa), violating sepulchres and giving vent to other expressions of bestial hatred. Actually all this is hard to understand for anyone who recalls the relative mildness, and sometimes the apparent obliviousness of the Caliphs of Damascus with respect to these claimants to the throne and their propaganda. Umayya's clan was wiped out, and his memory execrated. Only a nephew of Hishàm, Abd ar-Rahmàn ibn Muà-wiyah managed to save his life by an adventurous escape, and was bound to revive in Spain the fortunes of his people.

Syria was soon to regret the indifference with which it let its national dynasty be swept away, treated, as it immediately was, with an iron fist by the new masters. Here and there attempts at an Omayyad restoration took place, the greatest one of which was headed by a descendant of Muàwiyah, a scion of the first Sufyanid branch, who therefore was called as-Sufyani. After this movement, and others, were drowned in blood (751), the memory of as-Sufyani was preserved there with messianic and eschatological features, like that of an awaited restorer of justice and prosperity; this in the country which was forever degraded from the primacy which it had held for a century in Arab and Islamic history.

Of the other provinces, Persia could be considered as the mother of the revolution. Iraq finally saw its rivalry with Syria satisfied and, at least in part, its Hashimite legitimism, although the Shi'ite group were now thrown back into the opposition, and had henceforward to taste Abbasid repression and persecutions in forms which were certainly not milder than they had been under the Omayyads. Egypt changed masters gently. In the change of the dynasty and in the transfer of the center of the caliphate still further east (the Abbasids established themselves in loyal Iraq), North Africa saw a propitious occasion to loosen its bonds with the central power, and to pass on quickly to a substantial autonomy. Thus the very advent of the Abbasids coincided with the first displacement of the immense Empire which the Omayyads had succeeded, almost miraculously, in maintaining as a unity.

In the new phase that was now opening in Arab history, the language and culture of the conquerors (the latter being the fruit of a crossing between national elements and foreign cultures, under the sign of Islam) were to rise to a more splendid development, the outlines of which were barely visible in the Omayyad period. But the imperial moment of the Arabs had passed by. For those who study its history at the most authentic sources, the acme of ancient Arabism is not "in the golden prime of good Haroun Alraschid," as Tennyson put it, nor in the days of "Thousand and One Nights," but in the heyday of Muàwiyah, of Walìd and of Hishàm. The consciousness of having then reached the summit as a political force made headway only very much later even in the Arab world itself, when it began to contemplate its past no longer in the light of Moslem tradition, but in that of western historiography and ideologies.

5.

The Moslem Empire

IN Arabo-Islamic history the Caliphate of the Omayyads, which lasted less than a century, was followed by that of the Abbasids. They came to power by revolution in 750, and they maintained themselves in power with a dynastic and institutional continuity until 1258. But a comparison between the two periods based only upon the differences of duration would be wholly deceptive, because other more substantial differences contradistinguish them. The two dynasties had their ethnic origin in common (both were Arabs of the Quraysh tribe, but the second was closer to the Prophet because of its descent from one of his uncles, the eponymous Abbàs). But, as we have pointed out, the process initiated by the Omayyads, and developed and perfected by the Abbasids, of transition from a patriarchal to an absolute monarchy, on the model of the ancient Orient, was unique. With the Abbasids, however, the directing class of the State and of the Islamic community, which had been purely Arab under the Omayyads, lost this national character. And now, in addition to Arabs, it was broadly opened to Islamized non-Arabs (the *Mawali* and their descendants), Persians, Turks, Kurds, Aramaeans, and in the West, as we shall see, to Berbers and Spaniards. The common denominator of these various peoples, which really fused them and joined them like brothers, was the

Moslem faith, their feeling that they were members of a community which had its cradle in Arabia, its revelation in the Arab language, and which made use of this language to express its culture, which was a synthesis of genuine Arab elements with others of diverse provenience. This is tantamount to saying that Arab hegemony was transferred from the political field—where it had asserted itself under the Omayyads —to the cultural, setting its seal on all the Moslem civilization of the Middle Ages, and fusing the legacies of the more anterior civilizations, the Hellenistic as well as those of the ancient Orient, in a linguistic-cultural crucible. The antinomy between a national affirmation and a universalistic faith, from which the former nevertheless drew its legitimacy, had been a thorny issue in the Omayyad period and was resolved in the Abbasid era by the prevalence of the second element. In fact it established peace between the primordial people of Islam and all those who gradually came to accept the new faith, making them all equal in the political sphere as subjects of an absolute power.

But this political power, which in the beginning was personified by the new dynasty which inherited the Omayyad legacy, could not maintain its unitary character in the long run. The Arab empire had already arrived at its greatest limits of expansion in the middle of the eighth century, and the peripheral provinces would have ended up by slipping out of the hands of the Omayyads themselves, even if the Abbasid revolution had not destroyed them. As the other races found themselves the arbiters of their own destiny, within the frame of Islam, their special brand of autonomy was added to that of the Arabs. Thus the unitary Arabo-Islamic monarchy, at the very time that the second element of the equation was being emphasized to the detriment of the first, began to fall apart into a multiplicity of political formations which were held together (furthermore, not all of them) by a nominal bond of vassalage to the higher authority of the Caliph. This process began at the very moment of the advent of the Abbasids who from the beginning saw a good part of the Maghrib, along with Spain, slip out of their hands; it continued its course in the ninth century and was consummated in the tenth, reducing the direct power of the orthodox Caliph (other competing Caliphs were then to arise in Egypt and Spain) to little more than Iraq, which the Abbasids had elevated to the center of their Empire. Indeed at a certain point in Iraq itself the will and personality of the Caliph was no more than one of the elements of the game, played in cooperation or in opposition, with other political forces, Arab and non-Arab, who attacked or defended that remnant nucleus of what had been the great caliphal empire. Actual political control of the country then passed to other hands, the praetorian Turks in the second half of the ninth century, the Persian Buwayhids in the tenth, and again the Seljuk Turks in the eleventh. Finally, after some flashes of revival by the tenacious institution amid the waning of these successive hegemonies, the Abbasid dynasty and the Islamic caliphate received their death-blow from the Mongols in the middle of the thirteenth century.

In our project which is not an historical outline of that dynasty and of that caliphate but a survey of the Arabs as a whole, the Abbasids will be the protagonists only for the first phase of the long, checkered career of their dynasty, which was doomed to a gradual decadence. In fact the first great Caliphs of the house of Abbàs, no less than the Omayyads, were the leaders and representatives of the Moslem state, even in the aforementioned alteration of its base from a purely Arab one to one of a supra-national character. The premature decline of Abbasid power began from about the middle of the ninth century. Nevertheless Iraq, which had been thoroughly arabized, for about a century continued to be the center of the Moslem empire in the process of disintegration, just as the vicissitudes of Arabia, of Mesopotamia and Syria, of Egypt and of the whole Islamic west—which still today constitute the ethno-linguistic zone of Arabism—form part of a history of the Arabs. On the other hand the provinces east of Iraq, Persia and the territories further east (Sogdiana or Transoxiana) cut themselves off from the destinies of Arabism. They had played a part in the history of the conquests and of the Arab Empire, but the resurgence of the national conscience and language, and the successive domination by other foreign conquerors (Turks and Mongols) gradually reduced in these territories to a purely cultural function the imprint of Arabism, and they ended up by almost eradicating it there outside of the religious and scientific field.

ABU AL-ABBÀS AS-SAFFÀH, proclaimed Caliph in Kufa in November of 749, after the victory over the Omayyads and the pitiless hunt for the vanquished, did little more than inaugurate the advent of the "Blessed Dynasty," which has unreservedly won the sympathies of medieval Moslem historiography. Iraq which had been in the opposition for a century and had undermined the power of the Syrian dynasty with its revolts, offered itself as the natural seat of its supplanters. And this was sanctioned by the brother and successor of as-Saffàh, Abu Giafar al-Mansùr ("The Victor" i.e. by grace of God. All the Abbasid Caliphs have passed into history with a sobriquet attached to their name, an adjective or a participle which proclaims their piety, rectitude, faith in God and His favor). In Iraq Mansùr (754-75) created *ex-novo* as his residence the first nucleus of the superb metropolis of Islam, Baghdad, not far from the site of the Sassanid Ctesiphon on the west bank of the Tigris. Mansùr is the real founder of the

Abbasid state. He was a despot of frigid temperament who did not shrink from any cruelty or violence. At the same time, however, he was an energetic and intelligent organizer of the new order, placing the Caliph at the apex of an elaborate court and bureaucratic hierarchy, open equally to Arabs and non-Arabs. Naturally the backbone of the military and civil cadres were the Persian elements or Arabs of Persian origin who had made the revolution (the Khurasanians and the *Abnà ad-Dawla* or "Sons of the Dynasty," the faithful of the first hour). But when the principal Persian artificer of the advent of the Abbasids Abu Muslim, appeared to be disloyal to the Caliph and aspiring to personal ends, Mansùr did not hesitate to eliminate him. With the same lack of scruples he bloodily suppressed the Alidic revolts in Medina and Basra, where Ali's incompetent direct descendants belatedly realized that in the new Caliphs they had usurpers who were no less unscrupulous than the extinct Omayyads. In general, a deep overflow of politico-religious movements (the two terms are strongly intertwined in the history of ancient Islam) for a time accompanied and followed the advent of the Abbasid dynasty. Indeed, strictly speaking, this turbulence never managed to subside throughout all the five centuries of the dynasty's formal duration. If Kharijism entered into a distinct decline with the Abbasids, flaring up only sporadically, the Alidic Shiah did not admit defeat after the comedy of the "transfer of powers" from the one to the other Hashimite branch and it continued to redden the Moslem world with bloody revolts, in an infinite variety of nuances, some of which were singularly fortunate and fruitful, as we shall see. But under Mansùr and his successors a series of bizarre heretical movements proliferated as a result of the collusions between the extreme Shiah and ancient Iranian, religious and social doctrines. The precise doctrine and action of the Shiah is often all else but clarified by the contradictory data of the historical and heresiological sources, which modern historico-religious (and in fact historico-social) research is working hard to reconstruct critically. Mansùr found himself facing the fanatics of an extremist Iranian sect who claimed to adore him like a God, and whom nevertheless he blithely had massacred. Other movements with an economico-social, no less than a religious background, have had a greater impact on Moslem historiography and heresiology. In particular, these were the movements of al-Muqanna (778-80), the "Veiled Prophet" of Khurasàn under Mansùr's successor al-Mahdi; and later that of Babek (817-37), the rebel of Azerbaijàn, under Mamùn and Mù-tasim. The example of the successful Abbasid propaganda, during the course of which the most diverse tendencies of political opposition and religious heterodoxy had flowed together, was contagious. But all the aforementioned movements were drowned in blood, and the triumphs of heterodoxy were reserved to a less proximate future.

Under al-Mahdi (775-85), Mansùr's son, the suppression of the heterodox movements went hand in hand with the persecution of ideas, for which the Caliph created an apposite inquisitorial organ. These ideas were above all of Iranian origin, dualistic and Manichean in a special way, with which the Iraquian intellectual élite appears to have been permeated at this time. The poets Salih ibn Abd al-Quddùs and Bashshàr ibn Burd fell victim to al-Mahdi's persecution, just as the brilliant translator and stylist Ibn al-Muqaffa had been similarly executed under Mansùr. But al-Mahdi's Caliphate was no less important because of the foreign policy of the dynasty which sought to resume the military traditions of the Omayyad epoch, and restore Islam's aggressive drive. Since 751, on the morrow of the Abbasid revolution, a Moslem victory on the Talas river against a Chinese army had assured Islam's shaky destinies in Central Asia. Now, in 782, the Arabs, for the third and last time looked out on the Bosphorus, after having traversed the whole of Anatolia under the command of Mahdi's son Harùn (the future ar-Rashìd). The Empress Irene managed to send them back after entering into negotiations with them and paying a money tribute. The war with the Byzantines, regarded as the holy war *par excellence*, was vigorously continued under the major Abbasids (Harùn himself, Mamùn and Mùtasim, the last of whom distinguished himself by the conquest of Ammorium in 838). The *jihàd* on the Syrian frontier ceased to be the direct concern of the Caliphs of Baghdad, once the internal crisis of the Caliphate began, and it was continued by peripheral dynasties like the Hamdanids.

Harùn ascended the throne under the name of ar-Rashìd in 786, after his brother al-Hadi had ruled for hardly a year. He has passed into history, but perhaps more into legend and literature as the greatest sovereign of the Abbasids, almost as the incarnation of caliphal power and magnificence. In a strictly historical sphere, we would not know just how to justify this primacy (to which the late cycle of *The Thousand and One Nights* contributed more than all else), since neither does Harùn's personality present individual features of special value, nor is his reign marked particularly by memorable deeds. If anything, he has the dubious merit of being the first to sanction the dismemberment of the Moslem unitary monarchy, which had already begun, with the investiture granted in 799 to the Aghlabids of Tunisia, as sovereign tributaries and vassals, but in fact independent of Baghdad. The whole Maghrib west of Tunisia, and Spain, had already been lost to the Abbasids from the moment of their advent. The recognition of Aghlabid autonomy can also be considered as the only means that the Caliph saw to preserve some formal link with territories now practically withdrawing from his direct authority. Hence from the start of the ninth century, the political history of the Maghrib was totally broken off

he gallery, *Tower of the Infants, Alhambra* (*Arabic,* al Hamra—*the red
palace*]), *Granada, Spain. Erected in the fourteenth century by the Nasrid
ltans.*

Kazimain Mosque, Baghdad, Iraq. Abbasid dynasty.

*Dome of the Rock, Jerusalem. Erected in 691 by the Omayyad Caliph Abd-al-Mal
on the site of the Temples of Solomon and Herod.*

e Hegira: Mohammed's arrival at Medina, A.D.

Avicenna instructing a class in medicine.

Mosque of Sultan Qait bey, Cairo. Mameluke period, late fifteenth century.

Page from a thirteenth-century treatise on astrology.

Bedouins in the Sahara, Tunisia.

Street scene in Amman, Jordan, known in antiquity as Philadelphia.

President Nasser of Egypt with King Saud of Arabia at Mecca, 1954.

Prince Saud of Arabia with Emir Talal of Transjordan at Amman review, 193

e: President Bourguiba of Tunisia, King Hassan II of Morocco, and Ferhat s of Algeria at a conference in Rabat, 1961.

Below: Secretary-General Hassouna of The Arab League with Premier Kassim of Iraq at Baghdad, 1961.

King Hussein of Jordan with King Saud of Arabia. The Hashimite Hussein direct descendant of the Prophet Mohammed. The Saudi dynasty conquered unified the greater part of Arabia after the First World War.

from that of the Arabo-Islamic East, and for some time Egypt remained as the most western province of the actual Abbasid dominion. Even thus limited Harùn ar-Rashìd's Empire, stretching from Transoxiana to the reefs off Libya, is hardly comparable with what was to be a little more than a century later the constellation of peripheral states, linked to the nominal sovereignty of the Caliph of Baghdad who had been stripped of his authority. Harùn's reign, assisted by the intelligent energy of his vizier Yahya al-Bàrmaki (from a family of Persian origin who had already attained the highest state posts under Mansùr) certainly coincided with the highest international prestige of the Abbasid Caliphate in the East and the West, from the China of the Tangs to Charlemagne, whose diplomatic relations with ar-Rashìd are known to us, only, however, from western sources. In the interior (namely from now on "in Iraq") under Harùn's reign we can follow the development of an economic and agrarian policy, tending to the formation of vast landed estates, owned by the state and privately, but also an intensive exploitation of the soil with an elaborate system of irrigation. While taxation, the old problem of Omayyad times, had definitely been transferred from persons to real property, and was reorganized on more equitable bases (in the land tax, a percentage of the harvest was payable instead of a sum fixed in advance) every inequity between the Arab conquerors and the indigenous "customers" (*Mawali*) had now disappeared. It was then that the norms in regard to classic Moslem law were more fully elaborated, as reflected in the apposite manual on the land tax which the magistrate Abu Yusuf wrote precisely for ar-Rashìd. In the face of the importance of these political, economic and social problems, which only recent studies have begun to bring to light, there is only an anecdotal and picturesque value in the vast *adab* literature. This anecdotal literature, belonging to an older time than our *Thousand and One Nights,* describes for us in minute detail the splendors, gossip and scandals of Harùn's court with its musicians, singers and poets; or the pathetic episode of the fall of the Bàrmakids (803), in whose misfortune one might also look for some obscure political motive.

The succession of the "Righteous One" or the "Well Guided" (for this is the meaning of ar-Rashìd, whose moral personality does not seem to merit such praise) threatened to divide the Moslem Empire, which was already beginning to fall apart on its peripheries, at its very center. When Harùn died in 809, he was succeeded as Caliph by his son al-Amìn who quickly came into conflict with his brother al-Mamùn, who had been designated as the second successor, and governor of Khurasàn and of the whole Iranian part of the Empire. The whole Orient lined up behind al-Mamùn, who himself was Persian on his mother's side, while the weak and frivolous Amìn, after a series of defeats was reduced to a defensive position in Iraq and finally in Baghdad itself. A long and ruinous siege of the capital by al-Mamùn's forces put an end to the fratricidal war in 813 with the killing of al-Amìn and the general recognition of the victor. But it was only six years later that the new Caliph set foot in the metropolis of the Tigris, having been detained in the East by a series of politico-religious complications. In order to satisfy the Alidic legitimism, which was inconsolable because it had been sacrificed to the advantage of the Abbasids, Mamùn thought of designating as his own successor the Alid imàm ar-Rida (Ali's direct descendant and leader in his time of the *Ahl al-bait*). At the same time he presented him with his daughter as a wife (817). This was followed by a sudden revolt of the Abbasids who proclaimed another prince of the dynasty as Anti-Caliph in Baghdad; but everything ended in a general accommodation with ar-Rida's death, and that of Mamùn's vizier who had recommended the philo-Alidic policy. In 819 al-Mamùn finally made his entry into Baghdad and began the second phase of his reign which lasted until 833, and which in the intellectual and cultural field surpassed in importance that of his father ar-Rashìd.

In fact that intense movement of philosophical, scientific and medical studies, which showered fame on his caliphate and continued under his immediate successors, is due to the patronage of the Arabo-Persian Caliph. He let the treasures of Hellenistic philosophy and science seep into Moslem culture through translations from the Greek and Syriac. Al-Mamùn's personal contribution to this admirable cultural exuberance is difficult to determine but we are more certain of it than of ar-Rashìd's problematic cultural merits. The Caliph's keen speculative interests were manifested also in the position he took in the theological disputes of the times. Under the influence of the magistrate Ahmad ibn Abi Duàd he espoused the theories of the Mutazilite rationalist school with the related dogmas of human free will and of the creation in the course of time of the sacred Book. It was not a question of any Moslem "free thought," as was erroneously believed at one time, but of philosophical and theological doctrines which simply gave greater weight to rational speculation than to tradition. Its followers—like the true "free thinkers" of the 19th century—supported their ideas with an intolerant fanaticism, to which their adversaries hastened to reply in kind. In fact Mutazilism, which al-Mamùn declared a state doctrine in 827, prospered for almost twenty years; it created inquisitions and unleashed persecutions, and ended in turn by being persecuted itself when the opposite orthodox doctrine again prevailed under the Caliph al-Mutawakkil. Al-Mamùn died in 833, after launching a campaign against the Byzantines. Under him Khurasàn, which had been his base for the conquest of the kingdom, detached itself from direct dependence on Baghdad through the initiative of the formerly loyal general

Tahir. But the impressiveness of Mamùn's personality was enough to hold other centrifugal forces in check, and his conspicuous merits in the scientific field assured the most enduring fame to his caliphate.

Upon al-Mamùn's death still a third son of ar-Rashìd, al-Mùtasim, ascended the throne, reigning there until 842. He was a valiant soldier, whose mettle had been tried in many campaigns. Further, he also knew how to surround himself with able generals like the Persian Afshìn, who at last subdued Babek's long revolt and ended up as the victim of a dismal heresy trial. Also traceable to Mùtasim, however, is the initiative—which turned out to be fatal for the Abbasid dynasty—to give a great part in the army and its command to the Turkish element. Freshly Islamized, this element brought its roughness and martial efficiency to the islamic state, which quickly degenerated into undiscipline and tyrannical arbitrariness. With these Turkish praetorians, the Caliphs believed they could solve the military crisis which weakened the army cadres of elements which at first were pure Arabs, then a mixture of Arabs and Iranians, who had constituted its backbone under the first Abbasids. Likewise, the insecurity of the great Baghdad metropolis, which had profoundly altered and widened in character during the civil war at the time of al-Mamùn, induced al-Mùtasim to establish his own court residence in Samarra, less than a hundred miles north of the capital. Thus Samarra was the seat of the Abbasids for almost a half century, but then they again abandoned it in favor of Baghdad. Samarra's monumental ruins have been preserved up to our day, whereas only very scarce residues of Abbasid Baghdad have remained. The danger of the overbearing military power of the Turks was not slow in revealing itself, immediately after the energetic al-Mùtasim disappeared from the scene, and grew in all its seriousness under al-Mutawakkil (847-61), his second successor. This cruel, sensual and bigoted

Caliph, under whom the anti-Mutazilite reaction lastingly re-trieved power (harsh discriminatory measures, which had fallen into disuse, were newly applied against Christians and Jews) himself ended up by falling victim to his Turkish guard. And with his assassination it was possible to measure the gravity of the crisis that had struck the Arabo-Islamic state hardly a century after the advent of the "Blessed Dynasty." The caliphate, from a powerful and operating center of the whole Moslem community was on the way to becoming a figurehead at the mercy of the intrigues and acts of violence of a court clique, and its authority little by little was being re-stricted, from the enormous extension of Arab conquest, to the central nucleus of Iraq. Thus in four of the five centuries of its existence the history of the Abbasid dynasty gradually passed from the imperial to a merely local plane in Iraq.

THE caliphate was to reach the rock-bottom of this deca-dence only in the middle of the tenth century. The end of the ninth century and the beginnings of the tenth sparked the development of this process by the formation of ever new dynasties at the edges of the Empire: in Egypt the Tulunides (868-95) and, after a brief return to direct Abbasid admin-istration the Ikhshidids (935-69), in Syria and Mesopotamia the Hamdanids (929-1005) of whom we make mention later, in Persia the Saffarids (867-903) with other small local dynas-ties. Further still there were the Samanids of Transoxiana (874-999), the dynasty which played so important a role in the reformation of an Iranian national, or at least, cultural conscience. In all these regions and under all these sovereigns the higher authority of the Caliph of Baghdad was never denied in words, and the symbol of this was the mention of his name in the collective ritual Friday prayer. But subordination to the center was limited to such formal homage, to requested diplomas of investiture, and to the conferment of honorific titles (in some cases, also to the payment of a tribute). For the rest, these dynasties acted in full independence. An even more serious case was to be represented by the states which were not even formally to recognize the Caliph of Baghdad, as was the case with the Omayyads of Spain from the start, and with the Fatimids of Tunisia and then of Egypt from the beginning of the tenth century, the one and the other assuming the caliphal title in competition with the Abbasids.

In Baghdad this process of disintegration seemed to have been felt as fatal, but no caliph made a serious effort to arrest it. Indeed the defense of Abbasid authority and prestige was undertaken in the last decades of the ninth century by the brother and co-regent of the Caliph al-Mùtamid, al-Muwaffaq, an energetic soldier and administrator who loyally stood by the throne. He fought very hard to blunt the threat represented by the Saffarid emir Yaqùb ibn Laith, who had marched from the Orient against Baghdad (876), and he acquired merit above all by putting down, after years of tenacious struggle, a dangerous slave-war, the revolt of the Zanj. These Negroes had been imported from east Africa in order to work the salt-mines of the southern Babylonian provinces. They were exploited and tormented in the most inhuman manner by their masters. As a result they broke out into open revolt in 869. For fourteen years they drenched Iraq in blood, conducting a real war of maneuver which at one moment made them the actual masters of the Babylonian provinces which they subjected to a frightful pillage and plunder. Muwaffaq was the Crassus of the Abbasid repression which came to an end only in 883 with the storming of the rebels' capital, the ephemeral Mukhtarah (the "Elect") on the Tigris, from where the rebellion had been directed by an Alid agitator.

Muwaffaq's death in 891 marked the disappearance of the

only Abbasid who, because of his high qualities as a person and ruler might have been able to arrest the decadence of the dynasty. Nevertheless the capital that had been accumulated in the century and a half of ascendant Arab fortune was still so great that at the beginning of the tenth century the Caliph of Baghdad could still consider himself a potentate of the first magnitude in the Near East. Those were the years when from Italy, Bertha of Tuscany, the daughter of Emperor Lotharius II, turned to the Caliph al-Mùktafi (902-08) with offers of marriage and of an alliance, perhaps for an action against the common enemy, Byzantium. Thanks to Ibn Fadlàn's precious geographical and ethnographical report, we know about the embassy to the Volga Bulgars of Mùktafi's brother and successor, Mùqtadir (908-32). We also possess a no less precious description of the state revenues for one year of his reign, 919, with the exact tributary yield from each of the provinces. From this picture it appears that at that time, besides Iraq, Persia and Mesopotamia, also Syria and Egypt, and part of Arabia, Armenia, and Azerbaijàn were more or less directly subject to the caliphal authority. But the situation rapidly worsened. Immediately after Mùqtadir's death, Egypt and Syria definitely escaped from direct caliphal control, while in Persia the rule of the Iranian family of the Buyids or Buwayhids (932-1055)—who were to take the caliphate under tutelage—was being formed. The revolt of the heretical Qarmatians had been raging for some time in Iraq. In Baghdad viziers and generals like Ibn al-Furàt, Ibn Muqla and the eunuch Munis contended for power in a long series of intrigues and palace dramas, of which the Caliph was the actor or passive spectator and often the victim, accompanied by phenomena analogous to the most turbid periods of Byzantine history. In 936 a new figure appeared in the hierarchy and list of titular dignities of the Abbasid state, that of *Amìr al-Umarà*, or supreme commander. It was conferred for the first time by

Caliph ar-Radi on the governor Ibn Raiq with full military and civil powers, which reduced the Caliph's functions to those of a purely honorary post. And *Amìr al-Umarà* was the title that was conferred on the Buwayhid Muizz ad-Dawla in 945 when, coming from Persia, he entered al-Mansùr's ancient capital. Here he was hailed as defender and patron by the degenerate epigonus of the first great Abbasids from whom these faint-hearted successors often seemed to have inherited only their negative qualities. The Buwayhids had formed a family rule in Iraq, which was divided among the branches of three brothers, at once associates and rivals. After a series of recognitions from the Caliph, one of the brothers succeeded in installing himself in the capital itself (alternating this residence with the Persian residence in Shiraz). Thus was created the singular situation of an orthodox Caliph "protected" by an heterodox emir, since the Buwayhids were of the Shi'ite confession. Nevertheless such protection, which had an ironic ring for the heirs of the Arabo-Islamic Empire, was a necessity and a salvation for them. For at that time and later they had been reduced to dependence on the grace of rival emirs, and sometimes of mere adventurers or bandits (such as an al-Baridi, in Buwayhid times, or later, at the time of the Seljuks, an al-Basasiri). They were dragged and bandied about hither and thither in their quarrels, raised to power and deposed, mutilated and put to death. In this state of extreme degradation, from which the Abbasids were to rise only formally in some other less stormy period, the principle of the orthodox Quraysh Imàm as the successor of the Prophet and the symbol of the entire Islamic community nevertheless remained firm, albeit his powers had been reduced to merely "spiritual" ones. There has been much discussion about this limitation. It has been justly observed, for instance, that in the theory of Islamic public law such a distinction of powers does not exist for the supreme monarch of Islam. Indeed no spiritual and doctrinal powers may be attributable to him analogous to those of the Roman pontiff. If this is true in theory, it is no less true that in fact, once every actual "temporal" authority had passed into the hands of profane authorities, like emirs and sultans, the institute of the caliphate from that time on preserved and accentuated a religious aura about itself. It was considered as the first magistrature of Islam which was directly traceable back to the "lieutenancy" of the Prophet, and as the custodian of the faith, capable of inspiring reverence as an institution if not as individuals, even among the very persons who dominated and abused it. It was only three centuries later the Mongolian tempest effectuated the total dissolution of any organized power at the center of the Moslem world, and caused the Abbasid Caliphate to vanish from the scene, without arousing appreciable reactions in the Islamic world. But for the time being the shadows of caliphs who continued to reside in Baghdad under the tutelage of the Buwayhids always received the formal homage of these same heterodox groups and from the whole of orthodoxy. After almost a century they changed masters when in 1055, the last Buwayhids having been swept away, the Seljuk Turks made their entry into Baghdad. With these the third ethnic element on which medieval Islam leaned, and which had already looked out on Islam's history in the ninth century as the Caliph's praetorian guards, now installed itself at the center of the caliphate, supplanting both Arabs and Persians and assuming the functions of a guiding-people in eastern Islam.

THIS process of disintegration, and the tendency of some historical sources, risk reducing the history of the Moslem Empire of this period to the dynastic chronicle of the Caliph of Baghdad and to anecdotes concerning the palatine circle.

In reality, however, beginning even before the tenth century many other forces were operative on the edges of the Abbasid state: forces which the characteristics of oriental history also arrange into dynastic schema, in pure terms of political vicissitudes, or as an effect of politico-religious movements. In the constellation of more or less ephemeral dynasties into which the caliphate was gradually disintegrating, the history of the Arabs offers the Hamdanids of Mesopotamia and Syria as a typical example of the first case, whereas the Fatimids of Egypt exemplify the second.

In contrast to the Tulunides and Ikhshidids who preceded the Fatimids in Egypt, and to the minor and major Persian dynasties, the Hamdanids were pure Arabs of the tribe of the Taghlib, and they were among the first to rise as practically independent emirs within the very nucleus of the most ancient Arabo-Moslem state. The fortunes of the family began in 904, when the Caliph al-Mùqtadir nominated one of their members, Abu l-Haijà ibn Hamdàn, governor of Mosul in Mesopotamia. His son in fact became lord of the province, a phenomenon which became increasingly frequent in those times, and received the title of Nasir ad-Dawla in 941 from the Caliph. But the Syrian branch of the family rose to a much greater renown than the Mesopotamian branch of the Hamdanids, who were soon led back to a status of vasallage not indeed by the Caliph but by his Buwayhid "protectors." The founder of the Syrian branch and its most illustrious representative was Nasir ad-Dawla's brother Saif ad-Dawla (944-67) who founded his power in Aleppo. Here a task that was more important and honorable than the usual dynastic disputes awaited him; the prosecution of the holy war against the Byzantines, who were now in the process of escaping from the weakened grasp of the Caliphs. Saif ad-Dawla took on this task with Arab pride and Moslem zeal and carried it out until his death. The war was a series of rough campaigns, not all of which were victorious, against the traditional Christian foe in one of its periods of greatest efficiency (these were the times of the great military emperors Nicephorus Phocas and John Tzimisces). Saif ad-Dawla and his kin and successors experienced both victories and defeats on both sides of the Taurus mountains, and for a moment they even saw the Byzantines actually within the walls of their Syrian capital. But if these campaigns did not give enduring successes to either of the two contenders, and did not considerably modify the frontier between the two hostile worlds along the mountains of Cilicia, they did galvanize Arab national feeling and Moslem pride as in the days of their most epic feats, and they were celebrated as such by the poets. Saif ad-Dawla's martial achievements live on in the verses of al-Mutanabbi, the most outspoken champion of Arabism which was already in a state of decline, in those of the soldier-prince Abu Firàs, cousin of the emir of Aleppo, and in those of a pleiade of minor panegyrist poets. This occurred because Saif ad-Dawla's court in Aleppo, in addition to the honor of conducting the holy war also enjoyed the prestige of having been a distinguished center of culture and poetry. Not only the great Mutanabbi, but the philosopher al-Farabi, Plato's interpreter among the Moslems, the illustrious man of letters Abu l-Faraj al-Isfahani, compiler of the precious *Kitàb al-Aghani,* and many other poets and writers enjoyed the hospitality and rich patronage of the greatest Hamdanid emir. His heritage survived him for only a few decades, because his little state had already disappeared at the beginning of the year 1000, being absorbed by the Fatimids. His legacy to the Arab world was the remembrance of a luminous affirmation of the converging values of Islam and Arabism, which were attended to, if we may use the words of al-Mutanabbi, "with the sword and the pen."

For reasons that were either frankly political or religious, to an extent that we cannot exactly determine, the Hamdanids

of Syria declared themselves Shi'ites, and instead of the orthodox Caliph of Baghdad they recognized the Fatimid anti-
caliph of Africa and then of Egypt. The Fatimid dynasty and
state constituted the greatest political achievement of heterodox Arabism, which we have seen dissipate itself in a chain of
sterile revolts under the Omayyads and the first Abbasids, under the banner of Alidic legitimism. The imàms or Ali's direct
descendants of the Husayn branch, who were always recognized as the leaders of this legitimism, had succeeded one
another until the end of the ninth century in a state of ex-
pectancy which was as vain as it was messianic. The Abbasid
revolution had merely exploited them and used them as pawns
and al-Mamùn's attempt to consolidate them peacefully into
the caliphal state had soon failed. But the ferments, the expectations, the intrigues to realize or to exploit their aspirations as the symbol and pretext for the ambitions and doctrines of others, continued to operate in the form of an underground activity for more than two centuries, before culminating into movements which were historically conclusive.
Very soon the marching wing of the Alidic movement revealed itself to be that of the Ismailites or "Seveners," namely
of those who recognized an Ismail as the seventh imàm of the
series after Ali, with whom, in their reckoning, the chain of
visible imàms was terminated. Others, instead, continued it up
to the twelfth (hence the name of "Twelvers"). For the one
as for the other, the line of the legitimate Imàm (which in
this case was the synonym of Caliph, with a more emphasized religious and sacral connotation, alien to orthodoxy)
disappeared at a certain point from public notice (and some
of these imàms had in fact physically "disappeared," i.e. they
were to disappear from circulation through the machinations
of their enemies) in order to flourish later in accordance with
Messianic expectations, either in their own persons, or in that
of their declared descendants and representatives. A similar

historico-theological conception was fertile *humus* for every sort of subversive doctrine and movement, which from the second half of the ninth century flared up here and there. In their opposition to orthodoxy and loyalty towards the Abbasid Caliphs they sometimes really convulsed the political and social body of Islam.

The most serious of these movements in the heart of the central provinces of the caliphate was that of the Qarmatians, so-called after a Hamdàn Qarmat, which around 890 drenched Iraq and Syria in blood. It conducted agitation for a program of Ismailite legitimism, coupled with an esoteric interpretation of the *batin* or occult meaning of the Koran (hence the name of Batinites or "Occultists" that was given to all those sectarians), and egalitarian social doctrines. After being opposed and repressed, in these provinces, the Qarmatians succeeded in affirming themselves in the Arab peninsula where in al-Ahsa (modern Bahrain) in 899 they founded their own independent state, which was ruled by an oligarchic and comunitarian regime up to the first decades of the eleventh century. The practically republican form of the Qarmat state of Arabia (which in 930 conducted a successful raid on Mecca, and temporarily removed the Black Stone) at first sight seems to be in contradiction with the legitimist principle which to us will appear to be more coherently personified in the Fatimid monarchy. But on the one hand we know little about the authentic doctrines of the Qarmatians, and about their relations with the contemporary Fatimids, and, on the other hand, the principle of the legitimate "hidden" Imàm evidently gave every possibility of recognizing him or at least his incarnation in individual claimants, requiring in the meanwhile obedience to those who presented themselves as their temporal vicars. Another point to bear in mind in all these heterodox movements is that the "Imamite" principle, with its historical and genealogical implications was often only the point of departure for religious, philosophical, and social doctrines with which the pure and simple Alidic legitimism had no necessary genetic connection. It appears to us, rather, as the catalyst of such doctrines, in great part of non-Arabic origin but of late antique (neo-Platonic) gnostic and Iranian provenience, combining these elements in the most bizarre syncretism. For the tenth century the best known literary evidence of such esoteric doctrines is the so-called "Encyclopedia of the Ikhwàn as-Safà," a corpus of about fifty "Epistles" in which a sodality of initiates ("The good friends") with its seat in Basra expressed its view of the world and the *summa* of its culture which was precisely oriented in an Ismailite sense.

But in the political sphere the most successful of such heterodox movements was the Fatimid which, based on Alidic legitimism, could counterpoise itself to the Abbasid caliphate, as an equal. Its first affirmation would exceed the spatial limits of this chapter, and should be included, rather, in the history of western or Maghribian Islam. But the displacement which the Fatimid State effected by transferring from Tunisia to Egypt, and its successive gravitation towards the Orient, enlarging its dominions in Palestine and Syria, give it a more appropriate place in the frame of the dismemberment of the Abbasid Empire. At the beginnings of the tenth century a new power of Ifrìqiya (modern Tunisia) supplanted the Aghlabids whose autonomy had been recognized a century earlier by Harùn ar-Rashìd. The new sovereign, Ubaidallàh al-Mahdi, was or proclaimed himself an Alid, descendant of Ali and Fàtimah, Mohammed's daughter, hence the name of Fatimid for the dynasty, also called Ubaidids after the name of its founder. The substantiality of this genealogical connection was already disputed in ancient times and still is today. A modern theory denies that al-Mahdi was an Alid, holding him to be the son of an Ismailite agent, but in turn considers him as the "father" through an initiatic affiliation, of an authentic descendant of the imàm Ismaìl, the second Fatimid Caliph al-Qaim. In general all the origins of the Fatimid movement and of the related propaganda, which went from the sectarian central office of Salamiyyah in Syria to Mecca, and from here to its successful affirmation in Ifrìqiya, are wrapped in an obscurity that is almost impossible to dissipate. It is certain that Ubaidallàh, with the messianic title of al-Mahdi, came to power in 909 in Africa as the legitimate Imàm or Caliph of Ismailite descent. He got rid, Abbasid-style, of his adversaries and of his own Abu Muslim, the propagandist Abu Abdallàh ash-Shii, and with his new capital Mahdiyya he founded a dynasty and a state destined to have a great future. In a first phase the Fatimid expansion was more fortunate in a westerly direction, subjecting to its power a good part of the Maghrib to the point where it collided with the opposite imperialism of the Omayyads of Spain; but it early also had its eye on Egypt. Two attempts to conquer it under the first Fatimids failed, in the face of the resistance first of the direct Abbasid power, and then of the new local dynasty of the Ikhshidids. But in 969, under the fourth Caliph al-Muizz, his general Jawhar (a valiant man of arms and of affairs of Sicilian, Byzantine or Slavic origin), easily succeeded in making himself the master of the valley of the Nile, which had already been worked on by Fatimid propaganda. A short time later the Caliph himself transferred to the capital (which Jawhar founded at that time near ancient Fustàt) with the auspicious name of al-Qàhira ("The Dominant", i.e. Cairo). And in its new seat the heterodox dynasty initiated the most brilliant phase of its history.

After al-Mahdi the greatest Fatimid sovereigns were al-Muizz (952-75) and his son al-Azìz (975-96). The most famous was the son of al-Azìz, the violent and brilliant, half-insane al-Hakim (996-1020). When the caliphate of Baghdad was now but a shadow of its former greatness, under the

tutelage of the Buwayhid *Amìr al-Umarà*, the Fatimid caliphate of Egypt arrived at the apex of the parabola, rapidly
becoming a force of the first magnitude among the Moslem
and Christian states of the Mediterranean. Its conquest of
Palestine and Syria in part corresponded to the old aspiration
of every strong and solid Egyptian state, from the Pharaohs
to the Ptolemies, in part to the specific Fatimid program
of politico-religious expansion of wresting as many territories
as they could from their weakened Iraquian rivals. Thus
Fatimid Egypt became the guiding-state of Ismailite propaganda, even though the rise to power had created problems
of conservation and balance for the Imàmic dynasty which
restrained its original revolutionary drive. This is the sense in
which its fluctuating relation with the Qarmatians of Arabia
has been explained, who at one moment appeared as docile
satellites of the Fatimids, and at another assumed the attitude
of an extremist political opposition. But certainly in relation
to the Fatimid power and propaganda the whole tenth century, even outside Egypt, has been called Islam's "Ismailite
Century," because of the great number of political, religious
and philosophical ferments that welled up everywhere, influenced by Ismailite doctrines, traces of which have been
found even in the works of poets like al-Mutanabbi. Other
poets like the Andalusian Ibn Hani were among the pane-
gyrists and official propagandists of the Shi'ite dynasty which
in addition made use of a net of secret agents (*duàt*), spread
in almost all regions of the orient. Travelers and geographers
like the Arab Ibn Hawqal in the tenth century, or the Persian
Nasir-i Khusrev in the eleventh, seemed to have been won
over to its cause and to be under its influence, because of the
indoctrination absorbed and also because of the show of efficiency and of prosperity which Fatimid Egypt, in its halcyon
days, offered in contrast to the conditions of insecurity or of
virtual anarchy in which the regions of the eastern caliphate

were then floundering. There was a rich and splendid court, regulated by a pompous and minute ceremonial surprisingly similar to that of the Byzantine court, a magnificent capital and a florid economic and financial situation. The latter was also due to the unprejudiced employment of Jewish functionaries and technicians, like the brilliant vizier Ibn Qillis, to an army and, above all, to a most efficient fleet, capable of coping with its Byzantine and Spanish counterparts in the waters of the Mediterranean, as well as to an active maritime trade in the Mediterranean itself (among others with the Italian maritime republics of Amalfi, Pisa and Venice) and in the Red Sea and the Indian Ocean; finally to a crown of vassal possessions and states which stretched from Sicily to part of Arabia, to Palestine and Syria. Such were the features of the Fatimid state at the height of its power, which had been achieved with the conquest of Egypt and maintained for a good part of the following eleventh century, under the very long caliphate of al-Mustansir (1035-94). The latter's succession ushered in a dynastic crisis; the powerful vizier al-Afdal gave preference to the youngest son Mustali instead of to the eldest son Nizàr, which served as a banner for new secessionist developments of the Ismailite movement. But the weakening of Fatimid power was now evident through other signs, as was proved by the loss of the Syrian possessions which had already begun, confirmed shortly thereafter by the very weak defense of its remnant positions in Palestine and Syria, in the face of the onslaught of the Crusaders. Indeed the Crusaders took Jerusalem from the Fatimids in 1099. Conquered also were the ports along the seaboard where only the Turkish emirs, the heirs of the Seljuks, furnished an effective assistance to the Moslem defense. The Cairo Caliphate still dragged on for almost a century in conditions not unlike those of the Abbasids of Baghdad, where in the play of rival forces an adventurer for an instant succeeded in having the

prayer recited in the name of the Fatimid Caliph (1059).
Like the Caliph of Baghdad, the latter also ended up by being
reduced to a personage fit only for show; he was confined to
the palace and was a mere tool in the hands of the viziers and
military chieftains who succeeded one another in the seat of
power. And when the last Fatimid al-Adid died, or was
helped to die in 1171, Saladin was able to lead Egypt back to
the fold of orthodoxy without any opposition, re-establishing
the formal recognition of the Abbasid Caliph there. Ismailite
heterodoxy does not seem to have had any influence in the
lower strata of the Egyptian population; it remained an ap-
panage of the court and government élite, ultimately evapo-
rating into a mere lip-service to the reigning dynasty. Nevertheless the Fatimid period remains a felicitous epoch in
Egyptian history because of the aforementioned political
power and economic prosperity, to which must be added a
great cultural flowering. Ismailism acted everywhere as a
most notable leaven of culture and science, albeit in the service
of its bizarre theology and political philosophy. In Egypt, as
in the other regions where it made its influence felt, intellectual life derived a vigorous impulse from it, especially
through the intensified contact with the scientific-philo-
sophical patrimony of late antiquity. Just as the Fatimid caliphate represents a most notable page in the political history
of the Arabs, so does the great Mediterranean adventure of
Ismailism remain one of the most fruitful phenomena of
medieval Islam. It was extinguished in Egypt in the twelfth
century, but it flourished further in Syria, where we shall
find it under the Crusaders, and in Persia and in India.

WE have already seen how the Abbasid state, from the start,
broadened its bases from the Arab element to the Iranian and

then to the Turkish, thereby dissolving the hegemony of the Arabs in the equality of absolutism. It thus realized an objective which in reality the Omayyads themselves had aimed at, but they had been held back by the unruly individualism of the Arab tribal structure on which they had to lean for support. After having eliminated the latter as a political force the Abbasids could freely establish their absolute state on the Sassanid model, the memory of which was still alive in Persia and in Iraq, with a veneer of piety and Moslem religious conformism. By this statement there is not the slightest intention to deny that the Caliphs completely felt their dignity as leaders of the Moslem community, and that they displayed a profound reverence towards the pious and the doctors of Islamic law (orthodox Islam does not have a real clergy) and that they considered their "Blessed Dynasty," as the triumph of the theocratic ideal over the impious Omayyad "kings." But in reality reasons of state, along the lines of and with the methods of oriental absolutism, had the upper hand over that theoretical ideal which had to content itself with a formal homage and with a very approximative realization.

In the Abbasid state the Caliph in theory (and in practice as much as he could) was the absolute sovereign, whose power was limited only by the norms of the *sharia* or sacred Moslem Law, interpreted and fixed by the doctors. But the Abbasids never had a ruler like Omar II, and all of them without exception in practice departed from the strict observance of the Law, whenever policy or their personal interest so counselled them. The figure of the vizier appeared alongside the Caliph, from the beginning of the dynasty. This was a novelty with respect to the Omayyad period, even though it does not appear so certain that the word and the office itself are of Iranian derivation. The vizier was the prime minister, the right arm of the sovereign and the head of the whole civil and military hierarchy of the state. One of the characteristics

of the Moslem Empire under the Abbasids and their successors was the development of a vast bureaucracy, divided into
several offices (*diwàn*) minutely organized and corresponding to western ministries. First among them stood the offices
of finance and of the treasury '*diwàn al-azimma*), the caliphal
chancellory '*diwàn ar-rasail* or *at-tawqì*), the office of the
state postal service together with the information services
(*diwàn al-barìd*) which exercised the central power's control
over the peripheral administration. As in Omayyad times
these were directed by governors (*Wali, Amil, Amìr*) flanked
sometimes by the head of the financial and fiscal services.
With the centrifugal process already referred to, those governors often were transmuted into autonomous local dynasties, sanctioned by caliphal recognition. Judiciary power was
exercised according to the norms of the *sharìa* by judges
(*cadi*), who were nominated by the Caliphs. Police powers
were exercised by the state police (*shurta*), and by a magistrate typical of medieval Moslem society, the *Mùhtasib* who
attended to the application of the norms prescribed by the
sharia in the municipal field, in the market place and in the
sphere of public morality.

It was in this governmental and administrative structure,
of which we have traced only the bare outlines, that the
Arabo-Islamic society of the Middle Ages lived out its long
and active day. In its material and spiritual aspects the ascend-
ing line of the civilization did not coincide with that of the
central political power whose parabola we also outlined above.
For while we have been able to count only a century of
unity and efficacy with respect to the Abbasid Caliphate, with
its actual imperial function, the index of the economic and
spiritual productivity of the society over which it presided
continued to rise for at least two centuries, and maintained
itself at a high level beyond the year 1000. It was to decline
later only in the Seljuk era, and was to come tumbling down

with the Mongol invasion, together with the last semblance of
the caliphate which in the beginning had been its propelling
center and almost the symbol of its continuous ascent.

The society of the Abbasid era was distinctly urban: the
desert which had been the matrix of Arabism, and with some
reservations of Islamism, no longer was the generator of active
forces, which now by choice concentrated and developed
in the cities. Baghdad, the imperial metropolis, surpassed every
other, followed closely by the oldest Arab cities of Iraq, Kufa
and Basra, and the centers of mixed Arabo-Persian languages and cultures, such as Rayy, Hamadan, Isfahan, Merv,
Samarkand, Bukhara. It goes without saying that the holy
cities of Arabia, as the centers of religious studies (but no
longer of art and of poetry, as they had been under the
Omayyads), had a position unto themselves but they were of
little economic and political importance. The circulation of
persons, of goods and of ideas was very active, and not
hampered, in this vast territory which corresponded to a
single state as long as the Empire maintained its unitary
character, and then to several states in the political fraction-
ing in which it culminated. Indeed that dichotomy between
East and West which the different political destinies have
suggested to us has much less value in the economic and
cultural sphere because of the free, perpetual flow of ideas
and commodities which at this time circulated from one end
of the Moslem world to the other. Very seldom did the political borders change into rigid economic and police-like barriers. From the eighth to the twelfth centuries the intense
rhythm of the supranational life of medieval Islam pulsated
above such barriers. It can be said that this pace reached its
climax in the tenth century, which has been incorrectly but
effectively described as the "Islamic Renaissance." That same
tenth century which witnessed the greatest humiliation of the
orthodox caliphate, also marked the greatest creativity of

Arabo-Islamic civilization, whose habitat, along with the economic and social life, the usages, customs, monuments and local characteristics, have been described for us by the great geographers of the epoch, such as Ibn Hawqal and above all al-Muqàddasi.

From the ninth century on, every political distinction between Arabs and non-Arabs had been dropped and the competition between the individual races was to be reflected only in the cultural sphere, in the polemics of the non-Arab "peoples" (*Shuùb,* hence the name Shuubiyyah given the partisans of such an anti-Arab movement) against the primacy of the former conquerors. But the curious thing is that such a polemic came into being when that political primacy had already been liquidated. On the other hand the very adversaries of Arabism wrote in Arabic, thereby accepting the Arab legacy in the language and culture. On the economic and social level, urbanized Arabs and non-Arabs were now on a plane of perfect parity and together they collaborated in the great impetus to material and intellectual production and to trade and commerce that characterized this epoch. The geographical literature to which we referred was born of the itineraries (*masalik*) which were arranged for commercial as well as for political and religious needs, and which linked the various regions of the Empire together in a thick network of roads. These were the roads traveled by the merchants, the backbone of medieval economic life, who transported the products of Arabo-Moslem agriculture and industry from one end to the other of Islamic territory, and even beyond its frontiers among the infidels. Linen of Egypt, the cotton and silk of Persia, the valued rugs of Armenia, and the ceramics and the creations in metal, the perfumes and spices of Tabaristan were all transported. The ancient silk route in the heart of Asia, and the sea routes from the ports of the Indian Ocean (Basra, Obolla, Siràf), which absorbed the

greater part of the maritime traffic in the Abbasid era, acti-
vated the commercial relations of the Empire with India and
China, a reflection of which constitutes the background of
Sindbad's romantic adventures. No less intense was the import
traffic from eastern Asia (silk and spices, precious woods
and gems, animals and animal skins), from central Africa
(gold and slaves) and from eastern and even northern Europe
(furs and amber) as—in addition to the reports of the geographers—has been shown by the discovery of Moslem coins in
the Scandinavian peninsula. Although it does not seem probable that many Moslem merchants arrived as far as the Baltic,
their exchanges and their money must have reached that far
by way of the Slavs and Bulgars and Khazars of the Volga,
whose contact with Abbasid Iraq is attested to by, among
others, Ibn Fadlàn whose embassy has been recalled here.

A banking system corresponded to this ample volume of
production and trade. It had its center precisely in Iraq, and
its representatives in a real class of Arab and Persian, Moslem
and Jewish capitalists. The koranic prohibition of usurious
loans was evaded by technical stratagems and tricks (*hiyal*),
like that of the double sale (the *mohatra*, a designation and
a matter that have passed into western commerce). The great
Iraqian bankers of the tenth and eleventh centuries, like their
later colleagues in the West, became an essential element of
the political life and of the court ambience, subventing the
state coffers with their loans during the frequent financial
crises provoked by the dishonesty and inexperience of the
functionaries and by the abuses and dissipations of viziers and
caliphs. Another means which became altogether normal for
replenishing the caliphal treasury was by making high functionaries "cough it up" by persuasion and torture, once they
had left office or fallen in disgrace. The related procedure
(*musàdara*) was considered almost as an operation of routine
administration at every alternation. In general the spectacle

that this caliphal bureaucracy offers is that of an intriguing class, greedy and corrupt, intent more upon personal gain than working for the public interest; hence the rare cases of honesty and ability stand out more conspicuously, like Ali ibn Isa, the "Good Vizier" of the time of al-Mùqtadir, in whom historiography and anecdotal tradition have seen a *rara avis* to set in contrast to a technically and ethically disqualified majority.

THE science and culture of the Abbasid era remained its most enduring glory. There has been a dispute over whether the intellectual achievements of that time ought to be called "Arab" or rather "Moslem." In fact not only did pure Arabs participate in it, but the offspring of the most diverse races amalgamated with Islam and with its language, which was used also by non-Moslems (Christians of the Orient, of Egypt, and Jews). In other words we have the same phenomenon of the Roman imperial age, when Latin and its culture were adopted by writers, neither Latin nor Italic, but who just the same felt themselves as members of the Roman civilization, and they absorbed and enriched it with the fruits of their genius. That common denominator which in the Roman Empire was essentially political and civil, in the Moslem Empire was religious, and in both cases its means of expression was the common language, in the former the language of Rome and in the latter that of Arabia. Therefore we can speak not only of an Arab literature, even though non-Arabs contributed to it, but of an Arab science and culture, on the condition that this term be understood without any racial narrowness. We include therein all those who made use of Arabic as a means of intellectual communication even, as we have mentioned earlier, in order to attack polemically that

Arab predominance which in part had already waned. The urban character of Abbasid civilization even better delimited the orbit and setting of this science and culture. The desert for some time was still considered the depository of linguistic purity and richness, but science, culture and art flourished in the cities: in Baghdad, the city *par excellence*, and in all the major and minor Arab centers of the Empire.

From the first Abbasid century the fundamental fact was the opening up of the Arabo-Moslem culture to foreign cultures, after the first sporadic contacts at the end of the Omayyad era. The figures of the great Caliphs Mansùr, Rashìd, and above all Mamùn rightfully enter in this process as the promoters and patrons of culture. The brilliant Ibn al-Muqaffa who was the popularizer of the Iranian epic, of Indian narrative and fables, and perhaps also of the first Greek philosophical works to Arab culture, worked under Mansùr. Harùn seems to have more favored the study of poetry, and the first steps that were taken in the study of grammar and philology. But it was under Mamùn, the founder of the *Bait al-Hikma* or Hall of Science (a kind of Baghdadian library and museum, which recalls those celebrated Alexandrian institutions), that the work of translation and of the elaboration of Hellenistic science and philosophy was unfolded in full. The most illustrious name in the circle around Mamùn was that of the mathematician and astronomer al-Khuvarizmi (a non-Arab as his name indicates, but who composed all his fundamental works on mathematics, astronomy and geography in Arabic). This medieval Moslem culture above all sought and assimilated the philosophy, the medicine and the sciences of Greek culture, leaving aside its poetry, eloquence and historiography as uncongenial. Homer was known as little more than a name (there are some tenuous traces and echoes of lost translations). Completely unknown were the lyric poets, the tragic and comic dramatists (significant in

this respect were the muddled works of the Moslem philosophers who tried to write commentaries on and to adapt
Aristotle's "Poetics") as well as the historians and orators.
But alongside Plato and Aristotle, often contaminated, Plo-
tinus and Proclus, Porphyry and Sextus Empiricus were quite
familiar to Islam, along with a profusion of authentic and
pseudo-epigraphic writings of late Antiquity. Soon the translations were joined by reelaborations and original works.
The names of al-Kindi ("the philosopher of the Arabs," since
he was of pure Arab descent) al-Farabi and Avicenna were
well known in philosophy. In astronomy the famous names,
besides the aforementioned al-Khuwarizmi, were Abu l-Wafà,
Abu Mashar and al-Battani, in medicine the Syrian family of
physicians, named Bakhtishù which continued the old traditions of the Persian medical school of Jundishapùr. Above
them all, however, towered the versatile and original figure
al-Biruni (973-1048). He was great not only for the various
branches of science which he cultivated (astronomy and
cosmography, chronology and ethnography, pharmacology,
geology and geography) but for the interest displayed towards the extra-Islamic cultures of Asia, primarily the Indian
of which he gave a classical description. The Persian al-
Biruni wrote almost always in Arabic, and he praised the
Arabic tongue as the only language capable of expressing the
fruit of thought and of scientific experiment. Consequently
this greatest glory which racism would deny to the Arab
culture reaffirmed his loyalty to it.

Still closer to the spiritual patrimony of the Arabs than
the international scientific studies however, were the studies
concerning grammar and philology, and the original poetical
and literary production which enjoyed a marvelous flowering
in the Abbasid era. In the eighth, ninth and tenth centuries, a
legion of grammarians and philologists in Iraq reduced the
national language to a system, and carefully collected and

commented upon its ancient poetic monuments, also in the service of the linguistic study of the Sacred Book. Others gathered the ancient historico-legendary remembrances of Arabia, her genealogies, her proverbs. Others, for purposes of piety and edification, but also with intentions of a more scientific and objective character dedicated themselves to an organic compilation of the traditions on the life of the Prophet and of his companions, on the conquests and on the most ancient history of Islam. Thereby they laid the groundwork for a fruitful genre of Arabo-Moslem historiography, alongside which, with intentions of more normative, theological and juridical character, there developed the "science" *par excellence* of medieval Islamic culture, the research revolving around the establishment and elaboration of the canonical traditions or *hadîth*. The severity and sometimes the scholastic aridity and mechanics of these fundamental aspects of culture in the Abbasid era (which then were to perpetuate themselves ever more rigidly and scholastically in the subsequent eras) was tempered by the rich production of poetry and *adab*, by which name we understand the entertaining narrative and essayist literature. Classic poetry underwent a profound renewal in harmony with the altered social and cultural ambience. Nevertheless it never completely lost its traditional positions, and finally reaffirmed itself in a compromise with the modern poetry which gave place to a cold neo-classicism. But the Abbasid era saw the full development of scientific, semiscientific and merely literary prose. The first was cultivated by pure scientists some of whom we have mentioned above, the second and third by a swarm of men of letters and publicists, among whom in the ninth century emerged the brilliant and creative essayist al-Jahiz. In the tenth century he was followed by his ideal disciples Tawhidi and Tanukhi, considered today as classic models to the neo-Arab literature. While the Abbasid Caliphate already floundered and declined

in the political crisis that we have outlined, this lofty intellectual, speculative and artistic life effervesced around it with
a remarkable drive and enthusiasm. Thus, if we may lightly
touch on fields which are not germane to our study, the
activity of the figurative arts expanded into a splendid flowering, notwithstanding every partial limitation imposed by religious scruples (we refer to sculpture particularly and in
general to the representation of living beings, disapproved of
by the Law, a disapproval which in reality was often ignored
especially during this epoch). Further, the art of music and
song triumphed in Abbasid Baghdad at this time and society,
and attained a primacy perhaps never reached before. Musicians and singers, male and female, appeared as a social element
of the very first order.

An immense, disordered compilation, top-heavy with technical particulars and with a technique of transmission, in accordance with the custom of the time—but which at the
same time is rich with precious materials in poetry and prose
and on the artistic and social life of that era—has come down
to us in the *Kitàbal-Aghani* or "Book of Songs" of the aforementioned Abu l-Faraj al-Isfahani (died 967). As we leaf
through that collection of inestimable value, which not only
most vividly preserves the remembrance of ancient Arabism
and of the beginnings of Islam, but also that of the first two
Abbasid centuries, a most lively and faithful picture of this
society and this culture, at bottom Arab but wholly speckled
with foreign elements, parades before our eyes. It is here
rather than in the stylized and mannered reconstruction of
the *Thousand and One Nights*, that we must seek the authentic remembrance of the golden age, which was now cultural
and no longer political, of the Arab world under the Abbasids.

6.

The Arabs and the West

FOR the Arabs Maghrib, or the West, was the whole strip of North Africa west of Egypt. At one and the same time it was the point of junction and division between the two parts of the Arab diaspora: the eastern part whose destinies we have been following until now, and the western or Maghribian part, including the appendix of Spain. We have seen this zone first lose its political ties with the center of the Moslem Empire without, however, ever breaking those of faith and culture which kept it bound to the East. But the Arabo-Islamic faith and culture also had several particular marks in the West on the basis of which, within Islam, we can speak of a minor Maghribian unity just as we can speak of a Maghribian history and culture. In both cases it was the result of a special combination and reaction between the Arab ethnic element, with the Moslem creed which it imported from the East, and the pre-existent indigenous background, Berber in Africa, Visigoth-Romantic in Spain, with which Arabism and Islam proceeded to quickly amalgamate. Several constant characteristics of Maghribian history and the fact that it had been the object of Ibn Khaldùn's original view of history, bestow a special importance on this African segment of the Arab movement, almost as a proving ground for sociological theories. The account of the Arabs in Spain, conversely, has a specialist's value as the only real transplantation of Arabo-Moslem civilization on European soil. The Arab incursion in Sicily was a comparable episode, albeit of shorter duration and more limited extent.

We have seen the first Arab invasion in North Africa reach the ocean with Oqba ibn Nafi at the end of the seventh century, and maintain itself there with difficulty in the first half of the following century against the violent revolts of the Berbers. Total loss of contact between the Maghrib and the Syro-Iraquian center of the Empire was the natural consequence of the anarchy and revolution into which the Omayyad caliphate fell. The Abbasids, of course, succeeded in imposing their direct authority on Ifrìqiya, first with the energetic governor Yazìd ibn Hatim and, following his death in 787 with Ibrahìm ibn al-Aghlab who then became the founder of the autonomous dynasty of the Aghlabids. But west of modern Tunisia anarchy reigned with the collapse of every semblance of authority, or isolated independent emirates arose like the Rustemides of Tahert in Algeria (ca. 776-908), a petty Kharijite state which was the oldest autonomous formation of Maghribian Islam, and a little later the Idrisids of Morocco (788-985), a dynasty of Alidic origin which lasted almost two centuries in the far West. These Arabo-Berber states of Africa, like all those which succeeded them, represented many attempts to impose a political and social order on the anarchy welling up from the turbulent indigenous tribes, who at one moment were subjugated and held in check, and at another erupted in ever new revolts. Up to the advent of the Almoravids (middle of the eleventh century) these were "the dark centuries" of the Maghrib, understood above all as central and outermost Maghrib (modern Algeria and Morocco). It was an age of public disorders refractory to every stable and organized power, and of great economic and cultural poverty, where this part of North Africa was more an object rather than a subject of history, being contended over by the opposed hegemonies of the great and powerful Moslem states that had been formed in Egypt and in Spain.

But throughout the ninth century the Aghlabid state, which in contrast to the Kharijites and Shi'ites still recognized the nominal sovereignty of the Caliph of Baghdad, wedged itself between Egypt and central and outermost Maghrib in modern Tunisia. For Ifrìqiya the Aghlabid century was an age of power and prosperity, and especially under the first sovereigns of the dynasty it most brilliantly represented the adaptation of Arabism to African soil. At that time Islam dug its deepest roots in that country and experienced its first cultural flowering there. And from there in 827, during the reign of the Aghlabid Emir Ziyadat Allah I in Qairawàn, it crossed the channel of Sicily, thereby establishing an enduring foothold on the largest Mediterranean island. The Byzantines at first let themselves be defeated easily near Mazara, but then they put up a tough and long resistance—in part with the indigenous element—in individual cities (Castrogiovanni was taken in 859, Syracuse after a tenacious siege in 878, and Taormina only in 902). But the Arabs had already entered Palermo in 831, which with them became the chief town of the island. Here they began their dominion that was to last for two centuries.

From the beginning, Arab Sicily was an Aghlabid dependency, just as its conquest had been Aghlabid. But the island had hardly been subjugated to Moslem rule when the star of the Aghlabids eclipsed in Africa. This was the result of the aforementioned rise there, at the beginning of the tenth century, of the heterodox power of the Fatimids who also inherited the Sicilian province from their predecessors. When, however, after the first seventy years of their dominion in Ifrìqiya, the Fatimids transferred to conquered Egypt, their ties with Sicily—as with the Maghrib itself—were loosened, although both regions always remained included in their Mediterranean sphere of action and subject to their theoretical hegemony. The local governors in Palermo acquired an ever greater autonomy, by reflex. So much so indeed that they practically founded a local dynasty there in the family of the Kalbites. This was a local dynasty which acknowledged itself as a vassal of the caliph of Cairo, as the Aghlabids had been vassals of the caliphate of Baghdad. Recently published texts show that at least in some periods such vassalage was less formal than it seemed at first. Nevertheless it is certain that in the eleventh century, with the decline of the Fatimid power in Egypt, its links with Sicily also loosened. Rather, Sicily leaned for support on the lieutenants and then on the independent successors of the Fatimids in Tunisia, the Zirites. But almost at the same time Tunisia and a good part of North Africa were convulsed by the disastrous invasion of the Bedouins Beni Hilàl and Sulaim, which the Fatimids launched there in reprisal for the Zirite independence that had been proclaimed. In Sicily the brief Kalbite dynasty, which had given the Island its greatest prosperity of the Arab era, even bringing Moslem arms to the Italian mainland with victorious raids, ended amid civil strife.

After the fall of the Kalbites, the political power in Sicily was divided among rival lordlings. The politico-familial contest between two of them (the lordling of Catania Ibn al-Thumna and the lordling of Girgenti Ibn al-Hawwàs) from the start provoked an appeal for help to the Normans, who had already asserted themselves in southern Italy. The Christian reconquest of the Island, begun in 1061 by Count Roger with the capture of Messina, was practically accomplished by him in thirty years, although this time too resistance was prolonged in isolated fortresses.

Thus Moslem rule over Sicily ceased by the end of the eleventh century (there had been only brief settlements on the Italian mainland, at Bari and at Taranto, in the ninth century, and on the Garigliano up to 915, but then and later frequent and devastating raids throughout the South). Nevertheless the imprint of the Arabo-Moslem language, culture and civilization lasted in Sicily for still another century, the Norman century. The Rogers and Williams, in contrast to the Habsburgs in Spain, knew how to gather every positive element of the Moslem legacy and incorporate it into the composite culture of their state. Hence it is precisely that Norman era which has preserved for us the most vivid remembrances of the presence of the Arabs in Sicily, in institutions, deeds, documents, inscriptions, coins, scientific works like Edrisi's *Geography*, and the verses of court poets. Much less has remained to us of the authentic period of Arab dominion, either in the form of literary works or direct documents and monuments. The great scholar Amari reconstructed the history of that period by basing himself more on general and Western chronicles than on the lost Arabo-Sicilian historiography. The greater part of these chronicles are not contemporary but sometimes they preserve—given the compilational system of the Moslem Middle Ages—valuable materials that are even more ancient. Thus the material and spiritual life of the Arabs of Sicily is reassembled laboriously as in a mosaic with pieces coming from other territories and other countries, leaving free spaces that perhaps will always remain unfilled. Amari's description of Arab Sicily, traced with diligent and brilliant labor and still valid after a century, contains elements of a great economic and social value (an intense development of agriculture, and of small landed property), and traces of a rich cultural life which, unfortunately, escapes us in its concrete reality, just as does the possible Arab influ-

ence on the Sicilian origins of Italy's first literary language and
poetry.

THE Sicilian adventure remains a secondary episode in the
history of the Arabs of the West, regardless of the importance
it had for southern Italy. The presence of the Arabs in Spain,
where they were a prime factor in the political and cultural
history of the country, and of the whole Christian West in
the Middle Ages, was an event that was incomparably greater
and of longer duration. Seven centuries and a half yawn between the beginning and the end of Arab rule in Spain,
against the two and half centuries of their domination in
Sicily. And in this so much longer time and on this more
ample arena, Arabism was able to dig much deeper roots,
thereby giving rise to a civilization of which a greater number of remembrances and famous authentic monuments remain to us.

The easy crossing of the Pillars of Hercules tempted the
Arabs to make the passage into the Iberian Peninsula when
their dominion in the outermost western reaches of Africa
was not yet wholly consolidated. The first incursion occurred
in 710, under the Caliphate of al-Walìd which was witness
to the greatest expansion of the conquests in the east and
west. But the actual invasion ensued a year later under Tariq,
the freedman of the Omayyad governor of Africa. The Visigoth kingdom was in the throes of a full dynastic, political and
social crisis, and like the Sassanid Empire in the east it could
not withstand the shock of the young Arabo-Berber forces
unified in the Word of Islam. The battle of Wadi Bakkà
—the Rio Barbate at its mouth in the Janda Lagoon northwest
of Gibraltar (Spring of 711)—was decisive for the fortunes
of Roderic, the last Visigoth king who never recovered

from the defeat inflicted here, even though resistance continued for some time. Musa himself crossed the straits with new forces, and the two Moslem leaders, coming up from the south, rapidly moved towards the center of the Peninsula, joining each other near Toledo. Then with a vast wheeling maneuver they gained mastery of Saragossa and of the entire Tarragona region and pursued their attacks in the northwestern regions, Asturias and Galicia. Musa's and Tariq's amazing adventure ended here, since they were both recalled by the Caliph in Syria. Their successors fought to consolidate and enlarge the conquest, in the northern regions and by crossing the Pyrenees towards France. But here instead of establishing stable settlements, save for some colony of plunderers in Languedoc and Provence, they conducted only a series of raids. Celebrated among these is the raid at Poitiers (732) which Charles Martel brought to a halt.

The obscure period of the first governors of Andalusia, subject to Damascus, was entirely spent in struggles against the resistance of the natives, which gave the invaders many a headache, and no less in fierce internal disputes among the invaders themselves: Berbers against Arabs, Arabs of northern origin against southern Arabs. The same tribal rivalries flared up again here, at a great distance from the homeland, which in Syria and at the opposite end of the Empire, in the Khurasàn, wore out the race, and ended up by causing it to lose its hegemony. The African events caused new Arab contingents from Syria to land in Andalusia and in turn they scuffled with the first emigrants. The result of these discords was that an integral occupation of the Peninsula was never achieved. Sparse centers of Christian resistance, the nuclei and presages of the future reconquest, maintained themselves in the outermost northern regions (Galicia, Asturias, Cantabria). Pelayo's victorious resistance at Covadonga (around 720) was its semi-legendary and almost symbolic point of departure.

A dramatic personal adventure, shortly after 750, marked the beginning of new destinies for the Arabs of Spain. The Omayyad Abd ar-Rahmàn, a young nephew of the Caliph Hishàm, was among the very few who succeeded in escaping from the Orient when the family was massacred after the triumph of the Abbasid revolution. After five years of a wandering life in the Maghrib, in 755 he set foot on the Spanish soil. He himself was far from imagining how much of the future he was bearing with him, for his family and for his race. After moving in on the game of the rival forces with the support of the Syrians, he imposed his authority with a combination of astuteness and force on the local Arab chieftains. In July of the year 756, he had himself recognized in Cordova as the emir of Andalusia. Thus the Omayyad emirate of Spain was founded independently of the distant enemy Abbasids, and for two centuries and a half it was to give Spanish Arabism a unitary state and a splendid flowering of civilization.

Abd ar-Rahmàn I, "the falcon of the Quraysh" struggled for thirty years with indomitable energy to impose his unitary monarchy on the Arabs and Berbers and non-indigenous tribes who with rebellions and chain conspiracies vainly tried to get out from under his rule. One by one he got the upper hand over all of them, though not without harsh struggles which were inflicted on him by a gamut of foes ranging from the last representatives of Arab tribal particularism to Charlemagne himself whom a rebellious coalition had vainly appealed to for help. There was no need for Abd ar-Rahmàn to test his mettle with him because the revival of the Saxon peril in his rear induced Charlemagne to abandon the enterprise (here, upon his return to France in 778, occurred the famous episode of Roncesvalle with the attack of the Christian Basques against the rear guard under Roland's command). At his death in 788, the Omayyad who had arrived in Spain as a refugee (certain of his melancholy verses to a palm tree breathe all the nostalgia and bitterness of exile), left his son Hishàm a power solidly established all over the Iberian peninsula, which Musa and Tariq had conquered for his ancestors in Syria at the beginning of the century.

The fusion between the Arabo-Berber immigrants and the native element who to a great extent had embraced their faith, was carried out in the eleventh century under the Omayyad emirs al-Hakam, Abd ar-Rahmàn II and Muhammad. These *muwalladùn* or "adopted ones" demographically constituted the backbone of the Arabo-Spanish society, while the Mozarabs or "arabized" Christians, that is subjects of the Moslem state of Spain, remained outside Islam, but not outside the Arab language and culture. The Cordovan emirs tried to amalgamate and level these different forces under the regime of absolutism, as their rival Abbasids did in the East. Like them they soon surrounded themselves with a foreign guard (the "Slavs," former Christian slaves and mercenaries most of whom came from central and northern Europe, more than from eastern Europe) and with a court ceremonial that aimed to rival that of Byzantium and Baghdad. Under al-Hakam I they had to suppress savage revolts like the sadly famous ones of Toledo and Cordova, and public disorders caused by religious fanaticism, like the deliberate race to martyrdom of the Mozarabs under Abd ar-Rahmàn II. Finally, under Muhammad, the centrifugal forces rose frighteningly again and threatened to submerge the emirate. A series of native *caudillos*, although they had been Islamized for some time, assumed the airs of independent sovereigns in the frontier provinces, like the Beni Casi in Saragossa. But above all of them towered the true anti-emir, the Spanish *muwallad* Omar ibn Hafsùn, who defied the authority of the Cordova Omayyads for several decades from his eagle's nest in Bobastro. In the end he returned to the

Christian faith of his fathers and died still unsubdued in
917. Abd ar-Rahmàn's legacy was once more at stake at
the end of the ninth century, under the emir Abdallàh. But
the vigorous personality of that emir succeeded in overcoming his difficulties (the victory at Poley against Ibn Hafsùn,
891), and initiating the process of recovery of the central
power which his nephew and successor Abd ar-Rahmàn III
was to bring to its apogee.

The long reign of Abd ar-Rahmàn III (912-61) was the
golden age of the Omayyad monarchy in Spain. As is often
the case, it is difficult to determine how much the personal
qualities of the sovereign and those of his collaborators along
with the weakness of his adversaries, and sheer luck contributed to this. Certainly under his reign the anarchy of the
caudillos was entirely broken; Ibn Hafsùn disappeared without having succeeded in founding an enduring power on
his rebellion, and the authority of the Cordovan emirate
was recognized throughout the Moslem territory of Andalusia.

The Holy War (felt as such by both sides) flared up again
with the Christian kingdoms of León and of the Asturias
which in the course of the preceding century had pushed
forward up to the line of the Duero. This, for a long time,
was to remain the southern border of Christian Spain with
the Arabs. In this war Abd ar-Rahmàn experienced both
victories and defeats which for that matter did not greatly
alter the territorial and power relations between the two opposed worlds. And in 929, at the height of his fortune and
prestige he assumed the caliphal title, thus officially counter-
poising himself both to the Abbasids of Baghdad and to the
Fatimids of Africa. This was a purely formal manifestation
towards the distant Iraqian Caliphate which was in a state of
complete decadence. But with the Fatimids Abd ar-Rahmàn's
policy engaged in a close duel for the hegemony of the
western Mediterranean, competing in naval armaments and

in penetration of the Maghrib. After capturing Ceuta, he succeeded in having his sovereignty recognized by the Berbers of what is now Morocco and Algeria, although it cannot be said that there was an actual Omayyad dominion over these regions. Nor did the Cordova Caliph, amid so many ambitious plans, neglect the internal prosperity of his states: he promoted their agricultural and economic development, and also unfolded a grandiose building program. Alongside the capital rose the caliphal residence of Madinat az-Zahrà which recent excavations are bringing back to light. A patron of literature and of the arts, curious about science and culture, even of foreign provenience, he was the Harùn ar-Rashìd of the West. He also had the good fortune to symbolize in the name given to himself (an-Nasir li-din Allah, the Champion of the Faith of God) the greatest power of Moslem Spain.

State power and dynastic fortune coincided further with Abd ar-Rahmàn's son, al-Hakam II (961-76), who continued his father's imperial policy, keeping the Christian kingdoms of the north at a respectful distance, and fighting the Idrisites of Morocco through his valiant general Ghalib. It was precisely in this war in Africa that the rising star who was soon to become the arbitrator of the caliphate, the future Almanzor won his first laurels, which here were more diplomatic than military. The latter was an Arab of noble descent, Muhammad Ibn Abi Amir. While serving in administrative posts—and it seems he was also of service in more intimate connections—he had won the favor of the Caliph's wife, Princess Sobh. Here began his rapid rise, which reached its peak under al-Hakam's successor and a son of Sobh, Hishàm II (976-1008). During the long reign of the latter, Ibn Abi Amir with the title of *Hajib* or Prime Minister (the western equivalent of the Abbasid title of vizier) was in fact the absolute master of the State. After reducing the weak Caliph to a respectable exile in the palace, and neutralizing the opposition of his former patroness, Ibn Abi Amir became the dictator of Moslem Spain for twenty-five years. His imperious ambition did not make him shrink from any action, the shedding of blood included. As an example we can cite how, in order to gain the favor of the bigots, the *faqìh*, or doctors of the Law (who always exerted a great influence in Islam, particularly in Maghribian Islam) he did not hesitate—and he was all else but uncultured—to consign to the flames a part of the precious library of al-Hakam, a great bibliophile and patron of culture. Moreover Ibn Abi Amir, on behalf of the pious and of his own military glory, personally led a series of murderous campaigns against the northern kingdoms, to which he attended with the same vigorous impulse that he had given to the Holy War. From these campaigns, culminating in 997 with the devastation of the national Galician shrine of Saint James at Compostella, he acquired the proud surname of al-Mansùr ("The Victorious through God," in Spanish Almanzor) with which he passed into history. In the military field, he can be said to have been more fortunate than the great Caliph an-Nasir, if the final defeat at Calatañazor attributed to him by Christian tradition is a pious legend as it seems to be. In reality he died undefeated in 1002, on his return from one of his wars against the Christians, and he was buried with his head resting on a pillow, which had been filled with the dust gathered in his expeditions for the faith. His figure as a brilliant, magnificent and cruel tyrant still stands out in the annals of Andalusian Islam at the peak of its expansion.

After Almanzor the Omayyad Caliphate, which he had kept under tutelage and which Abd ar-Rahmàn III and al-Hakam II had made illustrious, fell into an inglorious decline. The abdication in 1008 of the faint-hearted Hishàm II ushered in a period of bloody internecine struggles in which five or six caliphs followed each other on the throne in rapid succession amid tumults, assassinations and interventions from rival dy-

nasties like the Hammudid Berbers, who had affirmed themselves in Malaga. Cordova, the proud Omayyad capital which
until then had rivaled with Baghdad and Cairo as a metropolis
of the Moslem world, was subjected to enormous plunder
and pillage and lost its primacy forever. The last trace of the
caliphate vanished there in 1031, when the city was ruled as
a municipal body. What had been the empire of the Omayyads
in Spain was dismembered into a constellation of small provincial states, each one of which was the seat of more or less
ephemeral Arab and Berber dynasties: the *Mulùk at-Tawàif*,
in Spanish *Reyes de Taifas* (provincial kings).

IN the history of Moslem Spain the eleventh century is precisely that of the provincial dynasties: Hammudids in Malaga
and Algeciras, Zirides in Granada, Tugibids in Almeria and
Saragossa, Aftasids in Badajoz, Dhu n-Nunids in Toledo and
Abbadids in Seville. As we already saw in the East, the line of
cultural development diverged from the declining political
line: in fact science, literature and art continued to flower
more than ever in this period, and they found as many
enclaves of cultural expression in the small emiral courts.
Seville of the Abbadids took the place of decadent Cordova
as a splendid center of art and poetry, and with the sultans
al-Mùtadid and al-Mùtamid it achieved a true intellectual
primacy. But the threat of the Christian reconquest now hung
over all these petty potentates. None of these small dynasties
could cope with it alone, now that Castile, united with Leon,
had placed itself at the head of the movement. This was the
era of Alfonso VI and of the Cid. Less than a century after
the feats of Almanzor, Christian Spain was on the offensive,
and Alfonso's capture of Toledo (1085) now revealed the
gravity of the danger. It was from this point that the history

of Moslem Spain was again intertwined with that of Africa, losing its autonomy.

After centuries of obscurity a great Moslem Empire, that of the Almoravids, had emerged in the outermost Maghrib in the middle of the eleventh century. These were Saharan Berbers of the tribe of the Lamtuna whom the activity of pious missionaries and of energetic leaders had pushed out of their desert towards the north, justifying their conquests by the sign of the faith. From the war-like vigils of the *ribàt* or redoubts for the holy war on Senegal whence they acquired their name (al-Muràbit or Almoravide actually means a warrior of the *ribàt*), they erupted into what is now modern Morocco as fanatical champions of Islam's recovery at a moment when its destinies seemed to be shaky throughout the western Mediterranean from Spain to Sicily. From his new capital of Marrakesh the fame of the Almoravid chieftain Yusuf ibn Tashufìn spread in Moslem Spain, and it induced its princes, first among these the Abbadids of Seville, to turn to him for help against the Christian menace. Yusuf crossed the Straits with his veiled warriors and slowed down Alfonso VI's advance at Zallaqa near Badajoz (1086), inflicting a serious defeat on him. But this intervention also marked the end of the independence of the Spanish *Reyes de Taifas*. When a few years later they again turned for help to the Almoravid sultan and the latter reappeared with arms on Andalusian soil, he was now determined to make himself its direct master. With the approval of the "doctors" (*faqìh*) who in a solemn pronouncement declared him worthy of replacing the incompetent emirs in the struggle against the infidels, Yusuf ibn Tashufìn smoothly reunified Moslem Spain in the last decade of the century, and he annexed it to his African Empire (the fall of the romantic al-Mùtamid of Seville, deported as a prisoner to Morocco, took place in 1091). Thus began the dominion of the Almoravids in Spain, which lasted for almost half a century.

For the Maghrib, the Almoravid Empire marked a progressive step in comparison to the pre-existent anarchy, and for the first time it gave an imperial and civil function to the Berber element. Yusuf and his successors, who dominated Morocco and part of Algeria, besides the Balearic Islands and Spain, assumed the title of *Amìr al-Muslimìn* or Prince of the Moslems, deliberately avoiding that of *Amìr al-Muminìn* (Prince of the Believers), peculiar to the caliph. In fact they recognized the theoretical sovereignty of the Abbasids of Baghdad. The power of the *faqìh*, the jurists of the Malikite school which had become dominant in the Maghrib grew enormously under them. This had particularly harmful consequences in Spain, where intellectual, scientific and artistic activity was sometimes fettered by their crude intolerance. It is true that *Andalusia capta* in turn conquered the rough African victors, at once civilizing them and robbing them of their vigor. Hence the rapid decline of their political power. The Almoravids corresponded only in a mediocre way to the task which justified their presence in Spain, that of resistance to the Christians. On the other hand the Christian kings, like Alfonse I of Aragon and Alfonse VII of Castile, kept up their pressure in the first decades of the twelfth century, even reaching as far as the vital centers of Moslem Spain with victorious raids.

The Almoravid Empire collapsed in Africa, by reflex in Spain, a few decades after having reached its ephemeral apogee with Yusif ibn Tashufìn. It was brought down and supplanted by a more vast revolt of Berber peoples (this time those belonging to the group of the Masmuda), which arose from the religious experience of a single man. The new Berber prophet (he can rightly be called such, although he remained

within the frame of strict Moslem orthodoxy, because of the
effective influence he wielded and the prestige he enjoyed)
was an obscure ascetic and doctor from the Atlas mountain
region, Muhammad ibn Tumart. A journey to the East led
to the ripening of his convictions on the necessity of a profound intellectual and moral reform of Maghribian Islam.
This was based on a rigorous observance of the Law in morality and customs, on the application in theology of the Asharite
speculative method, and on a return to the sources (interpretation of the Koran and of the Sunna) against the mecha-
nized routine of the Malikite *Faqìh*. This program culminated
in a more rigid reaffirmation of divine unity (*tawhìd*). The
Unitarians (al-Muwahhidùn, from whence derives our Almohads) became the battle-name of Ibn Tumart's followers. He
recruited them among the tribes of the Atlas mountain area,
and, after binding them tightly in an iron discipline and
hierarchy which in him recognized the messianic Mahdi, he
hurled them against the ruling Almoravids. The struggle was
continued beyond the death of Ibn Tumart (around 1130)
by his faithful ally Abd al-Mumin who succeeded in
leading the Almohad movement to victory. In 1147 he entered the Almoravid capital Marrakesh, and at the same time
his generals took over the mastery of Moslem Spain without
great resistance, where the local secessions and revolts had
already begun to nibble away at the rule of the last Almoravids. Around 1150 Abd al-Mumin, after proclaiming himself
the Almohad Caliph (thereby repudiating every subordination
to the Abbasids) had entirely supplanted the Almoravids in
Africa and Spain whose cause was defended further and for
a long time by the Banu Ghàniyah in the Balearics. In the subsequent years the Almohad Empire was extended further in
an easterly direction, reaching as far as the frontiers of Egypt
in Africa.

The new Berber Empire lasted longer than the one that had

preceded it, and it disappeared in Africa only in 1269, break-ing up into local dynasties. But it too enjoyed the true peak of its power for a little more than fifty years, under the founder Abd al-Mumin (1130-63) and his first successors, his son Abu Yaqùb Yusuf (1163-84) and his nephew Abu Yusuf Yaqùb (1184-99). These three great sovereigns really brought the greatest governmental formation of the Islamized Berbers, who were deeply arabized in their culture, to its apogee. For, in contrast to the Almoravids, the Almohads pro-tected and promoted intellectual life, especially the medical and natural sciences, and philosophy (Averroës, Ibn Tufayl and Ibn Zuhr did their work under them). As for the Almo-hads, their imperial capital was the African Marrakesh, and they always felt Africa to be the center of their power. But the obligation of the holy war continually recalled them to Spain, where Seville constituted their military base, and was frequently their residence in the struggle against the recon-quest now pushing relentlessly forward. Here the great ad-versary of the Almohads was Alphonse VIII of Castille, whose long reign (1158-1214) can be said to have been wholly a battle against the Moors. After having been defeated at Atar-quines and Santarem and above all in the grave disaster of Alarcos (1195), Alfonso was able to close his reign with the victory of Navas de Tolosa (in Arabic *Hisn al-Uqàb* in the province of Jaen, July 16, 1212). The disastrous rout here of the Almohad Caliph an-Nasir set off the rapid breakdown of the remaining Moslem positions in Andalusia, which were dismantled in the subsequent decades through the labors, above all, of Ferdinand III of Castille and James I of Aragon (Cordova was captured in 1236, Valencia in 1238, Seville in 1248, Murcia in 1269). Just as had been the fate of the Al-moravids in the previous century, so did the Almohads in the first half of the thirteenth century see their dominions in Spain break up into small pieces between the Christian reconquest and the formation of small independent Moslem kingdoms, the third and final flowering of the *Reinos de Taifas*.

One of the kingdoms, that of the Banu l-Ahmar or Banu Nasr of Granada, was allotted the good fortune of unexpectedly becoming and remaining for two centuries and a half the last refuge of Arabism and Andalusian Islam. Two-hundred fifty years of history, which school books all too easily summarize in a line, lie between 1232, when Muhammad al-Ahmar became the master of Granada during the afore-mentioned dismemberment of the Almohad dominions, and January 2, 1492, on which day the Catholic Kings of Spain, now practically unified, made their entrance into the Alhambra. The long survival of the outermost Arab strip on Spanish soil is explained by the vicissitudes of Christian Spain itself, by the cessation of the coordinated efforts for the reconquest which her sovereigns now felt to be practically accomplished, by the rivalries and crises which afflicted the various Spanish states in the fourteenth and fifteenth century, especially Castille which had been in the forefront of the war against the Moors. The Moorish peril now belonged to the past. After the Almohads were driven back to Africa, where they disappeared later because of the advent of minor kingdoms (the Merinids in Morocco, the Zayyanides in Algeria, the Hafsids in Tunisia), only a weak Moslem state remained in the extreme south of the Peninsula, a pawn in the policy of the Castilian kings vis-à-vis Africa and the other Iberian states. Thus it was possible for twenty Nasrid sultans to succeed each other on the throne of Granada in the fourteenth and fifteenth centuries, amid political intrigues and guerrilla wars, where they were to write the last glorious page of Andalusian Arabism in the flourishing culture and in the splendid architectural activity. Then the end came in the final years of the fifteenth century, which as usual was facilitated by dynastic discords. The union of Ferdinand and Isabella sealed the unity of Christian Spain, and Loja, Malaga, Baza, the outermost strongholds of Islam on Iberian soil fell between 1486 and 1491. At the beginning of 1492 the cross was raised on the Alhambra, and the last Nasrid Boabdil (Muhammad XI) left the land of his fathers, finding refuge in Morocco.

The end of the Arab dominion in Spain, illuminated by poetry, had a painful sequel in the destiny of the Moriscos, i.e. the Moslems who had become subjects of the Catholic Kings, and who had been vainly guaranteed freedom of their persons, possessions and cult at the time of the capitulation in Granada. Only ten years later they were forcibly faced with the choice between Baptism or expulsion: they underwent first the one and then the other, after long vexations, persecutions, and revolts. The last traces of Islam disappeared forever from Spain only at the beginning of the seventeenth century, with the definitive decrees of expulsion promulgated by the Habsburgs.

THE chronological terms at which we have arrived in this rapid survey of the history of Moslem Spain greatly transcend those over which we paused before in following the destinies of the Arabs of the East. But the argument itself involves such a disparity, since it treats of an ambience and a period concluded in themselves, with characteristics peculiar to them which exempt them from the periodization that is followed for oriental history. At the beginning of this chapter we spoke of Arabo-Maghribian historical unity, religious and cultural; and now we add that Spain constituted the summit of such a minor complex within Arab civilization, as the creator of original values and the transmitter thereof to European civilization itself. In comparison to al-Andalus the African Maghrib was very much less fruitful. It accepted elements of the superior Arabo-Andalusian society, and even achieved the political domination of Spain, as we have seen, but without bringing to Arab civilization a contribution comparable to that of Andalusia, nor to that which Africa, itself latinized, had brought to Roman civilization. The traces of that anterior civilization having been erased with terrifying rapidity, the Maghrib was thoroughly impregnated with the Arabo-Islamic religion and culture which sovereignly dominates there to this day. But it was much more receptive than creative, and the most valuable elements of such a reception came to it precisely from the other shore, from Andalusia.

Here on Iberian, Roman and Christian soil, the Arab settlement revealed itself to be amazingly fruitful. First of all a complex and profound ethnic mixture was realized between the conquerors and the natives, and between the various elements of the conquerors themselves. The latter were Arabs and Berbers. Among the Arabs, the aristocracy was reinforced by a strong contingent suddenly arrived from Syria, on which the Omayyad revival based itself, in the beginning. But the Syrian dynasty did not delay in admitting into itself, through matrimonial and servile unions, strong commixtures of romance blood. For political reasons it soon surrounded itself with a powerful military and civil bureaucracy of non-Arabs, composed either of natives (*Muwalladùn*), or islamized foreigners, Germans and Slavs (*Saqàliba*). All these eastern and western elements, to which the Jews were added in notable measure, found the bond that brought them together in fraternal community more in terms of the Arab language and culture than in the faith, as shown by the celebrated indices and testimonies from the Mozarabs themselves, i.e. the Christian subjects of the Spanish Arabs. The trace of Roman civilization, maintained as best as possible in the Visigothic period, was strongly attenuated although it did not disappear entirely as in Africa. Also preserved in Arab Spain was the Christian faith along with the romance language, which from the vulgar Latin evolved into the variety of Iberian dialects. It is to the credit of Spanish Arabistics that in recent times it has more effectively illustrated this survival which, in certain ambiences and periods, led to real bilingualism in Arab Spain.

The Omayyad emirate which gave the first unitary order to the Peninsula, at first naturally looked upon its homeland Syria as a model, and even before the emirate was established the bonds with Syria were reflected in the type and the very nomenclature of the settlements. After the consolidation of the emiral state, the cultural influences from the East continued (indeed in the ninth century the Iraquian influences were particularly stressed, despite the rivalry of the two dynasties) in the already mentioned brisk circulation of ideas, persons and things in every part of the medieval Moslem world. At the same time the Arabo-Spanish state came into contact with Byzantium (which indeed at a certain point tried to incite it against Baghdad, the common enemy), and with the Christian states of the West, ruled by the Carolingians and the Ottonians. The Omayyads knew how to maintain an intelligent balance in this double order of contacts and influences, distinguishing contingent political interest from an overt cultural receptivity. And even when the Omayyad power was eclipsed in the civil convulsions at the beginning of the eleventh century, the intellectual and artistic movement under the *Reinos de Taifas* was further accentuated in pace and performance. After waning somewhat under the Almoravids, it flourished anew under the Almohads, overflowing into the Maghrib and maintaining itself also in a considerable part of the Andalusian territory which the Christian kings were wresting away from Islam with the reconquest. In fact the centers of the great Arabo-Spanish culture were not only imperial Cordova in its halcyon days of the tenth century, but Toledo and Seville and Granada and the other provincial cities, some of them remaining so even after the Christian political reconquest. The intellectual movement in this era (from the tenth to the thirteenth century, with the long appendix of Granada) knew no national or religious frontiers, and remains a glory of Arab civilization and of its adaptation to European soil.

Most notable was Spain's contribution to Arab classic literature, either in *belles lettres* in the strict sense of the word or in the sciences, religious and profane, history, philology and philosophy. In some aspects of her literary activity, Spain with a provincial zeal, accentuated tendencies of classicism and neo-classicism of the East, as in the poetry and the ornate prose, where her authors competed with the most celebrated orientals. But other seeds and forms of art unfolded alongside this erudite and classicizing current on Spanish soil, new forms which are now at the core of linguistic, comparative and historico-literary interest. We are referring to the strophic poetry, either in the literary language or in dialect, which was a pure Spanish novelty, admired and imitated in the East. The name of Ibn Quzmàn, the brilliant author of *zajal* (strophic poetry in dialect) of the twelfth century is known today even to non-specialists because of the literary and social importance of his collection of lyrics and for his romance linguistic subtleties. Even more recently, whole lines of poetry in romance have been identified in Arabic, or also in Jewish in imitation of the Arabic, in the *Kharjas* or final stanzas of such compositions. They are a luminous confirmation of the bilingualism of Moslem Spain, and samples of a romance language and poetry in a stage that is prior to every document known until now. These discoveries have opened a new phase in the controversial question of the Arab influence on the forms and the spirit of the most ancient European, Iberian and Provençal lyric poetry, providing new data and arguments to the affirmative thesis. Whatever precise formulation is to be given to that thesis, linguistic and literary history, and according to more recent investigations even musicological history, converge in assigning an ever greater part to the Arab element in the dawn of the poetry and music of medieval Europe.

The Arabo-Spanish culture presents a profusion of great figures, worthy of being measured against the most eminent personages of oriental Arabism. These include the theologian, moralist and polemicist Ibn Hazm (eleventh century), the eminent historian Ibn Hayyàn (also of the eleventh century), and the philosophers Ibn Masarra (tenth century), and Avempace, Ibn Tufayl and Averroës, all three who belong to the twelfth century and enjoy a European fame. In the fourteenth century, the final Granadian period also presents us with the figure of an Arab man of letters of great stature, the vizier Lisàn ad-din Ibn al-Khatìb, an historic statesman and poet, whose stormy life and tragic end mirror the turbid, but not inglorious twilight, of Arabism in Andalusia. On the opposite African shore, the great Ibn Khaldùn was Ibn al-Khatìb's counterpart and rival. He was the only original thinker ever produced by the Maghrib, and he had diplomatic and business relations with both Moslem and Christian Spain. The Maghrib, at a later time (the beginning of the seventeenth century) was to give in the Algerian al-Màqqari the encyclopedist who, in a vast and precise compilation, fathered and embalmed, as it were, the historical and literary materials on the period of Arab Spain which had come to its close.

Very long before these notables, in the centuries of the political decadence which had already begun but which were also times of the greatest cultural flowering of this civilization, its contact with the Christian world revealed itself to be a fruitful medium, not only of Moslem, but also of ancient culture and science. The group of "Toledo translators" flourished in the following century under the patronage of the

Archbishop Raymond (1130-50) in Toledo which Alphonse
VI had wrested from the political but not cultural dominion
of the Arabs. This group consisted of enthusiastic interpreters
of the treasures of Arab science and, by way of the Arabs, of
Hellenistic science to medieval Latin culture.

The Italian Gherardo of Cremona stands out among these
men who, sometimes with the help of Jewish interpreters,
made known the works of Euclid and Ptolemy, Galen and
Hippocrates, and of the Arabs al-Kindi, al-Farabi, Avicenna,
al-Battani, al-Ghazzali and many others. He left his native
Lombardy for the specific purpose of studying at the fount of
ancient wisdom in Moslem Spain. Alongside him must be
mentioned the Spaniards Domenico Gundisalvi, Marco of
Toledo and Juan of Seville, the Englishmen Robert of Chester
and Adelard of Bath, the German Hermann of Reichenau, the
Slav Herman Dalmata. It was an amazing International of
medieval knowledge, the most precious fruit of that tolerant
collaboration among the races and faiths of which Spain was
then the sponsor. A century later, another center of such collaboration was the court of the King of Castille, Alphonse the
Wise (1252-84), the brilliant patron of arts, author and
promoter of culture. It is to his impulse, among others, that we
owe the translation of celebrated works of oriental genius,
such as the *Calila and Dimna*, the *Sindibad*, the *History of
Barlaam and Joshafat* and even edifying and popular Arab
texts like the eschatological *Book of the Ladder*, the most
direct Moslem precursor of Dante's *Divina Commedia*.

Hence the Arab history and culture of Spain, in which
pure Arabs and native Berbers and descendants of Iberians,
Visigoths and of Jews, collaborated, is not only a chapter that
ranks among the most brilliant in the Arab diaspora, but an
essential foundation of European culture itself. That which
the too brief settlement of the Arabs in Sicily did not permit
them to develop outside of a local plane (nonetheless here too

it fructified the composite Norman culture), in the Iberian Peninsula was able to yield an abundant flowering that enriched Spain. By reflex, it also enriched the Maghrib, which culturally was its tributary, as was also the whole of nascent Europe owing to that compenetration of East and West. For Spain, in the light of the most recent historiography (we are primarily thinking of the work of Americo Castro) the Arab period no longer appears as an exotic curiosity, an interruption and deviation from her Latin-Christian mission but precisely as a fundamental coefficient in the formation of her national individuality. To a great extent Spain became what she became, in both the good and the bad, through the effect of her Arab era, and through the assimilations, imitations and reactions to the customs and ways of life of the Arabo-Moslem-Hebrew civilization and culture which had flourished on her soil between the eighth and fifteenth centuries. The Arab world, *in situ* and in the very act of the process, had an imperfect consciousness of this exceptional result of its diaspora. It was preoccupied by the more deeply felt bonds of Moslem universalism, and at the end of its dominion in Spain, where Arabism was disintegrating. But in its modern resurgence the remembrance of the Andalusian triumph, instilled or revived in its consciousness by the science and philosophy of Europe, has become one of its greatest claims to glory.

7.

Arabs and Turks

THE political decadence of the Arab world of the East, which almost has its symbol in the decadence of the caliphate, was irreparably accentuated in the eleventh century. The Empire of the caliphs was now only a memory. From Syria to Transoxiana (not to speak of Fatimid Egypt and of the Maghrib whose destinies we have already followed) all was a proliferation of local dynasties, still Arab in Syria and Mesopotamia (Mirdasites, Oqaylids, Marwanids, Mazyadites) and Iranian in Persia (Buwayhids and minor dynasties of the Caspian). But in the Khurasàn province and in Transoxiana, at the very beginning of the century the Iranian Samanids had been succeeded by a Turkish dynasty (even though it was culturally Iranized): that of the Ghaznevids. And with it the Turkish element founded its first great Moslem state. The expansion of the Ghaznevid Empire was wholly directed towards the East, where it began the actual islamization of India. But other Turks, the Seljuks, towards the middle of the century, resumed the old movement of displacement of Turkish peoples from the East to the West, penetrating deeply into Arabism's area of expansion. From this moment on, the political and social history of the Arabs of the East was increasingly permeated by Turkish elements, leveled in the common faith of Islam, and in part won over to Arab culture (while on the other hand they assimilated and promoted the Persian culture, and then ended up by developing a literature of their own). From then on the Abbasids of Baghdad who managed to drag out their existence for another two centuries under Turkish tutelage, constituted the only Arab dynasty of some prominence on all the eastern territories of the caliphate. Everywhere else it was a continuous process of the formation and dissolution of large and small Moslem states ruled by Turkish dynasties, even where the language and culture remained Arab. But the dominant military aristocracy around the sovereign was Turkish, and the army cadres were also Turkish to a large measure. It was the Turkish power, much more than the Arab, which withstood the shock of the Crusaders, finally driving them back. And after the brilliant but ephemeral Ayyubid power (a dynasty which was neither Arab nor Turk in origin, but Kurdish), it was the Mameluke Turks who assumed the defense of Islam and of Arabism itself, against the Mongolian menace and every residue of Christian encroachment. Finally still another Turkish clan, that of the Ottomans, carried the banner of Islam in its last offensive against the West, and at one and the same time subjugated and incorporated into their own Empire all the countries with Arab populations, excluding Morocco. Thenceforth the Arabs ceased to be the subject of history, until their modern resurgence.

In the five centuries that this process lasted, we can still speak of the history of the Arabs, although they were politically and socially in a state of regression, because the bulk of the population of Egypt and Iraq remained Arab, just as its language and culture was Arab. Nor had the consciousness of the historic bond between Arabism and Islamism which united all these foreign hegemonies yet been extinguished. Moreover Turkish influence was still very weak west of Egypt, and here through the whole fifteenth century the ethnic contexture and the political power remained as they had been in the beginnings, while profound Turkish infiltrations took place only in the subsequent Barbaresque period. Therefore the alternations which we are about to describe belong to a history in which Arabs and other non-Arab Islamic peoples—primarily Turks—intertwine, without it being possible to make a clear distinction between them.

The eruption of the Turks as an organized governmental force in the ancient center of the caliphate took place, as we have said, around the middle of the eleventh century. The empire formed by the Seljukid Tughril Beg, at the expense of the Buwayhids and Ghaznevids in the eastern provinces, absorbed Iraq into its frontiers almost without resistance, when the foreign conqueror (the Seljuks were a clan of Oghuz Turks, who had not been islamized for long) in 1055 supplanted the Buwayhids as the protectors of the caliphate. Shortly thereafter he received the titles of sultan and "King of the Orient and Occident" from the Abbasid al-Qaim. The Seljukid state broadened further in the West under the successors of Tughril Beg, Alp Arslàn and Malikshàh (the first three "Great Seljuks), wrested Syria from the Fatimids, and with the victory of Manzikert in 1071 over the Byzantine emperor it forcibly established Islam for the first time in Asia Minor. From then on, and throughout the period of the Seljukid dominion in Iraq, there was a nominal diarchy in Iraq, sometimes also sealed by matrimonial unions, by which the caliph and the sultan in harmony watched over the interests of eastern Islam. In reality there were steady frictions and conflicts between the two powers in which the caliphs generally received the worst and their attempts to regain some freedom of action ended up by confirming their impotence. The great Seljukid empire did not maintain its unity for long. The principal line of Alp Arslàn's descendants was maintained in Iraq and in the Khurasàn province until the death of the sultan

Sinjiar (1157). Other collateral lines reigned over the dominions of Syria, of Kurdistan, and of Kirmàn, and one of particular political and cultural importance in Asia Minor (Seljuks of Rum, from the eleventh to the thirteenth centuries). But the most characteristic phenomenon was the withering away of the Seljukid state in a series of local dynasties, the so-called Atabegs. In origin they were Turks of servile descent (as was the case with a great part of the military chieftains of this Empire), assigned to the tutelage and education of the young princes of the blood. Often, however, they knew how to transform that tutelage into direct, active domination. At the beginning of the twelfth century, along with the same phenomenon of disintegration of the Caliphate of Baghdad, there was a constellation of small emirates at the edges of the ephemeral Empire ruled by these Atabegs. In theory they were the vassals of the Great Seljuk Sultan, but in fact they were independent: the Burids in Damascus, the Zendiks in Mosul, the Artuqids in Mardìn, while still other Atabegs were in Armenia, Azerbaijan and Persia. The Crusaders came up against these petty states of Syria and Mesopotamia (whereas they found Jerusalem and Palestine in the hands of the Fatimids of Egypt) from whence came the most effective Moslem resistance.

Despite the brevity of its duration as a unitary state the Seljukid empire has a great importance in the history of Islam, of Persia, and in part of the Arab world itself. In the religious field, it signified the victory of orthodoxy, which was vigorously sustained by all these neophyte Turks against all the heterodox politico-religious movements which had come to a head in the preceding century of the heretical caliphate of Egypt, and against whose propaganda the Seljuks reacted with material and spiritual arms. The soul of this revival of Sunnite Islam, threatened by old and new heresies (we shall presently discuss the Ismailite sect of Assassins) was the Persian vizier of Malikshàh, Nizàm al-Mulk. He was a great administrator and creator of a vast net of higher institutions of religious sciences (Mèdrese), among which was the celebrated one in Baghdad which was named after him Nizamiyya. He was also the author of a valuable manual on ethics and administration (the *Siyaset-Name* or "Book of Government") which is the source of much of our knowledge about the structure of the Seljuk state. In addition Nizàm al-Mulk was a vigorous champion on all fronts of the struggle against heterodoxy, of which he himself became a victim, succumbing in 1092 to an *attentat* directed against him. Alongside Nizàm al-Mulk in the specifically scientific and religious field, mention must be made here of the great thinker of Tus, al-Ghazzali (died 1111) who taught in the colleges of Nisabur and Baghdad, and who engaged in a lively disputation with the Ismailites. In contrast to his patron he died peacefully, after a life of profound intellectual and mystical experiences, which, among others, were expressed in an admirable autobiographical work. Al-Ghazali, the *Huggiat al-Islàm* (the living "argument" of its faith) was the true reformer of orthodox Islam: a Persian by birth, he wrote for the most part in Arabic, and had totally assimilated Arab culture. It is notable, however, that the administration and chancellery of the Seljuks, like the historiography and poetry which celebrates them, expressed itself more in Persian than in Arabic, attesting to the cultural prestige that had now been achieved by the second Moslem language and literature. On the other hand, the military and social organization of the Seljuk state, as we have said, was purely Turkish. It was based on the institution of the *iqtà* or military fief, the non-hereditary allotment of land to a feudal lord, with the right of direct collection of tributes and the correlative obligation to equip and contribute a given military contingent to the government forces. This Seljukid military feudalism for centuries was to remain the basis of the social and economic structure of the Moslem western Asia. From the Seljuks it was to pass on to the Atabegs, not without exerting influences even on the Christian states established by the Crusaders. The *iqtà* was later likewise to be inherited by the Mongol and Mameluke states, which developed and altered it further.

THE attack of the Crusaders or "Franks," as the Moslems called them, caught eastern Islam at a time when its forces were fragmented, following upon the disintegration of the Seljukid empire, and when the Fatimid state was already in a condition of advanced decay. The two rival caliphs of Baghdad and Cairo cut very mediocre figures in the defense of their respective territories. Coastal Syria and part of upper Mesopotamia were taken by the Crusaders from officials and petty dynasties, who were nominally vassals of the "Great Seljuk," who in turn theoretically was the right arm of the Abbasid caliph. Jerusalem and the coast of Phoenicia and Palestine were taken from the Fatimids of Egypt. Huge tumultuous demonstrations were mounted in Baghdad against the invasion of the infidels, but there was no talk at all of a direct caliphal intervention. After one of his expeditionary corps was routed near Antioch, the Seljuk Sultan Barqiyarùq could not and would not assume further direction of the resistance, leaving it to the Atabegs whose efforts at first were uncoordinated. Even weaker was the defense put up by the Fatimids in the south. The Egyptians were beaten at Ascalon, and they offered little or no assistance at all to their ports along the seaboard, which received some real help only from the Atabeg of Damascus, Tughtigìn. As a result of this politico-military decay, the first years of the twelfth century witnessed the establishment of three Frankish states along the

Syro-Palestinian coast (the kingdom of Jerusalem, the earldom of Tripoli, the principality of Antioch), with the earldom of Edessa as an outpost facing the East. Distinguishing themselves in the Moslem resistance of the first decades were the aforementioned Atabeg of Damascus, Tughtigìn, and the Artuqids of Mardìn, who inflicted a bloody rout at Danith (1126) on Roger of Antioch. But a real counter-offensive could only be hoped for from a unified effort. Here the task of the Holy War intertwined with the ambitions of the Atabeg of Mosul, Zenki, and of his son and successor in Aleppo, Nur ad-Din (the Nureddin of Christian sources), aiming at the control of all of Moslem Syria. Zenki eliminated the Frankish state of Edessa (1144) and in vain tried to make himself master of Damascus which was held by Tughtigìn's heirs. The latter did not hesitate to enter into an alliance with the Franks in order to resist him. His program was realized ten years later by Nureddin who, having become the ruler of both Aleppo and Damascus, was now able to unify the war-effort of Moslem Syria, and victoriously hold his own against the Crusaders. From Nureddin's retinue, but not from his family, later was to emerge the Kurd emir Saladin (Salàh ad-din Yusuf ibn Ayyùb) who was to become Islam's illustrious champion against the Christian invasion.

Saladin's career began in Egypt, where he followed his uncle, an official of Nureddin, who had been invited to intervene in the palace struggles for power during the death-agony of the Fatimid dynasty. After making himself the master of the country, in 1171 he put an end to the heretical caliphate, and brought Egypt back to a formal recognition of the Abbasid caliph. The death of Nureddin, who was his increasingly nominal lord, spared him an open rebellion, and the quarrels among his heirs helped him to gather Nureddin's material and spiritual legacy, and in the first place the religious obligation and political interest of the Holy War. Grown strong now, as a result of the unified Syro-Egyptian energies, he could now initiate those campaigns against the Franks culminating in 1187 with the victory of Hattìn, and the subsequent fall of Jerusalem and a good part of the Latin kingdom. The Third Crusade, as is known, buttressed the shaky Christian dominions of the Holy Land, with a powerful effort, and after a memorable siege it wrested St. John of Acre from Saladin. It led to the peace of 1192, which sanctioned the *status quo* of the moment between Christians and Moslems. Saladin died a year later in Damascus, dividing among his sons the barely formed empire, which included Egypt, Syria (save the residual Latin states), Mesopotamia and a part of Arabia.

The work of the great sultan, before whose greatness and spiritual value his very adversaries bowed, was interrupted by death, and had already been compromised by the massive intervention of the West, which accomplished its greatest effort in the Third Crusade. But still vivid in the Moslem world is his feat of recapturing Jerusalem (which is also a holy place for the Moslems), and of personifying the inflexible zeal and resurgent martial power of Islam before the infidel aggressor. For this reason Saladin's name has been inscribed in universal history, while that of the nominal head of Islam, the Abbasid an-Nasir, to whom he vowed homage and announced his victories is unknown to non-specialists. The character and the work of that great personality makes us at once aware of the difficulty of incorporating him, and of the impossibility of excluding him from a "history of the Arabs." In fact Saladin was not an Arab by birth, just as neither his state nor his army was exclusively Arab, nor did he fight and feel his cause only in the service of the Arabs alone, but rather of Islam, of all Moslems. Yet his mind was molded by the Arab language and culture, his principal civil collaborators were Arabs (the military, instead, were to a great extent Kurds and Turks), and the oriental remembrance of his feat has been transmitted to posterity in Arabic. As was the case with almost all the personages whom we must still discuss, he represented a synthesis between Arab and foreign elements, forged in the crucible of Islamism.

We shall not follow the vicissitudes of the adventure of the Crusade in the East which still lasted for almost a century. It will suffice barely to recall the two Christian attempts to bring the war to Egypt (in 1218-21 with John of Brienne, in 1250 with Louis IX) both of which were repulsed by the Ayyubids. And also to recall the peaceful crusade of Frederick II (1228-29), which was resolved with an ephemeral diplomatic success which exploited the quarrels between Saladin's heirs; and the final liquidation of what remained of the Latin states through the action of the first Mameluke sultans (Antioch was taken in 1268 by Baibars, Tripoli in 1289 by Qalawùn, Acres was the last to fall under al-Ashraf). Nothing remained of Christian rule in Syria and the Holy Land at the end of the thirteenth century, and all those territories now formed part of the Mameluke state of Egypt. But before referring to this and other important changes that occurred in the Arabo-Moslem world within that century, something must be said about the contact between the East and West which the Crusaders brought about, and on the forces—not only political—which the Crusaders found before them.

The coexistence between Latins and Orientals (Arabs and Turks above all) in the Holy Land without doubt gave rise to a whole series of reciprocal influences in which, however, the Crusaders took from the Arabo-Islamic world much more than they gave, for the reason that despite all religious hatred they felt Arab culture and civilization superior and worthy of imitation. The orientalization of the ways, life and customs of the Crusaders, their absorption of the language and elements of the local culture, are a well documented fact, of which there is no comparable counterpart in the opposite direction.

The Arabs and the Moslems in general showed themselves to be more impermeable to the mentality, the culture and the customs of the invaders, than the latter showed towards theirs. The reason for this was their very strong and—at that time—justified sense of superiority. At the close of the two-century old adventure, whereas the West had absorbed from the East some germs that enriched its own culture (in language, art, culture, economy; but on the whole in a more modest measure than in Spain and Sicily), the East could say that it had received almost nothing from that encounter, outside of destruction, tears and blood. It received no material goods, no thirst for knowledge nor tolerant sympathy, but on the contrary, a stiffening and an embittering of its aversion to that foreign creed and civilization which had vainly tried to introduce itself into Islam's orbit.

Of Islam, the Crusaders hardly knew the distant and impotent institution of the caliphate. As direct adversaries they first had the various local emirs, and then the powerful formations of the Ayyubite and Mameluke state. But there was another force with which they came into contact, the terrifying after-echo of which resounded along with the name itself in the West. The great adversary of the orthodox restoration effected by the Seljuks in Asia was the last offspring of Ismailism, the esoteric sect of the Batinites or Assassins. It came into being at the end of the eleventh century as a secession of its adepts from the Fatimid Caliphate, based as usual on a formal question of legitimism (the recognition as successor of the Caliph al-Mustansir of his first-born son Nizàr, instead of his other son who was recognized in Cairo with the name of al-Mustali). In reality, however, the dissidence inaugurated a wholly new and dynamic phase of activity of Ismailite extremism. This "new mission" (*dawa jadida*), as it was actually called, was brought by its promoter, the Persian Hasan ibn as-Sabbàh, to Iraq, Persia and Syria. And while the

Egyptian Caliphate was drowning in a political and ideological death-agony, the new Ismailite current vigorously grew and prospered in Asia as an underground movement, against which the Seljuk state found it difficult to mount an effective opposition. In 1090, Hasan ibn as-Sabbàh made himself master of the inaccessible fortress of Alamùt in northern Persia near Qazwìn, which he made into the central seat of his sect, while one of his lieutenants assumed the direction of the movement in Syria. From here, throughout the twelfth century, these "assassins" (from the Arab *Hashishiyya*, opium or hashish smokers) conducted a campaign of political terrorism more against orthodox Islam than against the infidels. The most illustrious Moslem personalities, for example Nizàm al-Mulk, and also Christian princes like Conrad of Montferrat, fell under the daggers of their fanatical cut-throats or *fidài* (a designation that has again come into use in connection with more recent phenomena of eastern terrorism). For the Moslem princes the struggle against this murderous subversive movement, which sometimes also worked for "third parties" was no less a source of concern than the holy war. Neither the Seljuks nor the Ayyubids got the upper hand over it; only the Mongols in 1256 succeeded in storming Alamùt, thereby destroying the headquarters of the movement, while its activity gradually waned in Syria in the course of this same century. Here the much-feared Assassins were reduced to becoming tranquil tributaries of the Mameluke sultans. The whole western medieval world picked up the after-echo of the "Old Man of the Mountain," and of the mysterious, unlimited power that he wielded over his fanatical followers. Modern research tends to put aside, perhaps too much, the dramatic and picturesque aspect of their political activity, and to study rather the ideological content of the movement that was based on doctrines of an oriental gnosis now at the outermost edges of Islamism. The fact remains, however, that the Batinite movement in the twelfth century was a political force of the first magnitude which had inserted itself—with ambiguous fortunes—in the struggle between Islam and the Crusades. But it did not succeed in creating anything enduring, except a sinister fame founded on its arcane initiation rites and on terrorism.

THE decrepit vegetation of the Caliphate of Baghdad was hardly disturbed by the struggle that unfolded on the shores of the Mediterranean in the twelfth and thirteenth centuries. Although he carried out his role, *pro-forma*, as the head of Islam, a dignity more symbolic than real, the caliph was now a pawn in the political game being played in Persia and Iraq. And it was on this limited chessboard that he now focused his true interest. This appears most clearly in the achievements of the last Abbasid of some worth who sat on the throne of Harùn ar-Rashìd and of al-Mamùn, the afore-mentioned contemporary of Saladin, an-Nasir. His very long reign was entirely dedicated to restoring luster to the caliphal institution, but even more to recuperating what was possible of his "temporal" power in the East. In order to obtain that the caliph aimed above all at ridding himself of the Seljukid tutelage, by cooperating in all ways in the liquidation of the surviving branch in Iraq, to which the great Empire of a century before had been reduced. Its direct liquidator was the sultan of Khwarizm, the new power that had been formed in the eastern marks of the ancient caliphal empire. The last Sel-juk of Iraq, Tughril II, was defeated in 1194 by the Shah of Khwarizm Tukush, and an-Nasir soon had to give thought to dealing with the latter and with his son, Alà ad-Din Muham-mad, who threatened to resume the expansionist program of the Seljuks on his own. Fortune came to an-Nasir's assistance, however. Although he was besieged by Alà ad-Din in Baghdad in 1217, he saw his new enemy forced to withdraw because of the rigors of an exceptionally severe winter. Thus the final hour of the Abbasids was postponed once more. The able caliph who, like some of his predecessors, privately nourished Shi'ite sympathies, had already obtained another diplomatic success with the recognition that had been rendered to him by Hasan III, the Grand Master of the Assassins of Alamùt (themselves in the process of domestication). An-Nasir's interests in the reorganization of the Islamic knightly order of the *Futuwwah* (a term equivalent to our concept of "chivalry"), were linked to this policy of the restoration of the caliphal authority. This Caliph proclaimed himself the Grand Master of this brotherhood, regulating and controlling its activity at close hand. But events beyond his control were now maturing in the East, namely the entry of the Mongols on the scene, representing a new element in the history of Asia and Islam, partly in that of the Arab world. According to some an-Nasir himself probably contributed to the unleashing of the Mongols in order to strike at the threatening Shah of Khwarizm.

The Mongol invasion of western Asia, beginning in 1219, is an event that greatly transcends the history of the Arabs; but it is also engraved on their destinies because of the deep repercussions it had in the whole Moslem world. In its first and most destructive phase under Ghengis Khan it swept over Transoxiana and Persia where it effectively destroyed the state of the Shahs of Khwarizm. But the cyclone which laid waste to those regions with terrible carnage and destruction spared Iraq for the time being, spilling over in a more northerly direction in Azerbaijan and Georgia, and from here into southern Russia across the Caucasus. Hence an-Nasir, at his death in 1225, could delude himself that he had resurrected the destinies of the caliphate, and recovered at least a minimal part of the inheritance of his ancestors. But this was only the last flicker of the flame. Thirty years later, a second Mongol wave hurled itself against western Asia, under the direct command of Hulagu, Ghengis Khan's nephew and the brother of the last Great Khan, Mangu. After sweeping away the remnants of the Assassins of Alamùt, this wave aimed directly for Baghdad. Mongols victoriously entered the ancient capital of the caliphs in January 1258, and the last Abbasid, the nephew of an-Nasir, al-Mustasim, who had vainly given himself up, was put to death. Thus did the caliphate come to an end.

For those accustomed to view this institution almost as the backbone in the history of Arabs and Islam (as in reality it was only for the first two or three centuries), its disappearance seems to have left a vacuum that could not be filled. But whoever has followed our description of its progressive, unarrestable decadence, will understand the relative indifference with which the Arabo-Islamic world accepted that disappearance. To be sure, a more or less authentic member of the Abbasid dynasty was received a few years later by the Mameluke Sultan Baibars in Egypt, where he and his descendants, the shadows of shadows, lived as the ornamental pensioners of those sultans, on whom they conferred a semblance of legitimacy. But the episode only has the value of a mere curiosity. In reality, Islam had now grown accustomed to doing without a unitarian politico-religious direction. It left matters of political power to the big and small sovereignties into which power relations had fragmented Islam. Religious matters were left to that ever more powerful caste of doctors of the Law (*ulamà*) upon whose consensus rested the elaboration of Moslem dogma and law. The disappearance of the Abbasid caliphate therefore did not mark any crisis in the bosom of the Moslem community. Rather, it sealed the crisis of Arabism, the ultimate displacement of its political and cultural center from the East to the West, and the removal of Iraq, where the Arabs at one time had left such deep traces behind, from the numbers of independent and civilized Moslem states. In fact, because of political and above all economic reasons, the country of the caliphs had for some time fallen very low in comparison to its flourishing heydey in the ninth and tenth centuries. The network of canals, which were essential for its agriculture, having been upset and neglected on account of internal disorders, its great urban centers, like Kufa, Basra, Wasit and finally Baghdad itself, having decayed, its wealth squandered and its security compromised, Iraq in the thirteenth century was but a shadow of its former greatness and splendor. After the end of the Abbasids, Iraq became a province of the Mongol Persian Empire, which under Hulagu's successors had its center in Azerbaijàn and northern Persia, of which Iraq was considered a mere appendage. Visiting the country in the fourteenth century, the Maghribian traveler Ibn Battuta found signs of depopulation and utter neglect everywhere. Turkish and Persian dynasties succeeded one another there. None of them, however, made Baghdad its capital, and the once proud metropolis of the high Middle Ages was reduced to the status of an impoverished provincial center. At the same time, indeed even before, intellectual and spiritual life retreated from Baghdad and from Iraq. Social life returned to a squalid nomadism. There the Arab element reverted to the economic and social conditions of former centuries, when it had first boldly looked out upon the Valley of the Two Rivers. But the charge of energy, which it had carried with it at that time was now exhausted, and Islam's urban culture was to continue its slackened course elsewhere.

For the time being the Mongols, who were to become islamized and accept the superior Moslem culture in its Persian form only at the beginnings of the fourteenth century, continued their drive towards the Mediterranean. In Syria the drama of the Crusades was now drawing to its end. But the outcome of the struggle might have been different if the plan that some people cherished in Europe had succeeded, namely that of placing Islam between two fires, the new Mongol threat from the East and the Christian threat from the West. The grandiose design was not carried out because of diplomatic ineptitude and even more because of the division among the Christian states, which practically left the defense of the remaining fortresses of the Holy Land to their own forces. By the time the Mongol wave had come within sight of the Mediterranean it had lost much of its drive and force. It was halted at Ain Jialùt in Palestine (1261), in a battle which was militarily of no great importance but which had decisive political consequences. The wave was stopped by those same Mamelukes of Egypt who shortly thereafter began the final dismantling of the Latin positions overseas. In fact for some time now Egypt had already gathered up Iraq's legacy as the ideal center of the Arab world in the three last centuries of its independent existence.

THE new phase of Egyptian history had begun with Saladin who built his fortunes there on the ruins of the crumbling Fatimid caliphate. The laurels which the great sultan won in the Holy War have led to a forgetfulness of the methods by which he rose to supreme power, which, for that matter, were no more peaceful nor honest than befitted the customs of the times. Nevertheless, the formation of the Ayyubite Empire must be judged as providential for Islam. Not only because of its struggle against the Crusades and its rigorous adherence to orthodoxy, but because at least in the person of the founder, it surmounted the difficulty represented by the political breakup of the Seljukid state, and welded Egypt and Syria again into a bloc that was destined to last for centuries beyond every ephemeral fragmentation. It is true that upon Saladin's death, the dismemberment of his Empire, stretching from Tripoli in Africa to Yemen and Mesopotamia, was resumed, breaking up into a series of minor rival states. But they also all remained in the hands of his descendants and kinsmen, among whom soon emerged the Egyptian branch with Saladin's brother, al-Adil (1199-1218), and the latter's son, al-Kamil (1218-38). The activity of these two sultans, the major ones after the founder in the intricate genealogy of the Ayyubite house, was directed towards the maintenance of a solid Syro-Egyptian nucleus on which all the other minor principalities could and should depend in the prosecution of the holy war inaugurated by Saladin. The bitter rivalries between some of these epigoni still allowed the Latins to achieve some successes. Thus their attack on Egypt, which coincided with the Mongol invasion in the East, gave Islam a momentary sense of loss which is reflected in the pages of the historian Ibn al-Athìr. But Adil and Kamil, who were wise and energetic rulers, knew how to cope with the danger. Near Damietta in 1219 al-Kamil listened courteously to St. Francis whom he received chivalrously and dismissed cordially at the very time that he was engaged in repelling the aggression of the Crusaders. The second Latin attack on Egypt, that of St. Louis thirty years later, no longer found "the Perfect King" (which is what al-Malik al-Kamil means in Arabic) on the throne of Cairo, but his son al-Malik as-Salih ("the Good King"), already afflicted with an incurable illness. This sultan died as the Crusaders were coming up the Nile from Damietta. The energy displayed by his widow permitted his distant son Turanshàh to come to occupy the throne and to inflict the decisive defeat of Mansura (1249) on St. Louis. Here the future Mameluke sultan Baibars distinguished himself for the first time, by his heroism in combat and by the cold ferocity with which a short time later he perpetrated the assassination of his lord Turanshàh, who was the last

Ayyubite of Egypt. In fact the one who succeeded him, by marrying the Queen-mother, was one of those military leaders of slave origin (Mamelukes) from which Baibars himself descended. Thus was a new regime of military feudalism inaugurated, destined to last in Egypt until the Ottoman conquest.

Unlike the Turks of the Abbasid and Seljukid era, these Mamelukes did not come directly from Central Asia, but from territories further to the West to which the Turkish expansion had extended. Mostly, they came from the coasts of the Black Sea, the Caucasus and from southern Russia. From here a regular slave trade had replenished the cadres of the Ayyubite guard, and in accordance with the usual process these praetorians had risen to the apex of the military and social hierarchy. Their access to supreme power was regulated now by successful violence, now by the consensus of their companions, now by a dynastic principle which created a sufficiently long genealogical continuity in the first series of these sultans (the "Bahri" or Nile Mamelukes from 1250 to about 1390), while it was much more fragmentary in the second series of the Burji Mamelukes which lasted from 1390 to 1517. These Turks and Circassians were rough soldiers whose education was often exclusively military; sometimes they were ignorant even of the language of their subjects. Nevertheless their rule over Egypt and adjoining Syria marked the last period in the history of the Arabs of the East, in which they were assured of political independence and untrammelled economic and cultural activity, albeit under the aegis of a foreign oligarchy. The Mamelukes who for a long time were still being imported into Egypt from the Black Sea never forgot the language of their birthplace, and they introduced Turko-Persian institutions, customs and titles into the military and courtly sphere. But they always maintained Arabic as the language of culture, they encouraged Arab

science and literature, and had a strong feeling for the independence of their Arab dominions which they defended with
the same passion. As we have seen they were the saviors of
the Near East from the Mongols and the liquidators of the
Christian states of the Holy Land, while at the same time they
put an end to all the surviving branches of the Ayyubites of
Syria. The one which maintained itself the longest as their vassal state was the principality of Hamàt, where the scientist
prince Abu-l-Fidà still ruled at the beginning of the fourteenth
century. When the sea again closed over the outermost surviving strips of Latinity in the Orient (St. John of Acre fell in
1291, the little island of Arados off Tortosa in 1305), Egypt
and Syria found themselves Moslemized again and entirely
subject to the sultans of Cairo. In the beginning there were
notable figures of sovereigns among which history counts especially the following: in the series of the Bahris, the aforementioned Baibars, the "Panther Prince" (1260-77), who was unscrupulous in his choice of means as much as he was a valiant
soldier, an active and able diplomat, and a great builder; or Qalawùn (1279-90), the conqueror of Tripoli and founder of an
enduring dynasty on the throne of Egypt. Among the Burji,
mention should be made of Qait Bey (1468-95), whose
name is linked to the architectural embellishment of Cairo,
and of Qansùh al-Ghuri, the penultimate Mameluke sultan,
who made a brave but unsuccessful stand in Syria against the
overwhelming Ottoman menace.

The Mameluke regime represented a development of military feudalism of Seljukid type, with a temporary allotment
of lands to the emirs in return for the obligation of an organized military service and contribution. One of the country's
greatest resources was the trade with foreign countries (numerous commercial treaties between the Sultans and the Latin
states of the Mediterranean, as well as with Byzantium have
been preserved). But this trade suffered a hard blow at the

end of the fifteenth century when Vasco da Gama opened the sea route to the Indies with his circumnavigation of Africa, and the Syro-Egyptian state ceased to be the normal route of transit between Europe and central Asia and the Far East. Moreover, at that time the days of the Mameluke Empire were numbered. In contrast to the Ottoman Turks it had delayed too long in getting to know and to assimilate the results of European technique, such as firearms, and this inferiority proved fatal in the clash with the new great Moslem power. Wholly medieval in structure and culture, the last independent Arab state had the irreplaceable function of providing a home for the Arab material and spiritual culture, which had completely died out in the East, and of preserving it for the future.

To be sure this culture was also being maintained west of Egypt in the Maghribian states that had sprung up in consequence of the dismantling of the Almohad Empire. These were the Hafsids of Tunisia (1228-1534), who repulsed St. Louis' attack in 1270, and who engaged in a brisk trade with the Italian and Iberian states; the Zayyanites or Abd al-Wadites of Tilimsàn who were absorbed by their neighbors the Merinids of Morocco at the end of the fourteenth century. This last dynasty (1195-1470), which was then continued by the cognate clan of the Wattasids up to 1550, had an especial importance in the outermost Maghrib because it had witnessed, along with ineffective attempts at help, the dying days of Andalusian Islam in its last Granadian refuge, and it had received a goodly part of its final flow of emigrants. But the capacity of Arabo-Berber Africa to unite in a great western bloc had been exhausted with the Almoravids and Almohads. The outline of its definite tripartition into Tunisia, Algeria and Morocco, a division which has substantially remained until today, was already manifest since the beginning of the thirteenth century. From the thirteenth to the sixteenth century the three Maghribian states likewise maintained their independence and Arab culture. But they preserved the latter in a more regional form than was the case in Egypt, and cut off from the eastern tradition.

The end of these independent Arab states, except for Morocco, came in the first half of the sixteenth century when the Ottoman Turks appeared on the scene. If the rise of this race was fatal for the destinies of Byzantium and of all the Christian peoples of eastern Europe, it was no less ruinous for those of Arabism, even though the community of religious faith at that time deadened the consciousness of the blow among the Arab peoples. For centuries they had grown accustomed to being subject to non-Arab dynasties, from the Seljuks to the Atabegs, from the Ayyubites to the Mamelukes. But whereas all these big and small dynasties had made Arab territories the center of their dominion, and had been almost all culturally arabized (only the great Seljuks preserved the seat in Persia, and favored Persian culture, as we have seen), the Ottoman conquest signified an aggregation of Arab countries to a Moslem Empire which had its center elsewhere, which preserved its non-Arab language and governmental structure, and leveled the subject peoples in a dull administrative and fiscal docility.

The Mameluke state was the first to fall, between the end of 1516 and the first days of the following year. After defeating the Sultan Qansùh al-Ghuri—who died during the engagement at Marj Dabiq near Aleppo—Sultan Selìm I from Syria rapidly came down into Egypt, where the last Mameluke sovereign Tumanbey made a vain effort to halt him. Tumanbey was hanged from a gate in Cairo in January 1517, and with this began the Ottoman dominion of Egypt which was to last three centuries. In the course of the sixteenth century it slowly but irresistibly extended to almost all Arab countries, from Arabia itself to the eastern and central part of the Maghrib. Since the high Middle Ages a fragmentation into various local dynasties had taken place in the Arab Peninsula itself. Notable among these were the heterodox dynasties, such as the Zaidite Imàmate of Yemen (893-1300, with its seat in Sada, and a modern continuation in Sana which has lasted until our days), the rule of the Ibadite Kharijites in Oman and that of the Ismailite Carmathians in Bahrein. The sovereignty of the Ayyubites and Mamelukes over part of western Arabia was now followed by that of the Ottomans, which was extended to Hijaz where from the ninth century power was exercised by a line of local Sharifs or "nobles" who handed it down to each other. The Arab states of the Maghrib instead sunk to the status of dependencies of the Porte because of the assaults of the great corsair captains (Uruj, Barbarossa, Ucciali), often operating entirely on their own, their undertakings then being sanctioned by Constantinople. In 1519 the territories conquered by Khair ed-din Barbarossa from the Moroccan Merinids were organized into an autonomous province of the Ottoman Empire; thus modern Algeria came into being. In 1534 the Hafsid dominion in Tunis disappeared, and after an ephemeral Spanish dominion Tunisia also definitively entered into the Ottoman orbit. In 1551 Dragut took Tripoli away from the Knights of Rhodes; and Tripoli, Tunis and Algiers began their notorious "Barbaresque" period. It was characterized by a high Ottoman sovereignty, exercised through a Pasha nominated by the sultan alongside whom stood the chieftains of the Janissaries and the captains of the pirate fleet (Turks, Arabs and renegade Europeans) who in Tunis and Algiers ended up by assuming an ever greater autonomy. From their ranks came those Beys and Deys whom the French found at the head of those Barbaresque states in the nineteenth century. In Tripoli the direct rule of the Porte alternated with the *de facto* autonomy of the local chieftains, the Caramamli who, however, were also of distant Turkish origin. And even in the times and places where the authority of Constantinople no longer made itself directly felt, the Turkish element infiltrated deeply into the ethnic structure, the language, and the political institutions of these Maghribian states, thereby profoundly differentiating the new period of their history from the preceding one which was purely Arab. It is more than a play of words to recognize a real return to barbarism in the Barbary era of the Maghrib, with its brutal regime of violence within and the roving piracy on the Mediterranean.

At the outermost opposite end of the Arab world, Iraq, worn-out and contended over by Persians and Ottomans, definitively fell into the hands of the latter in 1638. Since then remote Morocco, closed in archaic structure to penetration from Europe and the Orient, was the only Arab country to preserve its independence until the beginning of the twentieth century. Henceforth the Arabs, from the river Muluya to the Iranian plateau were now subject to alien masters, when they did not take refuge in the anarchic freedom of the desert.

THE centuries through which we have summarily traveled witnessed the political as well as the cultural decadence of that Arab civilization. The rhythm of the spiritual regression, however, was very much slower than the political. The Arab "Renaissance" still cast its brilliant rays for the first three centuries, up to the late thirteenth century, even though the creative summit of the preceding era was now surpassed. Indeed we saw the culture of Moslem Spain arrive at its apex in the same era of the political decadence (eleventh to twelfth centuries). But for the East the spiritual decadence became evident after the year 1000, despite the fact that great isolated figures still asserted themselves within a culture which tended to fall back upon itself becoming reflective and purely scholastic rather than original and creative as it once had been. There was no Arab poet of the East, except perhaps the blind Abu l-Alà al-Maarri of Syria (died 1057), who could express a new note capable of interesting us today. And the best artificer of the mother tongue in the opinion of Arab traditionalism, the celebrated author of the *Maqamàt*, Hariri of Basra (died 1122) seems to our modern taste to be a pure virtuoso of language, indeed the embalmer of a dead language. Alongside the great Ghazzali, the late Arab Middle Ages can count such outstanding figures like the Mesopotamian historian Ibn al-Athìr (died 1233), or the puritan Syrian jurist and theologian Ibn Taimiyyah (died 1328) whose passion and fecundity recall the Andalusian Ibn Hazm. But through all these centuries there was a very intense labor of systemization and compilation around these and a few other truly original personalities (without counting the Maghribian Ibn Khaldùn here), which made an inventory of the great Abbasid epoch, continuing, annotating, summarizing and rearranging it. This was *mutatis mutandis* the Alexandrian age of Arab culture which found its coronation in the Egypt of the Mamelukes. There in these three centuries, from the thirteenth to the sixteenth, in the last great independent Arab state, Arab learning erected monuments to itself with the encyclopedias and the treatises of the great compilers Nuwairi, Maqrizi, Qalqashandi, Suyuti. These are all names of men of letters who produced works that are well known to every Arabist, albeit of no significance to the layman who is not looking for valuable materials of scholarship but is rather seeking original values of thought and art. On the other hand the figurative arts continued to flourish in this period of slow regression. These were anonymous as almost always in the East, but always prodigal of beauty. It was the Mameluke era in Egypt and

Syria, when Iraq already was letting the monuments of its greatest past crumble into ruin, which developed the Seljukid legacy and created a style of its own, marked by a refined elegance which still gives the most characteristic imprint to the architectural aspect and to the creations of the minor arts in those two Moslem countries. Nor can we ignore the fact that the Mameluke era made a contribution of lasting validity also in the field of literature. This was the definitive elaboration of the *Thousand and One Nights*, whose later and precious narrative layer, often artistically superior to the older ones, mirrors the Egyptian society, high and low, of the fourteenth and fifteenth centuries. Unknown redactors and rhapsodists of Egypt have created several of the gems of the famous collection in comparison to which Harùn ar-Rashìd's tired, conventional evocations of Baghdad pale. With the thought and feeling of al-Ghazzali, who has appeared to some as a personification of Christian spirituality and finesse, with the yearning of the mystics who found their greatest poet in the Egyptian Ibn al-Farid (died 1235), with the savory realism of these best pages of the *Thousand and One Nights*, and the refined elegances of Mameluke art, Arabism of the East in those centuries showered its last gifts on medieval Islamic civilization. Then the springs of the spirit dried up, and the Arab world drowsily fell into a long state of torpor from which it was to awaken only through the violent and beneficent impact of Europe.

8.

Decadence and Rebirth

TURKISH rule which for the Arabs of the East lasted from the sixteenth to the twentieth century, marked the period of Arabism's greatest decadence. At first the Arabs submitted to it as though to the preordained dénouement of a process already in progress for centuries. Their hegemony had slowly been replaced in the Moslem world by that of the Turks: a people alien to them in race and language, but who shared their religious faith and who in part had absorbed their culture. A general spiritual and cultural decadence, a complete dissipation of the sense of nationality and a real social degradation corresponded to this apathetic resignation. Often a local aristocracy flanked the bureaucratic and military Turkish ruling class—sometimes actually opposing it in Egypt, as in Hijaz, and in Lebanon as well as in the Barbary states of the Maghrib. But this local element was itself sometimes also Turkish or Turkized (like the Cologhlis in Tripoltania, and the Janissaries in Tunisia and Algeria); and, even if it was Arab, it aspired to autonomy in a very instinctive way. From the seventeenth to the nineteenth century indeed there was no dearth of rebellions, even overt, against the central Ottoman authority. For example, there was that of the Druse emir of Syria, Fakhr ad-din (the "Faccardin" of our sources). He, in the first half of the seventeenth century, tried to free himself from subjugation to the Sultan, establishing relations with the Medicean court in Tuscany, but he was eventually defeated and executed in Constantinople. At the end of the eighteenth century, there was the case of the Mameluke Ali Bey, the unfortunate precursor in Egypt of Mohammed Ali; and then again in the first years of the nineteenth century the rebellion of the emir Bashìr ash-Shibabi in Lebanon. But in addition to the fact that all these attempts failed, they all constituted merely individual adventures, motivated by personal ambitions and resentments more than by an impulse consciously rooted in a conception of nationality. In general, the Arabs submitted to the feudal Ottoman regime, which continued that of the Seljuks and Mamelukes, but with an attenuation of its original military character. Being on a par with the dominant group in the equality of Islam, they theoretically had access even to the high posts of the Ottoman state, but very few Arab names appear in the annals of that Empire, which on the other hand often utilized the talents of persons of Greek, Albanian and Slavic descent. The spring of enterprise and creativity possessed by the Arab elements seems to have snapped.

Only one purely Arab rising, free of all foreign influence, shook Islam during these centuries of decadence. This was the rise of Wahhabism in Arabia itself. It was the last, and successful, aspect of that Moslem rigorism which in the beginnings of Islam had produced Kharijism, and which in the bosom of the community itself had found expression in the Hanbalite tradition of jurisprudence. In fact the origins of the Wahhabite movement, which was inaugurated in central Arabia in the middle of the eighteenth century by the doctor and agitator Muhammad ibn Abd al-Wahhàb (1703-92) are connected with Hanbalism (a school going back to the theologian and jurist Ahmad ibn Hanbal, the fierce adversary of the Mutazilites at the time of the Caliph al-Mamùn). This austere reformer, whose activity aimed at restoring Islam to its original pure faith by abolishing every superstructure of a secular evolution, had no aim whatsoever of an extra-religious character. Nevertheless the purely Arab and Bedouin ambience in which he operated, amid social conditions not very dissimilar from those of the times of Mohammed himself, gave his movement a national imprint, and almost represented a revival of that distant past. Muhammad ibn Abd al-Wahhàb found the support, which long before the Prophet had found in the Medinese community, in the person of Ibn Saud, the emir of Najd. From that time on the destinies of Wahhabism were linked to those of the Saudi dynasty and state. The culmination of its first victorious expansion came at the beginning of the nineteenth century, with the capture of the holy cities of Mecca and Medina, where the Najdian Wahhabites, in keeping with their aversion of the cult of saints and of the Prophet himself, did not hesitate to demolish shrines and mausoleums. Driven out of Hijaz after a seven-year war, conducted by Egyptian forces on orders from Constantinople, they reverted to indulging themselves in obscure dynastic squabbles in central Arabia. Here they vegetated until the beginning of the twentieth century when under a new Saudi emir, Abd al-Aziz ibn Saud, they initiated a second cycle of conquests which was to lead them to the establishment of the present Saudi monarchy, which now controls more than two-thirds of the Arab Peninsula. In the period of the Turkish hegemony, the Wahhabites had an unsavory reputation in the Moslem world as fanatical extremists who had to be fought with arms, whereas today they are regarded with respect and sympathy even by those Moslems who do not share their doctrines. This may be due to the fact that political exigencies have induced the Saudi dynasty to modify its original rigorism, or, even more, to the reborn Arab national pride which sees its archetypal affirmation in the patriarchal state of Arabia.

At the beginning of the nineteenth century Moslem orthodoxy and the Ottoman hegemony had a defender against the
Wahhabite peril in Mohammed Ali, who sent an army from
Egypt under the command of his son to liberate the holy places
from those fanatical puritans. The new phase of Egyptian
history had already begun, for about a year, with the cyclonic
Napoleonic expedition (1798-1801), which was as devoid of
immediate political results as much as it was a herald of that
country's future resurrection. From 1806 on, the restored
Turkish rule was represented by the rough warrior of Kavala
(Macedonia), who was to establish his dynasty there for
almost a century and a half. Mohammed Ali's rise to power
began with the massacre of the Mamelukes, organized in pure
medieval style, who still formed the oligarchy that had been
dominant in Egypt until then (1811). He gained prestige
through the services that he rendered to the Porte, of which
he remained the vassal, in the suppression of Wahhabism in
Arabia and in the struggle against the Greek insurrection
(1824-27). Finally he boldly opposed the Porte itself in the
war of Syria (1831-33) which was annexed for the *n*th
time to Egypt, from which it was taken away again only
through European intervention. These brilliant military successes, in which Mohammed Ali's son, Ibrahìm Pasha, distinguished himself, were the fruit of the organizational ability of
Egypt's new master and of his sagacious promotion of western
techniques to which he opened his country not only in the
military but also in the economic, agricultural and industrial
fields. It goes without saying that he remained an oriental
despot, Turkish by language and education and completely
alien to the ideals of a national Arab renaissance. But in order
to consolidate his state and make it powerful, he did not hesitate to solicit European help, and to surround himself with
western advisers. He also sent missions of Egyptian students to

the West. In short, Mohammed Ali laid the basis of modern Egypt which until yesterday had considered him as the progenitor of the national reawakening. Today he too seems to suffer from the *damnatio memoriae*, extended to his whole dynasty by the new revolutionary course.

The ties between the new Egyptian state and the Porte theoretically endured until 1914. The first successors of Mohammed Ali, who died in 1849, as well as his better-known nephew Ismaïl (1863-80), who acquired the title of Khedive from the Sultan, sought and obtained their investiture from Constantinople. Ismaïl, who was now distinctly arabized, resumed the work of his ancestor at an accelerated pace, opening the Suez Canal, and promoting the technical and intellectual progress of the country and conquering the Sudan. But the dissipations resulting from the oriental magnificence of his way of life ruined him, and he was forced to abdicate under the pressure of his European creditors. Under his successor Tewfik, British imperialism which for some time had been coveting a firm foothold in Egypt so as to ensure control of the route to India and its other Oriental possessions, seized the opportunity presented by a wave of xenophobia (the government of Orabi Pasha), and in 1882 it became *de facto* master of the country through military intervention. The Khedive continued to reign, like an Abbasid of the good old days, under the strict tutelage of a British High Commissioner. In those same years France established her protectorate in Tunisia, and she had already established a direct colonial regime in Algeria, after overcoming the stubborn resistance of the heroic and chivalrous Abd el-Qader. The early twentieth century saw the completion of the European colonial penetration of the Arab West (the Italian occupation of Libya in 1911-12, the French protectorate over Morocco in 1912). Thus did Turkey and England, Italy and France

divide between them the spoils of the Arab world on the eve
of the First World War.

IN this modern age the Turks had nothing more to teach the
Arabs, since they themselves were now in a phase of political
and spiritual decadence. But the case with Europe was quite
different. Together with its military and technical superiority,
it revealed to the East its loftiest intellectual and spiritual
achievements: its scientific, philosophical and political thought,
its literature and art. From the second half of the nineteenth
century on Turks and Arabs reached out for this culture with
hesitation and mistrust at first, then with an ingenuous enthusiasm. And the dual contradictory European influence of
political encroachment and spiritual illumination profoundly
affected the resuscitation of the Arab national consciousness,
by fashioning new goals and new ideals for it. At first the
renascence emerged in two countries, Syria and Egypt, which,
as we have seen, constituted the central nucleus of Arabism
in the centuries of its decadence, and were always the least
backward of all the Arab countries. Syria in a broad sense
(including therein Lebanon and Palestine) was, of course,
subject to the retrograde Ottoman regime, but the Europeans'
cultural penetration, above all French, made itself increasingly
felt in the course of the nineteenth century, and contact with
the Anglo-Saxon world was established in a large measure
through extensive emigration to America. Egypt had first
made contact with European science and technique with the
Napoleonic expedition, and then with Mohammed Ali's en-
lightened despotism. From 1882 on the British occupation
accelerated and intensified that process giving the country
an administrative, economic and educational structure of
Western type, which gradually imposed itself on the tradi-

tional modes of life. Everywhere acceptance of foreign material superiority attracted the young Arab generations to the fountainhead of such superiority, to contact with the ideas and political ideologies of the West. It was to this élite that the concepts of nationality, of freedom, and democracy, as they had been recently elaborated in Europe were revealed. None of these concepts were totally unknown to the Arab national tradition; indeed some precedents for democracy can be found in pre-Islamic antiquity and in the origins of Islam. But what certainly was unknown was a conscious longing for democracy, its theoretical justification, and above all the urgency with which its concepts operated in this new historic phase, on a terrain only now ready for their diffusion.

Thus between the end of the nineteenth century and the beginning of the twentieth, within the school of Europe, the Arabs learned love of country, budding up from the modern sense of nationality, along with its ultimate manifestation in nationalism. In the initial phase the ideal of independence from the foreigner was correlated in a Mazzinian manner with that of internal civil freedom and of democracy. Later, in the bitterness of the struggle, it lost these generous dimensions, becoming rigid, violent, and exclusive, as a result of the involution that those ideals then underwent in Europe itself. The first apostles of Arab nationalism, like Mustafa Kemal in Egypt and the band of Syro-Lebanese publicists who found refuge and a field of activity in Egypt, solidly intertwined ideals of freedom, independence and democracy along purely nineteenth-century lines. But when Europe set the example of breaking away from such a correlation, the Arabs, who were midway in their battle for independence, also sacrificed every other consideration to that single ultimate goal. They admired and aped the totalitarianisms of the twentieth century, and they associated themselves with the revival of democratic ideals after the Second World War only *pro forma,* without their erstwhile enthusiasm. The aspirations to independence which had been suppressed and disappointed for so long, the strenuousness of the effort to effectuate them, and the emergence of new disturbing factors in the ethno-political structure of the Near East (the establishment of Israel) gradually imparted to Arab nationalism that adamance and aggressive intransigence which has characterized its most recent phase, depriving it of its pristine afflatus of humanity.

Thus we have reviewed the ideological aspects of the Arab renascence, from the late nineteenth century to our day. We shall now summarize its concrete developments. Naturally the struggle of the Arabs was directed against their various tutors and masters: in Syria against the Turks, in Egypt against the British. The velleities of Syrian patriots for autonomy within the framework of the Ottoman state having been dissipated with the advent of the Young Turks, their aspirations assumed an ever more explicitly separatist and nationalist character to which Turkey reacted with sanguinary reprisals. In Egypt the struggle for independence was less violent, but its lines were no less tightly drawn. At first it was led by the founder of the "National Party" Mustafa Kemal (1881-1938), and immediately after the First World War by the "delegation" or party of the Wafd. The first great world conflict intervened between these two phases of the Egyptian movement for independence, along with the promises, hopes and disappointments, to which it gave rise among the Arabs. But the war also gave a decisive turn to their modern history. While the crumbling Ottoman Empire, with its proclamation of the Holy War, waved the banner of pan-Islamism (an ideology practically opposite to the national aspirations of the individual Moslem peoples), the Entente levered up Arab nationalism in order to goad it into an internal revolt against the Turks. This was the occasion of the notorious correspondence (1915-

16) between MacMahon, the British commissioner in Egypt (where in the meanwhile Great Britain had proclaimed a protectorate) and Husain, the Arab Sherif of Mecca. As a reward for the insurrection the latter was offered the dazzling prospect of a great Arab kingdom in the territories of the "Fertile Crescent," which at that time were all subject to Constantinople. Trusting in these promises, Husain raised the banner of revolt in the desert in 1916, which led his son Faisal and T. E. Lawrence to make a victorious entry into Damascus in the autumn of 1918. But MacMahon's assurances to the Arabs had already been compromised by the subsequent Sykes-Picot agreements which split the Arab territories of the Ottoman Empire into two zones of French and British influence respectively. The addition of the Balfour Declaration (1917), supporting the creation of a Jewish "national homeland" in Palestine, the nucleus of the future state of Israel, complicated the problem further. In this diplomatic imbroglio of the Entente, one can see that the role of ignorance had been no less prominent than deliberate bad faith. But it is certain that a disastrous impression was aroused in the eastern Arab world when the victorious conclusion of the war was succeeded by the imposition of dubious mandates instead of the promised freedom and independence. The Arab states formed out of the flotsam of the Ottoman Empire were in fact all subjected to this new form of European tutelage: Iraq, Transjordan and Palestine to Britain, Syria and Lebanon to France. Faisal who tried to resist the French at Damascus was driven out by French cannon (1920). Only a year later did Britain give him the Iraquian throne as dubious reparation, while his brother Abd Allah became the head of the emirate of Transjordan. Lebanon and Syria were proclaimed republics, but subjected to repeated administrative manipulations on the part of the mandatory power. Only Husain, the disappointed

Hashimite Sherif remained with the title of king of Hijaz. But under the thrust of reborn Wahhabite expansionism, his ephemeral throne was also doomed to speedy exantlation.

Such was the situation of the ex-Ottoman Arab territories at the end of the World War. In the decade between the two wars, all these young states struggled to free themselves from the tutelage of the mandate. The mandatory powers intended the abolition of the mandates to be accompanied by close ties of alliances. At first the results were purely nominal. The substance materialized only at the end of the Second World War. When the second world conflict broke out in 1939, the mandates had expired or were about to expire but none of the Arab states was yet in a position to conduct an independent foreign policy. To be sure, twenty years of unsolicited tutelage had brought them real advantages in the form of training in administration, of technical and cultural assistance and of real civil progress. But the more substantial this progress was, the more intolerable did foreign tutelage become, and recriminations against the colonial Western regimes became continuously more stentorian.

The condition of Palestine proved to be especially delicate. Here the governing powers were unwilling or unable to install even an attenuated form of self-government. Furthermore, Jewish immigration, which was alternately encouraged and curtailed, effected a profound modification in the ethnic composition and economic structure of the country, much to the disadvantage of the Arabs. Hence the Holy Land in the Second World War was rocked by rival terrorisms, and shaken by inflamed passions which British imperialism—after having imprudently aroused them—worked feverishly to restrain with futile police measures, or tried to reconcile in a concatenation of projects and conferences foredoomed to failure.

The struggle for Egyptian independence unfolded at the same time. It was fought outside the ex-Ottoman area, but it was directed against the same European imperialism. The end of the First World War found the country under a British protectorate, with a nominal "sultan" in the person of Fuad, a son of Ismail. But ineluctable public agitation headed by the nationalist leader Saad Zaghlàl compelled Britain, after the usual arrests, deportations and banishments, to recognize Egyptian independence in 1922, although the latter was modified by substantial politico-military reservations. The primary theme of the subsequent thirty year period of Egyptian history, including the interlude of the Second World War, involved the removal of these reservations. At first the essential stages of this process were Zaghlàl's governmental labors as such, which were conducted in most difficult conditions, between the authoritarianism of the Crown (Fuad had been proclaimed King of Egypt in 1922), and the return of British forces as in the crisis of 1924. When Zaghlul died, this task was resumed by his successor to the government and to the leadership of the Wafd party, Nahas Pasha. The latter's moral personality was very inferior to that of his predecessor but he was an able political strategist. With the treaty of 1936, he succeeded in terminating the British military occupation outside the Canal Zone but he could not avoid the treaty of alliance which Britain imposed as the price of her concessions. This led Egypt into the combat area in the Second World War; the war's victorious conclusion in favor of the Allies, however, created conditions which were much more propitious for total Egyptian and Arab independence than would have been the case if the outcome of the conflict had been otherwise. The final act of the Anglo-Egyptian duel was wrought in this post-war period by the withdrawal of British forces from the Suez Canal, the last strip of Egyptian soil in which the British had rooted themselves (a removal obtained by Egypt only in 1954 and terminated in 1956). Also, on this note was the question of the Sudan where Egyptian imperialism, suddenly reborn, tried to take the place of the British condominium in decline. But with this we arrive at political news of the day. Looking back over the last thirty years, we can observe in Egypt a no less keen internal struggle intertwine itself with the intricacies of political maneuvering. The leaders of the Wafd were spokesmen of a nationalism that was initially intransigent and dynamic and later became more accommodating and strategical. For this very reason they were ousted by new extremist views. They were opposed by the no less able strategist Fuad, in a conflict between Crown and parties which redolates the Italian *Risorgimento*. The work of this sovereign, who undoubtedly was a man of superior intelligence and tenacious will, certainly contributed, in a *concordia discors* with his various governments, in bringing Egypt closer to full independence, and into the camp of culture and civil progress. But like the precedent represented by the Savoy king to whom we have compared him, he no less aimed at the affirmation of his personal authority and prestige, even at the expense of strict loyalty to the constitution. Nevertheless, the whole measure of Fuad's worth, of his ability and prudence, is delineated by comparison with the abject failure of his successor Farouk, who succeeded him in 1936 in an aura of ardent popularity which then he was to squander so wretchedly.

THE Second World War found the Arab states much more along the road of actual sovereignty and of self-government than they had been twenty years before with the paternalistic and rather hypocritical systemization of the Near East that had been imposed by the victors at the end of the earlier conflict. But the bitterness and impatience of the Arabs, exploited by the propaganda of the Axis powers, engendered a mistrust of democratic ideals, leading to collusions between the Arab world and the authoritarian regimes which were entirely without precedent. The work of the Mufti of Palestine Amìn al-Husaini, of the Germanophile Ali Maher in Egypt, and above all of the Iraqian nationalist Rashid al-Kailani (1941), constituted the salient features of this political opposition, the dimensions of which were reduced and ultimately extinguished by the general course of the conflict itself. Between 1944 and 1945 the whole Arab world aligned itself on the side of the victors out of conviction and convenience, coupled with the feeling that now new destinies were in store for it. With America's massive intervention in the politics of the old world, European colonialism, even under the transparent mask of the mandates, was now in full liquidation in the Near East. Its last residues crumbled away precisely at the end of the war when Lebanon and Syria wrested their full independence from France with no reservation of military ties. Britain had abolished the mandate in Iraq in 1932, and in 1946 she abolished it in the emirate of Transjordan, which was elevated to the status of a kingdom. In 1946 Egypt regained total control of the national territory save for the Suez Zone, while the two principal Arab states of the Arab peninsula (Saudi Arabia and Yemen) had always preserved their sovereignty intact. In March 1945, all these independent Arab states joined in an Arab League in a solemn ceremony which promised much at the time of its establishment, but the achievements of which have since become very delusive.

The declared aim of the Arab League was that of coordinating the foreign policy of the various member states, and attending to the common social, economic and cultural interests of the Arab peoples. A federative intent was inherent in this broad program, aiming at a still higher and closer unity. But reality has shown that, alongside the pan-Arab ideal and the common problems and interests, there are strong causes for dissension, regional egoisms and particularisms. Among the Arab nations these are obstacles in the path of every great federal design. The work of the League has shown its effectiveness above all in the social and cultural camp, while successes have alternated with failures in the more specifically political field. Among the first successes can be counted its support of the claims to the total freedom of Syria and Lebanon. And later this was also true for Libya. (The possibility of returning Libya to Italy was removed by Great Britain's commitments to Cirenaica and by pan-Arab pressure. In fact Libya also became a sovereign state and member of the League.) But the great disappointment and the testing ground not only of the diplomatic but politico-military efficiency of this grouping of young Arab states has been the burning question of Palestine.

Here the efforts of the Arabs to reacquire integral control of the situation, and to reaffirm their historic rights to that land, arabized for thirteen centuries, collided with the new conditions that had been created between the two wars and assumed enormous dimensions in the period of Nazi persecutions, notably the accelerated Jewish immigration. Having become the first patron of the movement with the Balfour Declaration, Great Britain, perhaps, would have liked to halt the spirits she herself had conjured up, but the sweep of events, plus America's moral and material support of the Zionist cause made it impossible to reverse the course. A dynamic, bold element, equipped with the most modern techniques of warfare had now re-established itself in its ancient homeland, economically and socially reducing the primitive and indolent Arab population to a status of inferiority. The division of the country into two parts, sanctioned finally by the United Nations and the withdrawal of British military forces was immediately followed by the proclamation of the sovereign state of Israel, and by the attempt of the Arab states to hurl the new state into the sea through a combined military action (May 1948). But after a few weeks of hostilities the Arab effort bogged down, and the armistice which was laboriously negotiated left Israel in possession of the greater part of Palestine. It sanctioned only the advance of Jordan as far as old Jerusalem. It was a precarious armistice, not at all a resolution of the conflict, and it left the feud between the Arabs and Israel to smoulder indefinitely. It split the Holy Land in two, and perpetuated the problem of the 800,000 Arab refugees from Palestine, who had fled from their land in the face of the onslaught, and are now encamped in the neighboring states. To this day they constitute one of the most grievous and explosive problems of the situation. The defeat of the anti-Jewish action in 1948 brought about a deep sense of disappointment and a virtual inferiority complex in the Arab world. This has certainly not had a beneficial influence on its subsequent development in the domestic and international field. Egypt suffered the greatest trauma. Here the military fiasco, felt with a burning shame, was one of the major factors in the *coup d'état* of July 1952 which overthrew the monarchy of the discredited Farouk. But to some extent the Palestine problem has affected the life of all the Arab states, exacerbated by numerous vexations and incidents.

OTTOMAN rule in the West was much more indirect and intermittent than in the East. If it continued with hiatuses at Tripoli up to 1911, it had in fact ceased in Algeria and Tunisia when those countries were occupied by France in 1830 and 1881 respectively. Of the autonomous regimes that she found there, France totally eliminated the Algerian one of the

Deys, while the Beys of Tunis were maintained under a protectorate. Morocco, the last Arab country to preserve its independent sovereignty, lost it to France and Spain between the second half of the nineteenth century and the first years of the twentieth. The civilizing work of France in all the Maghrib contrasted favorably with the sterile Turkish rule in the East, and with the British politico-administrative hegemony in Egypt. It was accompanied by an intensive colonization and demographic penetration which in a special way made Algeria an appendage of the mother country. But it was not long before the very largesse with which France opened the resources of her civilization and her culture to these overseas territories led to the efflorescence there of the ideals of nationality, freedom and independence in a European sense, which as such had been unknown in the Barbary period. Maghribian nationalism smouldered under the ashes until its violent explosion in the second post-war period. It was encouraged by the example of the Arabs of the East, and by the independence attained by Libya, which in terms of civil maturity was certainly not superior to all the rest of the West. But here the tough colonial manner adopted by fascist Italy, and the war which she then lost, yielded the fruit of at least a nominal independence to the country. In the French Maghrib, the fortunes of the war, and the appearance in Africa of American military and economic power averse to colonialism, precipitated the crisis which now has finally been resolved in favor of Arab nationalism. In 1956 at the conclusion of a combined political and insurrectional action, in which the heads of state and the indigenous leaders knew how to make good use of arms against both the blandishments and hardening of French policy, Tunisia and Morocco were well along the road to recovering their independent sovereignty. There remained only the not-too-well defined tie of interdependence which could have kept those countries in the orbit of the French community. As a matter of fact, they have since become fully sovereign.

The problem of Algeria was the last to be resolved. It was a country without the least physiognomy of a state, a territory formerly assimilated to metropolitan France which the latter found it convulsive to abandon. What was at stake here was more than a century of labor, of wealth, of intensive European settlement. Hence the Europeans in Algeria were determined to defend their position by all and any means, not excluding counter-terrorism and sedition. It was inevitable, however, that the desire of the overwhelming Arab majority for independence should prevail; and after eight years of fierce military and political fighting, French accession finally occurred in the latter part of 1962.

Thus in a little more than a century, European colonialism has already exhausted its task vis-à-vis the Arabs, who had themselves once been conquerors and teachers of civilization, but who had declined to the point where they submitted to conquest and civilization in turn, and have now risen up again to claim equality of rights in the community of peoples. A glory more enduring than the technical progress imported from Europe to this world, and which it was quick to welcome, and sometimes awkwardly superimposed rather than assimilated and digested, is that of having radiated the light of its thought in the East, awakening consciences, and pointing out ideals of material and moral elevation to the common people of the East; ideals which among other things with a providential heterogenesis of ends, implied rebellion against political domination, and a struggle to bring it to an end.

IN a few decades the Arabs have once again become masters of their destiny. But the victorious outcome of the struggle for freedom from alien domination cannot make us forget the other grave problems that beset them, as they already have the peoples of Europe, as soon as external freedom is reacquired. In foreign policy there is still the exasperating and seemingly insoluble impasse of Israel which makes the Arabs susceptible to the blandishments of Soviet policy which is concretized in proposals of economic agreements and the provision of arms by way of the satellite countries. For obvious religious reasons this can never mean a full Arab alignment with the Communist bloc, but rather a barrier to every sincere understanding with the Anglo-Americans (witness the debâcle of the Baghdad Pact). While efforts are made to dismantle the last remnants of British influence in the Near East, American economic penetration (petroleum enterprises in Saudi Arabia) is accepted, divested of the abhorred aspects of colonialism, always insisting, however, on a jealous tutelage of political independence.

In domestic policy the experiments made by the free representative regimes in the still brief period of total independence have not in truth been very happy. In contrast to other states of the East like Turkey, which passed from a personal and party dictatorship to an ever more substantial democracy, the Arab states have shown a tendency (or the necessity) of resolving their crises by extra-parliamentary means, as is demonstrated by the Egyptian revolution of 1952 and its subsequent results, and the frequent *coups d'état* that have rocked Syria in the last decade. In these states which are in the vanguard of the Arab group, the dominance of the military over the civil elements has had a divisive effect inimical to political stabilization, frequently engendering the establishment of demagogic dictatorships. The position of Egypt is particularly delicate. It has replaced the monarchy with a dictatorship of socialist-revolutionary tendencies and it evidently aspires to assume direction of the whole Arab movement in realization of its potential international objectives. Its expansionist program suffered a setback in the Sudan, which in 1955 declared itself an autonomous and sovereign state opposed to every attempt at union with Egypt. Moreover, it obliged the Egyptian rulers to seek a success elsewhere to bolster their prestige. This was attempted in the nationalization of the Suez Canal, enforced against Great Britain and France in 1956, and in a union with Syria in 1958, sonorously entitled the United Arab Republic, which, however, was not successful and ended in 1961. Only the future will show to what extent this ambitious and adventurous foreign policy is reconcilable with the internal program of renewal that has been undertaken, and with the solution of the social problem which has not yet reached its most acute form in Egypt, as is also the case in the whole Arab world.

The dynastic problems that were eliminated with the *coup d'état* in the valley of the Nile were also felt in the Fertile Crescent. The Hashimites were overthrown in a particularly virulent revolution in Iraq in 1958, though they continue to rule Jordan. The ideal of a "great Syria" has been set forth several times which would unite in a single state Syria, Lebanon, Jordan and Iraq, thereby reconstituting the central nucleus of the Arab Empire in its most glorious period. But this, like every other project of larger, unitary and federative formations among the Arab states, collides against the regional particularisms and the egoisms of the minor national units, averse to being submerged in larger units. In this rapid survey of the single states of the East a unique position is held by the Saudi monarchy of Arabia: it is still an absolute state which the prudent and brilliant labor of its founder has consolidated, made powerful and surrounded with a political and religious prestige, not to be compared with the unpopularity and scandal of its distant Wahhabite origins. The possession of the Holy Places of Islam, the practical relaxation of Najdian rigor-

ism in Hijaz, the wealth brought by the petroleum concessions
and the reluctant but inexorable acceptance in high places of
Western techniques have converted the Saudi state into an
active and influential member of the Arab League, esteemed
second to Egypt in assuming positions of dynamic intransigence in Pan-Arab and international problems.

Political progress which in forty years has led the Arab
world from total subjection to alien domination to total independence has been accompanied by a cultural resurgence, a
nahda which has been a primary factor, and sometimes a real
determining element of the political liberation. In the beginning this cultural resurgence was fructified by contact with
European culture, but then it developed along its own paths,
linking itself once more with the most illustrious national tradition. The flowering of a modern neo-Arab literature in
Egypt, Syria and Iraq has corresponded to the purification and
modernization of the language, liberated from archaisms and
vulgarisms, and to the study and evaluation of the literary and
scientific heritage of Arabism. It tries new ways in poetry, in
narrative, essayistic and publicistic writing, attesting to an intense ferment of spiritual life in the élites. Indeed it is the cultural field where up to now the pan-Arabic ideal has realized
its greatest progress, unhampered by regional and centrifugal
forces: and international bodies like the linguistic Academy of
Cairo and the cultural section of the Arab League have given
excellent proof of the capacity for organization and collaboration of the modern Arab intelligentsia in the intellectual
sphere. Between the two opposite poles of traditionalism and
the mechanical imitation of the West, contemporary Arab art
and culture have shown that they pursue, and have often obtained, an intelligent balance. Just as in the political field the
names of the leaders of resuscitated Arabism, yesterday a king
Faisal and an Ibn Saud, today an Abd an-Nasir (the "Nasser"
of the journalists), have become part of general international

culture, so in the literary and cultural field the fame of a Taha Husain, of a Taimur or a Tawfiq al-Hakìn, has acquired a more than oriental renown, entering the circle of world literature. Thus Arabism unfolds fresh energies from all sides which show that its mission in the Mediterranean and the Near East is all else but exhausted.

We could not conclude this rapid survey of the past and present of the Arabs without reproducing here the words with which the eminent orientalist and historian, Bernard Lewis concluded his "The Arabs in History" (1950). They contain an acute synthesis of the present-day reality, and a prognosis of the future.

"In these problems of readjustment the Arab peoples have a choice of several paths; they may submit to one or other of the contending versions of modern civilization that are offered to them, merging their own culture and identity in a larger and dominating whole; or they may try to turn their backs upon the West and all its works, pursuing the mirage of a return to the lost theocratic ideal, arriving instead at a refurbished despotism that has borrowed from the West its machinery both of exploitation and repression and its verbiage of intolerance, or finally—and for this the removal of the irritant of foreign tutelage is a prerequisite—they may succeed in renewing their society from within, meeting the West on terms of equal cooperation, absorbing something of both its science and humanism, not only in the shadow but in substance, in a harmonious balance with their own inherited tradition."

Bibliography

Arnold, T. W., and Alfred Guillaume, eds., *Legacy of Islam.* New York: Oxford University Press, 1931

Asad, Muhammed, *Principles of State and Government in Islam.* Los Angeles: University of California Press, 1961.

Atlas of the Arab World and the Middle East. New York: St. Martin's Press, 1960.

Childers, Erskine B., *Common Sense About the Arab World.* New York: The Macmillan Co., 1960.

Dermenghem, Emile, *Muhammed and the Islamic Tradition.* New York: Harper & Bros., 1958.

Donaldson, Dwight M., *Studies in Muslim Ethics.* Naperville, Ill.: Alec R. Allenson, 1953.

Doughty, Charles M., *Travels in Arabia Deserta.* New York: Doubleday, 1955.

Frye, R. N., ed., *Islam and the West.* New York: Humanities Press.

Gabrieli, Francesco, *Arab Revival.* New York: Random House, 1961.

Hamady, Sania, *Temperament and Character of the Arabs.* New York: Twayne Publishers, 1959.

Hitti, Philip Khuri, *History of the Arabs.* New York: St. Martin's Press, 1937.

Hole, Edwyn, *Andalus, Spain Under the Muslims.* Chester Springs, Pa.: Dufour Editions, 1958.

Howarth, Herbert and Shukrallah, Abraham, *Images From the Arab World, an Anthology.* Chester Springs, Pa.: Dufour Editions, 1944.

Khadduri, Majid, *Islamic Jurisprudence: Shaffi i's Risala.* Baltimore: The Johns Hopkins Press, 1961.

———, *War and Peace in the Law of Islam.* Baltimore: The Johns Hopkins Press, 1955.

Kritzeck, James, and A. B. Winder, eds., *World of Islam; Studies in Honor of Philip K. Hitti*. New York: St. Martin's Press, 1960.

Landau, Rom, *Islam and the Arabs*. New York: The Macmillan Co., 1959.

———, *Philosophy of Ibn Arabi*. New York: The Macmillan Co., 1959.

Lewis, Bernard, *Arabs in History*. New York: Harper & Bros., 1960.

Mahmud, S. F., *Story of Islam*. New York: Oxford University Press, 1959.

Nicholson, R. A., *Literary History of the Arabs*. New York: Cambridge University Press, 1930.

O'Leary, De Lacy, *Arabic Thought and Its Place in History*. New York: Humanities Press.

Partner, Peter, *Short Political Guide to the Arab World*. New York: Frederick A. Praeger, 1960.

Smith, Wilfred C., *Islam in Modern History*. New York: New American Library, 1959.

Thesiger, Wilfred, *Arabian Sands*. New York: E. P. Dutton, 1959.

Index

The Author and His Book

Francesco Gabrieli was born in Rome in 1904. He is one of Italy's most distinguished scholars, having held the positions of professor at the Istituto Orientale in Naples, editor of the Enciclopedia Italiana, and since 1938 the chair of Arabic language and literature at the University of Rome. During the academic year of 1960-61, he served as visiting professor of history at the University of California. He is the author of numerous works on Islam and the Arab world, of which the present volume is one of the first to be translated into English.

Professor Gabrieli is married to the former Giovanna Santomassimo and makes his home in Rome.

THE ARABS (Hawthorn, 1963) was completely manufactured by The Colonial Press Inc., Clinton, Massachusetts. The body type is Janson, with chapter headings set in Civilité.

A Hawthorn Book